"I told you I should have stayed home," Catherine murmured.

"Nonsense. You have as much a right to be here as they. More, for your breeding is better."

"Reputation surpasses breeding. Leave me before you tarnish your own. Dance with Laura."

"No. I will lead you out." He could not dance with Laura first, but he could dance with each of his host's sisters in turn.

Or so he hoped. In truth, he had ached to touch Catherine since succumbing to temptation in the library that morning. His fingers tingled whenever he recalled that brief contact.

It was the situation, he assured himself. Once his task was finished, these feelings would fade. The only reason he was turning into a maudlin fool was because his vow forced him to think of her day and night, yet spending time together would hurt her. No wonder she invaded his dreams to suggest ways he could brush against her as they moved through the patterns of a country dance.

Don't feed the gossip, warned his conscience. . . .

The
Notorious
Widow

Allison Lane

A SIGNET BOOK

SIGNET
Published by New American Library, a division of
Penguin Putnam Inc., 375 Hudson Street,
New York, New York 10014, U.S.A.
Penguin Books Ltd, 27 Wrights Lane,
London W8 5TZ, England
Penguin Books Australia Ltd,
Ringwood, Victoria, Australia
Penguin Books Canada Ltd, 10 Alcorn Avenue,
Toronto, Ontario, Canada M4V 3B2
Penguin Books (N.Z.) Ltd, 182–190 Wairau Road,
Auckland 10, New Zealand

Penguin Books Ltd, Registered Offices:
Harmondsworth, Middlesex, England

First published by Signet, an imprint of New American Library,
a division of Penguin Putnam Inc.

First Signet Printing, November 2000
10 9 8 7 6 5 4 3 2 1

 REGISTERED TRADEMARK—MARCA REGISTRADA

Printed in the United States of America

PUBLISHER'S NOTE
This is a work of fiction. Names, characters, places, and incidents either
are the products of the author's imagination or are used fictitiously,
and any resemblance to actual persons, living or dead, business
establishments, events, or locales is entirely coincidental.

Chapter One

As a gust of wind ripped the bonnet off the woman emerging from the confectioner's shop, Blake froze, one foot in the air. She had the most striking coloring he had ever seen. Glossy black hair. Creamy face. Rosy lips. Blue eyes rivaling the plumage of that parrot his cousin had brought back from the Caribbean.

Another gust tugged the dangling bonnet. "Good heavens!" she exclaimed as one hand jammed it back on her head. "We might blow away."

Dry leaves swirled across the cobbles.

Laughing, she turned her face into the wind, exhilaration setting her apart from the women scurrying heads-down along the street. Such uninhibited joy was rare.

Blake resumed his walk. She was striking, yes, but not truly beautiful, he decided. Her slender neck lacked the curve that might draw comparisons to swans. Both height and shape seemed average beneath the plain cloak. Even her features were rather ordinary—straight nose, wide mouth, pointed chin—but they blended into a pleasing whole turned positively exotic by those eyes. Eyes that sparkled in the afternoon sun. Eyes that promised wit and humor. Eyes that could mesmerize a man as he drove into—

He cursed, cutting off the inappropriate thought.

"Definitely inappropriate," he muttered as a girl in a bright blue coat emerged from the shop to claim the woman's hand. Her blond curls danced as she tilted her head to ask a question. The woman met her gaze with a smile so tender it made him want to weep. The girl was fortunate in her governess. Not many actually cared for their charges.

Slowing, he savored the sight—her protective gestures, the child's pleasure, the unusual rapport between them—then stifled a kick of desire. He would do nothing to jeopardize her position.

Yet the thought had hardly formed before a sense of wrongness overpowered it. The scene depicted the perfect governess taking her charge on an outing—except that she was too attractive. Hiring a comely governess always led to trouble—unless the household lacked men.

He frowned. The long war with France had produced many such homes, though he would never wish that fate on the charming sprite in the blue coat. Picturing her without father or brothers twisted his heart.

Maybe the woman is married.

"No!" A flash of pain sped his feet away. He did not want to imagine her married. A matron without even a maid to accompany her on errands would have a miserable life—long hours mired in menial chores, sleepless nights wondering where to find even the bare necessities, the constant temptation to try unacceptable occupations, the dark moments when despair made every effort seem useless. He had escaped that fate recently enough that he would wish it on no one else, particularly a vibrant woman and a cheerful child.

But he doubted she was married. The two looked nothing alike, and several ladies had hurried by without a word of greeting, firmly relegating his black-haired Circe to the ranks of the insignificant.

Oddly relieved by this conclusion, he entered the stationer's shop and switched his thoughts to business. He had extended his stay in Devonshire to stand up at his friend Max's wedding. Now on his way back to Rockburn Abbey, he'd stopped in Exeter to look at a map.

Man's changing perceptions of the world had fascinated him for as long as he could remember, though he'd been unable to indulge his interest until his finances had improved. But at last his collection of ancient maps and charts was taking shape.

Mr. Cavendish, the stationer, claimed to have a fifteenth-century Italian map based on Ptolemy's *Geographia*. Blake hoped it was in good condition. Acquiring a Ptolemaic view of the world would compensate for his dreary room at the White Hart Inn.

"Can we feed the squirrels today?" Sarah asked, tugging on Catherine Parrish's hand.

"As soon as we finish our errands." Catherine shifted her grip on a length of wool and packet of paper, wishing she'd brought Annie along to carry parcels. But the maid had other chores today. Postponing this expedition had been impossible, for Sarah needed a warmer gown for winter, and this might well be the last sunny day until spring.

"What else must we do?" asked Sarah.

She smiled down at her daughter. "Your Aunt Laura needs pins and some Milk of Roses."

"For her skin," murmured Sarah, nodding. "Did she give up on cucumber wash?"

"No, but last month's hothouse accident left us short of cucumbers."

Sarah giggled. "What else?"

"Aunt Mary's books should be in. Uncle William is out of tooth powder. And Mrs. Moulding wants Balm of Gilead for her rheumatism. We also need more wax candles."

She frowned. Candle consumption had risen alarmingly in recent months. Mrs. Moulding swore that none were wasted, yet not even the shortened days of November could explain why they were burning so many. Perhaps they should switch to tallow everywhere but the drawing room. They had to cut expenses if they hoped to take Laura to Bath.

She exhaled in a silent sigh. Laura was beautiful, accomplished, and very sweet. But no serious suitors remained near Exeter. A London Season was far too expensive, so Bath was her only hope. And it had to be soon. Laura was already twenty.

Yet Laura was not her only concern, she admitted as she responded to Sarah's chatter. Mary was also of an age to wed, though her shyness kept her from attracting gentlemen.

Then there was Sarah. Her daughter was growing fast. What would become of her? Harold's death had left them penniless, without even a modest widow's portion. While her brother had welcomed them into his home, his own finances were strained. How would Sarah find a suitor without a dowry? They could hardly ask William to provide one. He could not even scrape up enough to take Laura and Mary to Bath, let alone fire off a niece. Even if he attached a wealthy wife, her dowry would provide for his own children.

She shivered at the image of William married, though she had always known that running his household was a temporary duty. She could only hope that he would choose a wife she could befriend.

Suppressing her blue-devils, she headed for the apothecary shop. This was neither the place nor the time to contemplate the future. Today might be Sarah's last visit to Exeter until spring. The sooner they finished their errands, the sooner they could enjoy it.

Half an hour later, Catherine spotted the visiting gentleman emerging from the stationer's—hardly a surprise, for Exeter was not large. So why did the sight of him pool warmth in her womb?

She rarely noticed appearance, though his was certainly striking—tall, with tawny hair, amber eyes, and well-tailored clothes that emphasized broad shoulders and shapely legs. He radiated the power and confidence typical of high-ranking gentlemen, yet she detected none of the arrogance usually found in such men.

His eyes locked with hers across the width of High Street, sending a jolt clear to her toes. Then he looked at Sarah and smiled.

Her heart melted on the spot. Pride stirred. Few men tolerated children, especially girls, but this one clearly saw the beauty of Sarah's soul. That explained the excitement tumbling through her system. Her instincts had known that he was an unusual gentleman and had recognized the opportunity his visit to Exeter offered.

Dreams closed her eyes to her surroundings: Laura meeting the handsome stranger—who would be titled and wealthy—falling in love, and marrying. He would take Laura's family under his wing, resolving their most pressing problems. Mary would get a London Season, William would receive the funds he needed to update the estate, Andrew could purchase that promotion to captain, Thomas could attend Oxford when he left Eton, and Sarah—

"Kate, my love. You look stunning today, as always."

Jasper Rankin. She crashed back to High Street with shattering speed. Pulling Sarah closer, she glared at her nemesis before turning away.

"Now what manners are these?" he asked teasingly. "You weren't so cold last night."

"As if you know." Again she sought to leave, but he grabbed the back of her neck, sliding his fingers beneath her bonnet to squeeze behind her ears. Pain exploded.

"Do not let guilt cloud your reason," he warned. "I've no objection to keeping secrets, but if you cut me, others will guess the truth."

"What truth?" she hissed. "Leave me alone. How dare you accost me on a public street!" As her mind searched for an escape, her hand warned Sarah to remain silent. Struggling was futile, for he was dangerous when riled and would enjoy subduing her. She cursed herself for bringing Sarah today, though he had never before been this bold.

"If you cared about appearances, you would never have started this, sweetings." His malicious smile increased her terror, but screaming would do no good.

He would take advantage of the confusion to do something worse. Yet submissiveness was not her nature.

"I started nothing," she protested, thankful that only the stranger was near enough to hear.

"No?" His grin stretched. "A look. A gesture. A meeting alone. But it matters not. You are no innocent, Kate." He casually turned his back to the street, then twisted his face into disapproval so severe that for a moment she was sure he would strike her. "This is your last warning, Mrs. Parrish," he snarled in a much softer voice. "Either mend your ways or be ostracized from polite society."

His sudden change from pretend lover to stern judge confused her. What new game was this? "You can't—"

"Silence," murmured Jasper, tightening his grip to inflict new pain. "If you say a word, I'll wring your neck."

Stunned, she could only comply.

Mrs. Hawkins flounced past, sweeping her with a contemptuous stare before disappearing into a shop.

The moment she was gone, Jasper shifted to face her, reverting to false intimacy. "Do you wish everyone in town to know about our little affair?" he asked, again raising his voice.

In a flash of insight, she realized that he was playing out this farce for the stranger's benefit.

"What would they think?" he demanded, smirking. "How long would they let you look after Sarah if the truth came out?"

She gasped. "But William would never believe—"

"No one attacks me with impunity," he whispered, his lips grazing her ear. "Harold's relatives would be shocked to learn of your exploits. They would remove Sarah from your care in a trice." He scowled and again raised his voice. "I am jealous, love. You called on Albert Smith and Ben Higgins last week. I don't share."

"That had nothing to do with—" She chopped off the protest, cursing herself. Every exchange made her appear guilty of impropriety—as he must know. He was manipulating her reactions just as relentlessly as he was controlling the pain that kept her at his side. Her temper snapped. "Spread your lies if you must. I can't stop you. But in the end, others will see you for what you are."

"They already do." He flicked one of Sarah's curls. "Everyone knows I am the soul of honor and the most benevolent protector this area has ever had."

He'd won. Sagging, she hugged Sarah closer, praying the girl would remain silent. He was as irrational today as she'd ever seen him. The way he'd touched Sarah raised her terror to heights she hadn't known existed, but she dared make no protest. She could not even curse him in her mind. He would know, and he would strike.

"Exactly," he murmured in satisfaction. "Everything has consequences. It is not just yourself you risk when you defy me."

Tears pricked the backs of her eyes, but she refused to let them show. Silence was her only weapon now. She could never win a war of words with him. His threat against Sarah changed everything, just as he'd known it would. Who knew better than she how far he would go?

With a final squeeze, he sauntered away, but the damage had been done. The stranger's eyes blazed with disdain. Miss Ander stood in the stationer's doorway behind him, her disapproval clear—not of Jasper's seeming caress, but of her own apparent acceptance of it.

Catherine clenched her fist. This was the second time she had threatened to expose Jasper, though they both knew it was impossible. How could she have been so stupid? His position in society was invulnerable, but her feeble threat gave him yet another grievance. Even worse, her instinctive protection of Sarah provided a new target.

"What did he mean?" asked Sarah, tugging her hand with trembling fingers.

This time Catherine let the curses parade through her mind, but she could not tell Sarah the truth. Even a precocious seven-year-old would not understand the threat. "He was trying to be funny, sweetheart, but he's not very good at it," she said lightly. "That was our last stop. Are you ready to feed the squirrels?"

Sarah nodded, but the sparkle had vanished from her eyes. "He wasn't joking, Mama," she whispered. "He's a bad man. Papa said he never learned to turn the other cheek, so he hurts people."

"Oh, sweetheart." Sarah's perspicacity often startled her, but this was a dangerous conclusion. "Papa was right, but never mention that to others." She turned toward the cathedral grounds, where a dozen squirrels played in the oak trees. "Mr. Rankin is more powerful than we are. Don't give him a chance to prove it."

That had been her mistake, she admitted ruefully as she handed Sarah a chunk of bread before settling under a tree. His one true charge had been that she'd brought this on herself. If only she had stopped to think that day. But she had been too furious to remember how dangerous he was. So she'd insulted him.

She shook her head. How could she have revealed her contempt? He had been persecuting her ever since, spreading rumors that she was a light-skirt. There wasn't a gossip in the area who believed her virtuous. Some looked askance at her sisters, distrusting the notorious widow's influence. And now he was turning on Sarah.

Her hand shook. She couldn't let him hurt Sarah, yet only leaving would guarantee her safety—an impossibility. Without funds, she could not even afford a remote cottage.

Again she cursed herself for exposing Sarah, though this attack made little sense. He could have threatened Sarah without staging a scene in the middle of High Street. By confronting her in such an intimate fashion, he'd risked exposing his part in the rumor campaign.

And all to convince the stranger that she was his mistress. But why?

She bit her lip to keep from crying. The stranger must be every bit the powerful lord her imagination had conjured. Perhaps he was pompous enough to complain to William about her presumed misdeeds, in which case her situation would soon worsen. But that seemed unlikely. Few gentlemen would intrude on total strangers.

Maybe Jasper had seen the man's interest in Sarah and thought he might form an alliance with them. Yet that worked only if Jasper recognized the stranger and feared his power, something she could not envision. Jasper feared no one.

Did he hope to spread news of her downfall beyond Devonshire? It would be pointless. She rarely traveled beyond Exeter, so disapproval in distant places could not harm her.

It didn't matter. This incident exposed her dreaming as the fantasy it was. Her family was doomed. No prince would appear to raise them from impoverished obscurity. Visiting Bath would do no good. Jasper would never allow an alliance with anyone desirable. Her flash of temper had condemned her sisters to spinsterhood.

Fighting back tears, she watched Sarah coax a squirrel to her hand. Sunlight glinted on the cathedral's rose window, reminding her that at least one power knew the truth. But it was unlikely that she would find vindication before Judgment Day.

"No," she swore, spurning despair.

She unclenched her fists, drawing peace from the scene. And strength. Somehow, she must fight back, expose Jasper as the source of these spurious rumors, and discredit his word. It was the only way to salvage Sarah's future.

Fury dimmed Blake's vision as the dandy bade farewell to his paramour with yet another blatant caress. If they were so lost to propriety as to make public spectacles of themselves, that was their business. But exposing an innocent child to their sordid behavior made it everyone's business.

The woman behind him agreed. "Scandalous!" she snorted, adding pithier remarks as she stalked away.

Society should protect its children from scenes like this one. But Exeter society had clearly failed to do so. Why had no one protested when that girl's family had hired a courtesan as her governess? If her father stood before him right now, Blake would demand satisfaction. Such disregard for morality was unconscionable.

No wonder the woman had evoked such lurid images in his mind. His instincts had seen past the charming façade to the temptress beneath. She was no better than the whores who importuned him whenever he left a London theater. Had she earned this post by seducing the girl's father? Perhaps she hoped to extract an offer from the fellow, though entertaining others would jeopardize a more respectable future.

Cursing, he headed for the bookseller's.

The girl had seemed frightened and confused by the suggestive repartee, but it would not be long before she understood what her governess was doing. Intelligence had lurked in her eyes. Already she was asking questions. The answers would forever strip away that charming innocence, replacing it with harsh disillusionment. And he had no doubt she would find those answers. The dandy was the sort who would enjoy providing them.

Again he cursed, launching a mental diatribe against the girl's father that pointed out the importance of choosing good teachers, moral teachers, pillars of propriety. How would the girl find a husband after being raised by a wanton? He visualized the father's horror, his shock, his determination to rectify the mistake—

It was an exercise that had often relieved frustration after his own father had dissipated the family fortune. But this time, his mental curses had no effect. How dare she accept the care and teaching of an innocent, then slip away to consort with rakes? If she wanted to be a courtesan, why pretend propriety?

Imagining her black hair spread across a pillow, her witch's eyes laughing up at him, increased his fury. Circe, indeed. She certainly knew how to attract attention. So why saddle herself with a respectable position when she could do so much better on her own?

The questions filled his mind, as did the rage he could not explain. So he clung to the memory of the child—warm, intelligent, and oh so innocent. Her silver eyes and blonde curls stirred protective instincts he hadn't known he possessed—which was why his temper shattered when he left the bookshop an hour later and ran the woman down.

"You should be ashamed of yourself," he snapped.

Her blue eyes widened as she stepped in front of the girl in a mockery of protection. The wind billowed her cloak, molding her gown around delectable legs.

"How dare you flaunt your liaisons on a public street?" he continued, ignoring the rise in his temperature. "It is bad enough to espouse indecency, but you have no right to expose a child to such vice."

"You are mistaken, sir," she protested, but her cheeks darkened in shame.

"I am not mistaken. I saw that disgusting display. You and that popinjay may go to perdition however you choose, but I cannot let you harm others. Who is your employer? Does he know that he hired a wanton?"

Anger blazed in her eyes, increasing his own. "Do you always jump to ridiculous conclusions, sir?" she snapped. "Surely a gentleman would discover the facts before heaping insults on a stranger. You are as dishonorable as those you condemn."

"You overstep your place," he growled, fisting his hands to keep from shaking her.

"How would you know?" Her free hand poked him in the chest. "You must be one of those arrogant lords who never admit fault. Why else would you demand that I bow to your misguided wishes? Well, you can go to perdition, sir. I don't take orders from cads. And I never obey blithering idiots." She turned to leave.

"This isn't about me." He grabbed her arm, then cursed as heat sizzled into his hand. Wanton, indeed. Circe herself could not incite such yearning.

"Isn't it?" she demanded. "Look at yourself. You know nothing about me, yet you create a public spectacle by accusing me of fictitious crimes. You hold me captive while you abuse me, then blame me for your lack of control. I won't stand for it." She glared at his hand. "Release me or I will throw a fit guaranteed to mortify you for years. I've never encountered such a pompous fool."

"Who is your employer?" Rage burned red around the edges of his vision.

"None of your business!"

A whimper distracted him. The girl peered around the woman's side, tears shimmering in her eyes. His heart contracted. Circe was right. He was behaving as badly as she.

But he refused to abase himself to a wanton. Abandoning the argument, he stalked toward his hotel. He would discover her direction elsewhere. The situation must be rectified, but subjecting the child to a public brawl was unacceptable.

So is hurling insults into a stranger's face.

He frowned, cringing as he reviewed his behavior. He should not have lost his temper—would not have done so if he hadn't already been furious. The map had not been at all as advertised. In fact, it had been a complete fake, and discovering that the governess was wanton had done nothing to decrease his lust. He'd spent the last hour alternately cursing himself for wanting her and wondering whether the stationer was a forger or merely a fool. Now tomorrow would be worse. Instead of leaving for home, he must discover the girl's parents and see that this so-called governess was turned off.

And what then? taunted his conscience. *Will you offer her your protection?*

Chapter Two

William Seabrook drained his glass and headed for the door. His horse should be ready by now.

The White Hart Inn was not one of his usual haunts. He found its massive beams and dark paneling oppressive and its flagged floors cold. His own taste ran to the Golden Stag, as much for its lower prices as for its warmth. But the White Hart was useful when he wished to avoid acquaintances. Like today. He'd needed an afternoon with a certain widow, but had to avoid his sister, who was also in town. How could he explain that he sometimes experienced urges he could not control? Not only had he long criticized others for indulging their unseemly desires, but rumors made this a bad time to pursue the baser pleasures.

He shook off his guilt, setting his hat firmly on his head. It was done. He'd seen no one he knew. Now relaxed for the first time in days and fortified against the chill of the approaching storm, he was heading home.

As he stepped into the hallway, the outside door burst open on a gust of wind, admitting a swirl of leaves and a gentleman. It took a moment to place the face, for he hadn't seen it in twelve years.

"Blake Townsend!" he exclaimed before recalling that the man was now an earl. "Or Rockhurst, I should say. What are you doing in Exeter?"

"Passing through." Rockhurst smoothed a frown from his forehead.

William's mind worked furiously as they exchanged pleasantries. He had met Townsend at Eton, though the man had been two forms ahead of him, so they had not been close. But perhaps he could turn this encounter to advantage. Might Rockhurst be interested in his sister?

He couldn't ask, of course. Rockhurst would be accustomed to fending off title seekers and matchmakers. Only a plausible excuse would entice the man to the manor.

Fortunately, he had one. Blake Townsend was a fair-minded champion of justice. At Eton he had used his standing as heir to an earldom to prevent the stronger, higher-ranking students from harming the timid or baseborn boys, most notably in the Easley case.

Reginald Easley, a solicitor's brilliant son, had been a favorite of the tutors, which had irritated an unprincipled group of students headed by Lord Dabney. One day Easley was called upon to correct Dabney's wrong answer to a simple question, an insult worsened when Dabney's friends ridiculed him for his mistake. Easley turned up head-to-toe bruises the next morning.

Townsend had been furious. He believed lords should protect those beneath them, so he'd arranged to have Dabney permanently sent down. The tutors never learned who was really behind the incident, but the other students knew. They soon discovered that Townsend did not tolerate persecution. Honest competition was one thing, abuse of power quite another.

His reputation as a champion of the downtrodden did not endear him to some, but he refused to ignore his principles. Woe betide anyone who preyed on the weak, abandoned honor, or planned a prank that might cause injury. Current rumor speculated that Rockhurst had contrived the recent exposure of Dornbras as a procurer for London brothels.

Townsend had also been intrigued by challenges, which explained his insistence on taking personal charge of his inheritance after his father had died. He had been gone from Eton two years by then, but everyone knew the story. Blake had found the estate on the verge of ruin. Instead of returning to Oxford, he had fired his father's advisors, hired Easley to rescue his investments, then taken up the reins of the estate himself. Reportedly, he had rebuilt his fortune several times over. Some hinted that he had done it through unscrupulous means, but William refused to believe it. That did not fit his character.

As he followed Rockhurst into a private parlor, he smiled. What more could he want for his sister? Rockhurst had a title, wealth, a pleasing appearance, and a history of fairness.

"Will you be here long?" he asked as Rockhurst poured wine.

"A day or so." He shrugged. "I only stopped to see if an ancient map Cavendish is offering would fit my collection."

"I doubt Cavendish has anything of interest unless he printed it himself," he warned.

"So I believe. He shan't make that mistake again." His expression sent shivers down William's spine, though it confirmed that the man had not changed since school. Cavendish would be on the next ship to Australia.

If anyone could champion Catherine's cause, it would be Rockhurst. And if helping Catherine placed him in Laura's company, the man could hardly cry foul. Laura's charm would soon bind him. No gentleman could ignore her. If only she weren't so particular. She'd sent every one of them packing.

"If you can remain a few days longer, I need help." William drained his glass, then stared at the fire, projecting an image of despair. "My sister is being unjustly persecuted, but I am powerless to counter the villain's plot. Perhaps your greater standing could rescue her."

"What tale is this?"

William paused. He had only one chance to win Rockhurst's interest. "Catherine married our vicar some years ago. They made a formidable pair, working tirelessly to aid the poor, protect the innocent, and bring the unscrupulous to the attention of those in authority. Even after Harold's death, she continued that work—our new vicar is more interested in hunting than in his duty to church or community."

"Not unusual," murmured Rockhurst, pouring more wine.

William sipped. "All was well until a neighbor began twisting her work to destroy her reputation. His rumors impute a more nefarious purpose to her visits."

"Fomenting rebellion?" Rockhurst frowned.

"Debauchery." He cursed himself. Of course Rockhurst would think first of political scheming. It was much on the minds of many men in these turbulent times. He forced the details past his lips—it always upset him to imagine his sister engaging in such sordid activity. "The rumors credit her with liaisons enough to weary a courtesan. Despite her denials, too many gossips believe him."

"Who is spreading the tales?"

"People cite a score of sources, though Catherine claims every rumor originated with Jasper Rankin. His father is the highest-ranking lord in the vicinity, so Jasper wields great power. No one would question his word."

"But why would he launch an undeserved attack on a vicar's widow?" asked Rockhurst, clearly suspicious.

William shrugged. This was the point where his own thinking always stumbled. "I have no idea, and frankly it does not fit his image. He is the darling of local society and quite generous to the victims whenever he or his friends cause trouble. Beyond saying that he is avenging an insult, Catherine won't discuss it. She swears anyone who knows her should recognize that the tales are lies, and she insists that the furor will fade in time."

"So your claim that she is being unjustly persecuted rests solely on her word," said Rockhurst. "Do you believe her?"

"Jasper is a gentleman." As usual, he was torn between loyalty and his own confusion. No matter how much he needed to entice Rockhurst to Seabrook Manor, he could not exaggerate Jasper's faults. "He is prone to high spirits and enjoys pleasure, but I've no evidence of worse—certainly nothing that might explain this sort of attack. On the other hand, I've never known Catherine to lie—certainly not about something this serious. Nearly everyone of stature has cut her, and our invitation to the squire's harvest ball was rescinded."

"So what would prompt an honorable man to lie about an honorable woman?" He almost sounded sarcastic.

William shrugged. "A misunderstanding, I presume. She was upset about damage he did to a tenant's field last month. Perhaps someone overheard them arguing and drew the wrong conclusions. But whatever the cause, the tales are too ingrained to disappear on their own. It will require someone of your stature to stop them."

"It does not sound promising."

"I know that Catherine cannot have indulged in such perversions," swore William, fearful that his doubts had made the task sound impossible—or unimportant. "And this is affecting everyone on the estate, even the servants. Sir Richard had offered one of my stableboys a position as groom, but he withdrew the offer the moment the rumors started. Come to Seabrook Manor and see for yourself. Once you understand how unfair the situation is, you will want to help—just as you did in the Easley affair."

Blake drained his glass, then walked to the window and back, pondering Seabrook's tale. Rankin's father couldn't be more than a viscount if Seabrook thought an earl had enough power to influence him, especially an earl whose own reputation was suspect—he grimaced at how unthinking he had been when he'd first descended on London. But there had to be more to this story than Seabrook was telling. Not only did his sister outrank the local gossips, but viscounts' heirs did not attack barons' sisters without cause. Seabrook was not even sure that Jasper was guilty.

The situation intrigued him. Perhaps Catherine had committed some indiscretions that were now being exaggerated—despite his claims, Seabrook clearly thought it possible—but if she was telling the truth, this was another case of the strong preying on the weak. And the cause might well be absurd. It wouldn't be the first instance of eccentric reasoning. He knew one gentleman who had banned all glassware from his house after cutting himself on a sliver from a broken figurine. He ate only from silver plates, drank from silver goblets, and refused to try the new Argand lamps because they required glass chimneys. But his edicts hurt no one.

Blake made another circuit of the room. He was bored. He hadn't faced a serious challenge since rescuing his inheritance. This one might well be impossible, of course. Gossips lived by the dictum *Where there is smoke, there must be fire.* Exposing a rumor as an outright lie would require considerable evidence, and even that might not sway the most vicious. They preferred to believe the worst.

There is nothing you can do, warned a voice in his head. *Failure will make it harder to succeed in other cases.*

Yet turning his back on injustice would make him a coward. His conscience was already pummeling him over Dornbras. He had known for years that the man was no good, yet he had never investigated his activities. Thus Dornbras had continued abducting virgins until Max had exposed him, only last month. How many girls had suffered because he had ignored his instincts?

Those instincts were again stirring. There was more to this case than Seabrook had revealed. Investigating it would take time, but he had plenty. He wasn't due back in London until spring, when he must seriously consider securing the succession. His steward could manage the Abbey without his oversight. November was hardly a busy month.

"When did the rumors begin?" he asked, leaning against the mantel.

Seabrook frowned. "I'm not sure, for I did not hear the stories at first. At least a month ago. Perhaps longer."

"You say no one else knows that Rankin started them?"

"Not to my knowledge. You must realize that few people discuss this with me. Catherine is family."

"Yet she swears she is innocent." He rubbed the back of his neck. "Didn't you press her for details?"

"Of course I did, but she swears they don't matter. A more stubborn wench never lived."

Blake returned to the window. The situation was muddled. Seabrook bounced from certainty that the tales were false to admitting that his only evidence was the unsubstantiated word of his sister. If he believed her, why had he not called Rankin out? Or did he expect that this request would decide whether a challenge was necessary?

He didn't like being used, but he could hardly form an opinion based on the word of one muddled baron. And the tale raised enough questions to warrant an investigation. "I cannot promise success, but I will look into the matter," he said over his shoulder.

Seabrook's face lightened. "Thank you. This weighs heavily on Catherine's mind. Will you join us for dinner?"

"No. I must discover what rumors are current." And he must also deal with Cavendish and that unsuitable governess. His conscience would not allow him to ignore such problems. "I will join you in two days."

Blake paced the parlor for another hour, pondering Seabrook's request. It was decidedly odd. Despite having had no contact in years, five minutes after meeting, Seabrook had bared a family disgrace most people would lock firmly away.

He shook his head, for this tale was too similar to

that which had led to his own reputation. Rebuilding his inheritance had been so exhilarating that he had gone a trifle wild when he finally reached London, acquiring a name for debauchery that would not help Catherine. And her problem was as difficult as they came. Gossips rarely believed denials, instead twisting them into evidence of guilt—*the lady doth protest too much*. Catherine must know that the more she argued, the guiltier she seemed—which explained why she was hoping silence would make the rumors go away.

Not that they would. Even if no one was feeding them, her being a widow worked against her. She could never prove innocence, for she was no longer a virgin. Besides, a wellborn widow could conduct discreet liaisons with impunity. Even wellborn wives entertained lovers. A vicar's widow might be held to a higher standard, but not to the point of ostracism. So what would provoke such scandal?

He frowned. There had to be more to the tale than a few intimate encounters. Rather than try to prove her innocent, he would be better served by forcing Rankin to recant. In the meantime, he would question the innkeeper. Tomorrow he would talk to those who knew more than Seabrook. Reaching into memory, he recalled an acquaintance whose elderly aunt lived in Exeter. If she wasn't a gossip, she could at least introduce him into local society.

"You what?" Catherine stared at her brother.

"A school friend will arrive in two days. I want Laura to make a good impression. He is of an age to marry."

"You actually invited a man to court Laura? Why would he agree? She has a minuscule dowry." She wanted Laura wed, but on her own terms. Arranged marriages often put the wife at the mercy of a brutal man.

William frowned. "I am perfectly capable of assuring my sisters' futures, Catherine. You need not fret. Just see that Laura is presentable."

"Yes, your majesty," she murmured, collapsing against the back of her chair. His high-handedness shocked her more than his announcement. Never before had he treated her like a servant.

He stared a moment, then his shoulders slumped. "Forgive me, Catherine. I did not mean to sound ungrateful for all that you do. Laura's future has long bothered me, for we both know I can never take her to town. My relief that I can actually address it made the words come out wrong."

"Perhaps, but did you consider the consequences of bringing him here now? Even if he is amenable to taking her, he must surely flee when he hears the rumors. What will that do for her expectations? He would spread these lies throughout England."

'Give me a little credit," he snapped. "My invitation did not mention Laura. The Earl of Rockhurst has long been a benevolent and fair-minded knight who defends the weak against injustice. I asked him to put a stop to the rumors. He must stay here, of course, but no one will expect anything further. And if he decides that he likes Laura, who am I to argue? He is wealthy enough that even you must approve?"

"That sounds sordid."

"I phrased that badly. Rockhurst is honorable, virtuous, and selfless. Laura would be perfect for him. He must produce an heir; she has excellent breeding. He loves music; she plays well and sings like an angel. He needs a hostess; she loves people, can converse intelligently, and is well trained in running a household."

She had to agree with this last statement, for she had overseen that part of Laura's education herself. And she knew that Laura yearned for London society.

William relaxed. "We are only introducing them, but think of the benefits if they reach an accommodation. He could give Mary a London Season and aid Andrew's career."

"To say nothing of financing your estate plans." Her temper flared, in part because she had spun similar dreams that very afternoon before discovering how unrealistic they were. Jasper would make sure that no one of power formed an alliance with her family.

"All you have to do is convince him that you are innocent and answer a few questions, Catherine. He is a paragon with credit so high that the gossips will have to accept you."

Catherine clamped her mouth shut in despair.

Convince him that you are innocent—devil take it, she *was* innocent, though it was clear that even William thought otherwise. His priggishness was already warring with family loyalty. Would he throw her out if Rockhurst failed to redeem her? Jasper's threat against Sarah suddenly loomed larger.

Answer a few questions—Did William have any idea how violated she already felt at the prospect of exposing her soul to a stranger? The situation was far worse than he could imagine. No one had enough credit to improve it.

She closed her eyes. It was barely possible that the Regent was powerful enough to stop the gossip. Maybe. But stopping gossip wouldn't make the tales disappear. They would remain in whispers behind fans and under stairs, in drunken confidences in the clubs, in rambling letters to correspondents. And they would grow all the more titillating for being suppressed. How could she invite such a future by asking for help?

Yet Laura deserved an introduction to the earl. Hadn't she been fretting over her family's future when that arrogant fool had accosted her in Exeter? Her fists clenched as she recalled his attack. If Rockhurst was a fair-minded knight who decried injustice, then the stranger in Exeter was his opposite.

"Very well." She met William's eyes. "We will make his stay comfortable. I will talk to Laura, and perhaps you can devise some entertainment. Does he hunt or shoot? You might be able to set up an evening of cards if people know that I will not attend. Mrs. Telcor has vowed to avoid any gathering that includes me."

"You will chaperon Laura." His voice was firm.

"Rockhurst's presence will force Mrs. Telcor's acceptance. She will never eschew meeting an earl."

"Dreaming again, William," she said gently. "If he utters one word in support of me, she will denounce him to all and sundry. Jasper cut me in front of her last week. You know she hates anyone who contradicts him. Didn't she take his part after people blamed you for the haywain fire he set when you were boys? You still do not understand our peril. Why do you think his lies spread so quickly and with so little scrutiny? Because he tells them first to her."

Leaving William to consider her parting shot, she sought out Mrs. Moulding. How many servants would Rockhurst bring? Should she add another course to dinner, or would additional removes suffice? What about linens? Did the green bedchamber's chimney need cleaning?

The questions buzzed through her mind, but she knew they were just distractions. She did not want to think about what this scheme might cost her family. William was a simple man who accepted the world at face value. He would never understand Jasper's ruthless cunning, which was one reason she hadn't revealed the confrontation that had started this. But in his ignorance, William thought it was all a misunderstanding that would disappear in time. So he had invited a man to stir the pot.

It could only create new trouble, which must again be laid at her door. But it was too late to cancel the invitation. Instead, she must convince Rockhurst that pursuing Jasper would ruin more lives.

Chapter Three

Blake shifted in his carriage seat, wondering for the hundredth time why he was here. After two days of talking to people, he understood Seabrook's ambivalence. Even knowing a fraction of the rumors would raise grave doubts about his sister's innocence. All was not well with the widow Parrish.

Yet he had promised to investigate the matter, and Seabrook deserved his best efforts. The lad had been well liked at school, though his dreams had been basic—improving the yields on his family estate, exercising good stewardship over the land and its dependents, and producing the heir who would carry on in the future. Nothing had changed, if the condition of his estate was any indication. The grounds were unpretentious but well kept. Hedges were tidy and the fields tended. Seabrook cared for his land, putting his meager resources into maintenance rather than squandering them on his own pleasure—which set him apart from the dandies who frequented London. Such a man would do whatever he could to help his sister, even if he suspected she might be guilty of at least some impropriety.

That might explain why he had not yet challenged Jasper. No matter how much the combatants tried, news of duels invariably became public. Whatever the outcome, it would attach another unsavory episode to Catherine's name. Or maybe Seabrook did not believe Jasper was responsible for the rumors. No one else had mentioned his name in that regard.

Again he shifted, resting one foot on the opposite

seat. He had to keep an open mind, at least until he'd spoken with Catherine and interviewed any witnesses. If the tales were false, or even exaggerated, he would try to temper people's outrage. Seabrook was right that the gossip was hurting more than Catherine. Learning that he had young sisters explained his request. William had to contain the damage before he could bring the girls out.

But Blake couldn't dismiss the possibility that Catherine was innocent. Evidence supported that conclusion as well, starting with the sheer volume of rumors—not merely the fact that the notorious widow's escapades were on every tongue but that every tongue cited a different tale. Then there was Seabrook's own behavior. Could a man who cared deeply for the land and its people keep a wanton in charge of his house and family? Apparently she had oversight of both.

As the carriage topped a rise, a modest manor appeared briefly in the distance, protected by a hill from the storms that swept in from the sea. The façade remained Tudor, hinting that the family had never been wealthy, but it offered welcome and the promise of peace.

Yesterday he'd called on his friend's aunt, Mrs. Crumleigh. She had been hosting an at-home, so he'd met a dozen of the local gossips. Without asking a single question, he'd heard tale after tale about Catherine Parrish—she seduced any man she could find, even servants and youths; she taught seductive arts to every young girl she met; she flaunted her disdain for propriety everywhere.

Mrs. Telcor's comments had been typical. "Shocking, absolutely shocking. I've never encountered such moral turpitude in one body. You would think her brother would turn her off to protect those girls from harm." She'd continued with a vehement diatribe condemning several of her exploits.

"Who is her current protector?" he'd asked when she paused for breath.

"She doesn't have one," she'd said, sniffing. "Few would mind if she did. A discreet affair is not unheard of. But she flouts every rule. Godless. The dear vicar would turn in his grave if he knew how his wife was conducting herself. And what that brother of hers is thinking to condone such behavior, I don't know. How is he to fire off those poor girls with this scandal in the family? No one would offer for someone corrupted by that woman's evil influence."

The gentlemen's club had also echoed with rumors—her visits to Torquay and Plymouth, where she had bedded half the seamen based at those ports; her trip to Taunton, where she had exposed a dozen schoolboys to her perversions; her calls throughout the parish that recruited participants for satanic orgies reminiscent of the old Hellfire Club, with her in the role of priestess.

Blake shook his head. Seabrook was puritanical. If he'd heard that last claim, he would have called out the speaker, then banished Catherine forever. He had nearly killed a fellow student at Eton for poking fun at the church. Anything hinting at blasphemy put him in a frenzy.

But the tales raised serious questions. None contained specifics. Where had the liaisons occurred? With whom? When? Who were the witnesses and why had they remained silent until now?

"No gentleman brags of his conquests," the White Hart innkeeper had insisted when asked to name one of Mrs. Parrish's paramours.

It was a lie, but Blake had not pressed. Though he'd learned to keep his own contacts private, he knew many gentlemen who graphically compared courtesans, opera dancers, widows, and matrons. Devereaux and Millhouse openly competed for ladies' favors. The betting books were crammed with their wagers naming this female or that.

So this lack of names was odd. The notorious widow entertained rakes, caroused with seamen, bedded students, tenants, servants, parishioners . . . Yet not one gossip had witnessed unsuitable behavior. Not one gentleman admitted sampling her charms.

How had she become so venal without anyone noticing? Even in London, everyone knew everything almost immediately. Servants rarely kept secrets.

If she was innocent, then her other claim must also be true—which meant Jasper Rankin was both clever and cunning. He had kept people so shocked that they hadn't noticed the lack of evidence. Fury had provoked public condemnations no one could easily abandon. The image of an immoral, unrepentant Catherine Parrish was now firmly ingrained. People might conclude that the tales were exaggerated, but they would fall back on the gossips' creed—*Where there is smoke, there must be fire*. The only way to change their minds was for Jasper to confess that he'd lied.

His carriage drew to a halt. A footman let down the steps.

Like the park, the manor showed attentive maintenance. The corner blocks of the sandstone building had been replaced sometime in the past century. As the carriage had swept up the drive, he'd glimpsed a half-timbered stable, its outside neatly whitewashed. And the paneled entrance hall was well proportioned.

"Welcome to Seabrook, my lord," said the footman, gesturing toward the stairs.

Blake looked, then froze as the bottom dropped out of his stomach. A woman was descending. Black hair. Blue eyes. Way too familiar.

He cursed under his breath. Here was that governess again, the one he'd had no luck tracing. Was her charge one of Seabrook's sisters? Perhaps rumor was crediting Catherine with the governess's exploits.

"You!" she snapped. Her hair was looser today, curling provocatively around her pale face. "How dare you follow me home!"

"I warned you I would discover your employer," he replied, though in truth, no one had recognized his description.

"*Threatened* is closer to the truth, sir. Why don't

you hold up a carriage or burn down a stable or two? It would be a less onerous way to amuse yourself."

"Rag-mannered baggage. I can't believe you pulled the wool over Seabrook's eyes."

"Shall I summon Lord Seabrook, madam?" asked the footman uncertainly.

"That won't be necessary, Rob." She inhaled deeply, then gestured toward a drawing room.

Blake followed, silent as he hurriedly rearranged his impressions. *Madam?* The footman's manner proclaimed that this woman was in charge.

"Who are you?" he managed once she shut the door.

"At last. An intelligent question." The drawing room's faded carpet made her coloring seem even more vibrant. "Mrs. Parrish, Lord Seabrook's sister. I will accept your apologies now, though only a empty-headed nodcock would have behaved so disgracefully. Parading your ignorance in public caused my daughter considerable distress."

He winced. "Forgive me, but—"

"Nothing here needs your attention. You will understand that I cannot offer refreshments. Perhaps in the future you will think before drawing unwarranted conclusions or intruding into business that does not concern you." She turned toward the door, clearly ready to escort him out.

"Not so fast, Mrs. Parrish," he said, crossing arms and ankles as he leaned against the mantel. Their eyes clashed across the width of the room. "I am not the only one prone to unwarranted assumptions. Perhaps you should summon your brother after all. I am here by his invitation."

"Damn! You must be—" She blanched.

"Blake Townsend, Earl of Rockhurst." He proffered a card.

Clearly dazed, she snatched it from his hand, then retreated to the window. "Dear Lord." She stared at the card as if it might bite. "Why did William drag you all the way from Oxfordshire? He has never mentioned you before."

"He didn't." Unsure what shocked her now, he decided to leave no room for further misunderstanding. "I was in Exeter on business. When I returned to the White Hart after our last meeting, I ran into Seabrook. I had not seen him since Eton, but he described your problem and asked me to investigate. I did not realize he was discussing you, of course."

"Of course. But what was he doing in Exeter?" she murmured, clearly bewildered. Before he could respond, she shook her head. "It matters not. What made him think you could help? I've never met anyone so eager to condemn without examining a single fact."

He could feel his face heat. "I beg your pardon, Mrs. Parrish. I cannot imagine why I behaved so badly. That was Jasper Rankin with you?"

She nodded. "He is adept at pretense, not that his acting excuses you. But no matter. William was mistaken. A man of your credulity cannot help me. Are you always so hasty to judge?"

"Never." His head reeled. Had he actually allowed someone to manipulate him into hurling lurid accusations at a lady? He never jumped to conclusions. He never accepted the unsupported word of one man as truth. He never—

But you did, reminded his conscience. *You were so furious that this intriguing a woman had feet of clay, that you lashed out without thought.*

He ignored it, unwilling to believe it. "I wronged you. It does not matter that it was an isolated incident. I must atone by exposing Rankin for the liar he is."

"Words." She stalked closer in a swirl of skirts. "Promise the moon, why don't you? It is just as attainable."

"Hardly."

"Do not be so quick to commit yourself. You know nothing of the situation."

"I know that rumor makes Jezebel seem pure com-

pared to you. I know that protesting your innocence
will accomplish nothing. I know that forcing Rankin
to confess is your only hope."

"Do you think that would work?" Her tone implied
that he was a simpleton as well as gullible. "Jasper is
as persuasive as Eden's snake and just as sly. Even he
cannot reverse opinion now. Words won't erase the
suspicions he cleverly planted. Evidence can prove
guilt, but it can never prove innocence. People will
believe that I am immoral and that he is conspiring
to keep the evidence secret."

"Not if he reveals his part in starting the tales." He
approved the way pacing swirled her skirt provocatively around long legs and raised color in her cheeks.
Admiration pulsed in his chest. She was a warrior. He
could picture her leading an army against injustice.

Yet her next words snapped the image as despair
crept into her voice. "You don't understand. His confession would merely identify him as the anonymous
l-lover I've supposedly been meeting. They will think
that a spat led him to revile me, but that we have now
reconciled and are trying to cover up our affair."

"You are the one who is ignorant," he said, but
gently. Her stutter as she choked out so innocuous
an indiscretion was additional evidence of innocence.
"Have you no idea how sordid the tales are? No lovers' spat would result in such revelations."

"What can be worse than liaisons with a dozen
men?"

"Plenty, and I doubt I heard everything yesterday.
The tales are clearly meant to destroy. But they can
be erased if Rankin admits the truth."

She laughed without humor. "You don't know Jasper. Nothing would compel him to do such a thing,
but even if you succeeded, it would do no good. No
one will believe him guilty of anything beyond high
spirits."

"Was it high spirits that prompted this campaign
against you?"

"Of course not. I insulted him. He seeks revenge. That is his way."

"Then we have a starting point. All things are possible, Mrs. Parrish. I will redeem your reputation. I owe you that much in atonement for my own insult."

Catherine closed her eyes, wishing that Rockhurst had turned out to be anyone but this man. How could she trust him after that confrontation in town? Granted, he had apologized, but she had seen first-hand how judgmental he could be. *Benevolent and fair-minded.* If William truly believed that, then she must question his judgment as well. Which might be a good idea. What had he been doing in Exeter? He had claimed vital business with the steward, then given her half a dozen errands, all of which he could easily have handled himself. So why had he gone to town? Were there other times he had lied?

Idiot!

It was obvious in retrospect. He must have followed her to see if the rumors were true. But clandestine surveillance was not his strength, so when he'd met Rockhurst, he had recruited the man. Under the guise of helping her, Rockhurst would assess how much damage she was causing so William could decide what to do with her. This was another instance of his priggishness overriding his sense. He had long decried the moral laxity so many men espoused.

She paced to the corner so she could blink back tears unobserved. If William had charged Rockhurst with spying on her, he would do so, regardless of where he stayed. It might be better to keep him close.

Then there was Laura. She had been so excited at the prospect of having an earl in the house. William's description of a fair-minded man blessed with both wealth and compassion had stirred her imagination. She was determined to win an offer.

Catherine flinched. Whatever her own impressions, Laura deserved a chance to judge Rockhurst for herself. They all knew the harsh truth. Raising enough money to visit Bath was unlikely, so this would probably be her last opportunity to snare a respectable husband—especially if Rockhurst was right and the rumors were worse than she'd heard. But Laura could attract him only if he were here.

So she must ignore her misgivings and let him undertake the impossible task of redeeming her reputation. Stifling a sigh at the necessity of baring her stupidity, she returned to face him. If only he were not so well set up.

"Try if you must," she said, shaking her head. "Not that I believe it is possible. Jasper has been avenging insults for years, but he has such a glib tongue that no one of consequence believes him capable of evil. And to be honest, I am his first victim from the upper classes."

"He preys on servants and the like?" He gestured toward the couch.

He could not sit until she had done so, she realized, chagrined at her lack of hospitality. "Would you care for wine?" she asked as she took her seat.

"No. How did you insult him? Even grave bodily injury hardly justifies this sort of spite."

"For you and most other men, perhaps, but Jasper's sensibilities are unusually tender." She clasped her hands, searching for words that would not cause worse trouble. "He cares for only two things—pleasure and himself. His father is the area's most influential man, so he grew up believing that he was better than the rest of us. If he wants something, he takes it. If the victims object, they pay. He allows no disrespect."

"I've met others like that, though usually with higher titles."

"That is in London. Jasper prefers to remain here, where he has little competition for power and glory." She paused, berating herself for allowing passion into her voice. Rockhurst already had a low opinion of her. Sounding like one of the Furies would not improve it.

She forced her hands to lie quietly in her lap. "He has always been quick to take offense and avenges even the slightest insult, no matter how inadvertent. His reprisals appear accidental, and no one can prove otherwise. Spirited young lords injure inferiors every day, merely by being their arrogant selves. In my case, I cannot even prove he started the rumors."

"You sound bitter, though I can hardly blame you. What insult triggered his attack on you," he repeated.

"He decided that he wanted me in his bed," she said bluntly, hurling the words out before she lost her nerve. She had never revealed the cause, fearing William's reaction. "I had ignored his innuendo and tried to avoid him, but he cornered me in the orchard one day and pressed his attentions." She shuddered at the memory of groping hands and slobbering lips. "When he refused to accept my rejection, I lost my temper and struck him."

"Where?"

She paused, searching for the right words.

"You applied a judicious knee where it would do the most good, I suppose," he said, flinching.

She nodded. "It was stupid, for it worsened the insult. I knew he would retaliate, but I couldn't help myself. Even worse, I threatened to reveal his reprisals unless he left me alone."

"You actually threatened a man who takes offense at any insult?"

She sighed. "Not the most intelligent thing I've ever done, but I was desperate to escape. If William had not appeared in the distance just then, Jasper would have overpowered me. As it was, he vowed that I would be sorry, so I wasn't surprised when he decided to ruin my reputation. You saw for yourself how he does it. His behavior is proprietary when he has an audience from the lower classes, implying that I am in league with him."

"What does that accomplish?"

"If they suspect my integrity, they will stop sharing information with me, which will prevent the upper classes from learning his vices. I have no recourse, for he is adept at manipulating impressions. If I rebuke him or deny his implications, I seem guilty and secretive. If I ignore him, I seem guilty and complicit. At first he used only suggestive words, but now he is pushing harder. I don't know what his purpose was in Exeter, but he staged that scene for your benefit. I'm sure it appeared intimate, but he was inflicting so much pain on my neck that I could not move."

His mouth thinned. "Why did you not protest the first rumor? Surely you could have raised doubts then. You are not the only person who knows his true character."

"No, but I do not visit town very often, so the story was firmly planted before I heard about it. And he has protected himself well. The gossips never question his statements. In their eyes, he walks on water. Those who understand him are from the lower classes, but no one would accept their word over his."

"You are not from the lower classes."

"That no longer matters. I should have considered the consequences that day. Once he realized that I saw past his genial façade, he had to destroy my credibility. It is the only way to retain the respect he craves."

"So we will reveal his attacks on others, forcing people to question his integrity." Rockhurst was frowning.

She shook her head. "You don't understand. These rumors are the only reprisal that he would deny. If we accuse him of destroying a tenant's crops, he will don an expression of great sorrow and agree that it was a most unfortunate business. He and his friends had consumed far too much wine that night and should never have attempted a cross-country ride."

"I see. He passes it off as high spirits, makes a token payment for the damage, and everyone believes him a fine fellow who has his dependents' best interests at heart. No one can prove his motive."

"Exactly. The victims know, for he always vows revenge at the time of the insult. But there are no witnesses to that threat, so no one can prove it. Since they are from the lower classes—Jasper is enthusiastic about keeping people in their place, which is one reason he pursues even the slightest insult—few people even hear of the incidents. I know about them only because I continue visiting members of Harold's parish."

"Seabrook mentioned that the current vicar prefers hunting."

She nodded, but declined to share her views of a church run by doddering fools and younger sons who wanted nothing but the income from their livings.

"Doesn't Rankin care that his actions affect others besides his victim? In your case, it is hurting your entire family."

"Why should he? It increases my punishment, for he puts all blame on my shoulders. It is my fault that William's courtship is faring badly. It is my fault that few people call and that our invitation to this year's harvest ball was canceled. If I had not turned him down, none of us would suffer."

"He should be stopped."

"I agree, but there is nothing you or anyone else can do. Jasper has no regrets and no remorse. He believes he is upholding the social order. Disrespect for their betters can push the lower classes into unrest and open rebellion. We wouldn't want England to go the way of France, now, would we?" Again she paused to restore her composure. "Personally, I think he is unbalanced, but nothing can be done. Trying to change him will only cause worse damage."

"His father?"

"Ignores him. Lord Rankin did his duty by producing an heir. That left him free to pursue his own pleasures, which do not include devoting time to his family. I doubt he even noticed when his wife died. He was in London at the time and did not return for the burial." She thrust aside her disgust over the cold life at Rankin Park. Jasper had come by his selfishness honestly. "Face facts, Lord Rockhurst, there isn't a threat you could make that would force Jasper to confess. And most of the gossips would dismiss such a confession, for they would know it was coerced. William doesn't recognize or understand evil, so he believes a little pressure in the right quarter might help, but nothing will rectify this situation."

She rose. Continuing this discussion could only lead to tears. Despair already threatened to overwhelm her.

Turning him over to Mrs. Moulding, she informed Laura that he had arrived, then headed for the nursery. Sarah must learn that the man who had frightened her in town was now a welcome guest in the house.

This was not one of her better days.

Chapter Four

B lake had wanted to scowl since Mrs. Parrish had
all but thrown him out of the drawing room, but
he wasn't able to indulge himself until he finally got
rid of the overly enthusiastic housekeeper. Where had
his sense gone?

I will redeem your reputation.

Twice he had uttered that vow—not to try, but to
succeed.

Fool!

He had always been careful never to promise what
he couldn't deliver. The integrity of his word lay at
the core of his honor as a gentleman. Now he had
sworn to accomplish the impossible.

Manipulating public opinion was not one of his
skills. He was a straightforward man who faced problems head-on and preferred the unvarnished truth.
That was how he had rescued his inheritance from
ruin and recognized Dornbras as evil when Max had
not. And it showed him just how futile his efforts
would be this time. Jasper Rankin was a master of
manipulation and deceit. Defeating him would require
a great deal of luck and skills he neither possessed
nor admired.

But he had to try, he admitted, peering out the window. A small formal garden gave way to lawn, then
to a lake with a Roman folly perched on its shore. He
had given his word. Failure would damage his reputation less than reneging would.

At least he now understood why Catherine had refused to tell William the full truth. She knew her brother well.

William had been well liked at Eton, but his classmates knew better than to provoke him. He had a wicked temper when anyone threatened someone he valued, and he didn't always think clearly when his blood was up.

Terror had flashed in Catherine's eyes when she'd recounted the confrontation in the orchard. *He would have overpowered me . . .* She was not a hysterical woman prone to dramatic charges. Nor was she the sort to imagine danger where none existed. Thus she must already have been under attack when her brother appeared. If the attack had continued, Jasper would have ravished her.

So she had remained silent. William would have challenged Jasper—might still do so if he discovered the truth. A duel, or even the offer of one, would make the situation worse as Jasper twisted it to his own purpose. The gossips would assume that Seabrook had caught the pair *en flagrante* but was bent on defending the indefensible, blood being thicker than water. Thus a challenge would make her look even guiltier.

Beyond that, Seabrook was no marksman, unless he had developed a sudden interest in pistols since leaving school. He had always refrained when his classmates competed, claiming that a pistol's recoil aggravated an old break in his hand.

On the other hand, the lack of challenge could also play into Jasper's hand by proving that Catherine had remained silent. Would he twist her reticence against her? If people assumed that William knew about Catherine's lovers, they would see his equanimity as proof that the stories were true.

Blake dropped into the chair nearest the fire, frowning as he gazed into the flames. Speculating on who might think what and why served no purpose. He was no good at it and would doubtless get it all wrong anyway. It was more important to plan his next move.

He should not have let her send him away. He needed details of the other cases she'd mentioned and more information about the Rankins, both father and son. Her explanation of Jasper's motives didn't make sense, so there must be more behind this than she was saying.

An angry, unbalanced man might strike back harder than the situation warranted, but not to this extent— unless he was terrified. But what could Jasper fear from Catherine? She was the first to admit that baring his other revenges would do no good. Even crying rape would harm her far more than him. A widow could hardly claim compromise to force him into marriage.

He needed to find out when the first rumors had appeared. If it had been immediately, then perhaps Jasper's initial purpose had been to stave off a duel by proving that a challenge was unnecessary because Catherine had no virtue to defend.

He shook his head. Catherine would not know the timing—she'd admitted that the rumors had been established before she'd heard them—but there were other questions he should have asked. Would have, if he'd not still been reeling over her identity. His mind had wandered too often to the stunning combination of black hair and blue eyes, to the way her skirts swirled as she stalked about the room.

Again he cursed himself for a fool. Distractions would make the task even worse. Only by concentrating on business would he have any chance of success.

When the flames reminded him of how her eyes sparked in anger, he jumped up. Pulling out his writing case, he began a list of everyone he knew who had connections near Exeter. He needed information about the Rankins beyond what Catherine might know, but he had met neither of them himself. The viscount had not attended London social affairs, visited Brighton, or occupied his seat in Parliament since Blake had been in town. Jasper had attended neither

Eton nor Oxford. According to Catherine, he rarely left the area.

Two hours later, Blake sealed the last letter and summoned his valet. It was time to dress for dinner.

He had come to one decision while writing. He could not question Catherine during meals lest he trigger William's temper by revealing facts the man did not know.

Cursing his valet for making him late, Blake rushed downstairs. Between tardiness and his outburst in town, Catherine would think him completely rag-mannered. Yet he hated to argue with Harris. He owed the valet for accepting a host of menial chores while Max corrected problems at his understaffed estate. And he hated to damage any man's pride. Harris had been with him for fifteen years, even remaining during the lean years following his father's death. So when the man had refused to allow him out of the room until his cravat was properly tied, Blake bit his tongue and said nothing. Harris's credit in the servants' hall would be diminished if his master displayed inferior dress.

But his tardiness didn't matter. Catherine was not yet down.

"Rockhurst!" exclaimed Seabrook, clasping Blake's hand and thumping him heartily on the shoulder. "We are so grateful that you agreed to help us."

"Seabrook." The effusive welcome was alarming. Even his rash vow to salvage Catherine's reputation should not elicit this much warmth. He hadn't felt this uneasy since last Season.

The feeling intensified when he glanced around the old-fashioned drawing room. A lady stood by the fireplace. She had to be all of twenty and was dressed to the nines in a gown more suited to a ball than a family dinner. As she caught his eye, she fluttered her fan and smiled.

Matchmaker!

His heart sank. Seabrook's sisters were not young girls. The baron might wish to prove Catherine's innocence, but his real motive was to find a suitor for this sister.

He cursed his blindness. Given Seabrook's age and that of Mrs. Parrish, he should have suspected that any other sisters were ripe for marriage. Between a limited dowry and the recent rumors, this one would be hard-pressed to attract an offer. Which made her dangerous.

More curses filled his mind.

This cast grave doubts on Seabrook's other claims. The man probably believed the rumors but claimed Catherine was innocent to improve this sister's chances. If his honor remained intact, he would be content with introducing them.

Don't make assumptions, he reminded himself. Desperation could tempt even good men to dishonor. Installing an eligible gentleman in the house would provide opportunities to force the issue.

Had Catherine condoned this plot? He had believed her innocent after today's meeting, but now he had to reconsider. He had judged her in part on her kinship to William, but he had not seen the baron in years. Men could change, and many did. And their siblings did not always reflect the same character. He need look no further than Dornbras, who was evil to the core, though his numerous siblings were stodgy paragons of virtue.

Was Catherine lying? Perhaps she had terminated their meeting so abruptly because her control was slipping. She had yet to arrive in the drawing room—odd for a woman whose future supposedly rested on his ability to divert gossip.

He stifled his rising fury. Dishonor did not invalidate his vow, so he must remain here long enough to discover the truth. But he must keep his wits about him if he hoped to emerge intact. He could trust no one.

"Forgive me for being out when you arrived," continued Seabrook. "I trust your room is comfortable?"

Blake nodded.

"I don't believe you've met my sister, Laura." He smiled, pulling Blake closer to the girl.

"My lord." She fluttered her lashes.

"Miss Seabrook," he said coolly, keeping his face neutral.

Seabrook's smile faltered, but Laura ignored the rebuff. "We are delighted that you could visit, my lord. November is usually quite dull, but I am convinced that everyone will flock to meet you." The fan waved coquettishly, giving her smile the same predatory look as that of Miss Coburn, the most blatant of last Season's fortune hunters.

"I am here to investigate your sister's difficulty," he reminded her.

"Of course, but that will hardly consume much time. William mentioned your success at vanquishing tyrants. You will have no trouble bending others to your will."

This time he made no response. Her lighthearted dismissal of Catherine's problem irritated him. He backed a pace as she leaned closer, then noticed that William's cheeks were pink. At her mention of his praise or at her unwarranted flattery?

She widened her smile. "I don't know why people believe these tales, anyway. They even contradict each other, as I pointed out to Helen Hawkins last week—she's the squire's daughter and usually thinks quite clearly, but this time she wouldn't listen. She has a hopeless *tendre* for Jasper, poor thing. Not that he would look twice at her, being so high in the instep. He would never settle for less than a duke's daughter, and it wouldn't surprise me if he thought himself worthy of Princess Charlotte, for all she's only fifteen."

"Then he will be disappointed." He kept Seabrook from slipping away by nodding toward another girl, who was reading in the corner. "And who might that be?"

"That's just Mary," said Laura, dismissing her with a shrug. "She always has her nose in a book. I don't know how she expects to make her bows to society when she ignores everyone who calls. I've told her and told her that she must learn to speak up and be noticed, but she invariably hides in the corner."

"Another sister?" he asked, for it was not clear from the girl's dress whether she was a member of the family or a poor cousin. She was ignoring his arrival.

Seabrook nodded, obviously irritated. "Mary," he snapped. "Put the book down and welcome our guest."

Mary jumped, then hastily shoved the book out of sight. "Forgive me, William. I did not hear you come in."

"Obviously, or you would not again be reading in the drawing room. Have you no manners at all?"

Mary blushed.

Blake coughed into his hand to hide a grin. This girl was more intriguing than her flirtatious sister—not that he was interested; she could not be above eighteen. But his cousin Jacob might find her much to his liking.

Setting that thought aside until he knew her better, he waited while Seabrook made formal introductions, then kept all three talking, cutting Laura off when she grew too voluble, asking Mary questions when she became silent, and preventing William from leaving. He wanted no tête-à-têtes until he divined everyone's goals. Only Catherine was safe. Even if she harbored secret motives behind that supposedly innocent façade, he could meet her without fear. She could hardly cry foul without further ruining herself.

But where was she? His list of questions was growing by the minute. Had she used his concern for victims to elicit the vow that chained him here? Was her absence deliberate, to let Laura monopolize his attention? Would she join them for dinner or eat later?

The mantel clock struck five, with no sign of a butler to announce the meal. He ground his teeth, for Catherine's absence would force him to escort Laura into the dining room. Precedence demanded that he accompany the highest-ranking female, as he was the highest male. Catherine was both the eldest sister and the nominal hostess.

"Forgive me for being late," Catherine said, hurrying into the drawing room. "We had a small crisis upstairs."

"Oh?" Seabrook frowned.

"Annie injured her ankle."

"Oh, no!" Mary's hand flew to her mouth. "Why didn't you call me?"

"There was no need. It is only a minor sprain." Catherine joined the circle, filling the space Blake created by stepping away from Laura.

"Is Sarah all right?" asked Mary.

"Why wouldn't she be?" snapped Laura.

Mary lapsed into silence, but Blake could see that the question had reflected genuine concern.

Catherine must have understood. "Rob carried Annie up to bed, but merely as a precaution. Sarah made sure she was comfortable, then returned to the nursery to eat dinner. Hannah is with her."

Mary relaxed.

"I take it Annie is a favorite?" said Blake, holding Catherine close with the question so Laura could not push her aside.

"She has cared for Sarah since birth, coming with us from the vicarage."

"Very important, then." Blake stifled a pang for his own nurse, who had been dearer than his mother when he was young. Might still be if she had not succumbed to a fever when he'd been fifteen.

"But not worth this much attention when we have a guest," said Laura, managing to excise most of the sharpness from her tone. "You were telling us about your business in Devonshire, were you not, my lord?"

He was not. He had been listening to Mary's description of Exeter cathedral. Fortunately Rob arrived to announce dinner, saving him from a rude retort. He wondered what Laura would say if he admitted that his original business had been accompanying sev-

eral courtesans to a celebratory house party. Granted,
that had been a month ago, and he had since discovered better reasons for remaining, but painting himself
as a rakehell might make her reconsider attaching him.
Of course, it would also make his investigation more
difficult. Laura did not strike him as someone who
could keep information to herself.

"Mrs. Parrish?" He offered his arm.

Catherine's frown closed Laura's mouth, which had
begun a protest, but he didn't know if she was ob-
jecting to Laura's rag manners or to her pursuit of a
guest lured to the house under false pretenses.

Seabrook shrugged, offering his own arm to Laura
and leaving Mary to bring up the rear.

Catherine smiled as Rockhurst seated her in the
hostess's chair. She had suspected that a man of such
impeccable reputation might be a stickler for protocol,
but it made little difference. As the highest-ranking
male guest, he sat at her left. Laura sat on William's
right, which put them side by side, making conversation easy.

"We need to discuss Jasper in detail," he murmured
before assuming his own chair. "I have a number of
questions."

"Tomorrow morning," she promised. "I must spend
the evening with Sarah. Hannah has other duties."

"She has no governess?" The question was casual,
but his mouth twitched as if he wished the words back.
Might he be embarrassed at the reminder of their
first encounter?

"Mary and I share the schoolroom duties, and
Annie looks after her other needs. She is—"

"I was not criticizing." His interruption made her
realize that she'd sounded defensive.

"Of course not," she agreed, though plenty of people did. Some thought William should provide one,
though he lacked the means. Her sisters' governess
had left four years ago and not been replaced.

Rockhurst pulled her from the gloomy memories.

"May I call on Sarah in the morning? I owe her an apology for frightening her. Even had my outburst been justified, accosting you in front of her was wrong."

"She will expect you."

To prevent further conversation, she issued a spate of unnecessary instructions to Rob so Laura could claim Rockhurst's attention. But his admission warmed her heart. She had been fighting trepidation since he had arrived, but this proved that William was right. Rockhurst would make Laura an excellent husband—assuming he chose to make an offer. She would give them every opportunity to become acquainted, but she drew the line at coercion.

Laura needed to remember that, she decided a few minutes later. Her behavior bordered on the unladylike as she exerted herself to appear fascinating. Even William was working too hard at extolling her virtues.

"Laura is a remarkable musician," he declared over the soup. "I had to buy her a pianoforte so she could explore the nuances of that German chap's work."

Laura choked. "It had nothing to do with nuances, William. I've explained that often enough. Beethoven's music demands emotion. It demands passion. It cannot be performed on a harpsichord. Surely you understand what I mean, my lord." She laid a pleading hand on Rockhurst's arm.

"So I've been told," he said stiffly, then reached for his wineglass with his left hand, breaking the contact.

"What can you tell us of the king?" Catherine asked to divert his attention from the unbecoming frown flashing across Laura's face. "Is there any hope of recovery?"

"I doubt it." He shook his head. "He showed signs of improvement last spring, even managing a ride about Windsor Park in May, but he suffered another relapse in July. The doctors recently padded his room to protect him from injury."

"Poor man. I suppose the Regency will become permanent, then?"

"If nothing changes by January, when its restrictions lapse, giving the prince all the powers of the monarch. It is not yet clear how he will use them."

"You refer to his abandonment of the Whigs."

He nodded, but before he could explain, Laura again claimed his attention. "Tell us of the Season. You must miss the excitement."

"Hardly. London is quite exhausting." He sounded bored.

Catherine tried to frown Laura into curbing her enthusiasm, but she could not catch her eye. Not good, she admitted, tensing. Laura's moods could be quite volatile, which created tension in the family and did not impress suitors. They had thought she'd outgrown the tendency, for she had been even-tempered for several months, but tonight she was unbecomingly aggressive.

"How can you call it exhausting?" demanded Laura, bridling at his statement. "It must be exhilarating. Tessa Umber was in London last Season and can talk for hours and hours about balls and routs and Venetian breakfasts and theater and opera and her visit to Vauxhall Gardens. She met the most diverting people and swears she was busy from morning to night, receiving so many invitations that she could attend half a dozen events a day."

"Exactly. And after a time, every gathering seems like every other one. The same people. The same gossip. The same food. Utterly exhausting." Rockhurst turned away to accept a serving of fish from Rob.

Catherine gestured for Bill to fill his glass, then counted the side dishes to make sure everything had been served. By then, Laura had the conversational bit firmly between her teeth and was running with it, regaling Rockhurst with Tessa's favorite tales and repeating London gossip that was at least six months out of date. She was also making grandiose plans for his stay, trying to fill the days with activity enough to rival London and ignoring that fact that they were ostracized from local society. Even William was frowning.

"I doubt that a picnic will be possible," Catherine commented, interrupting a description of the home wood's excellence for alfresco dining. "Last week's warmth is gone. Charlie claims it will rain tomorrow and remain cold for at least a week afterward. You know he is rarely wrong."

"Well, pooh." Laura pouted prettily. "But at least we can attend Saturday's assembly in Exeter."

"Must we?" protested Mary. "A new theater company arrived yesterday, and I was hoping to watch a performance. If we go to the assembly, the sticklers will cut us."

"No one would dare cut an earl," swore Laura. "He would be the highest-ranking man there. And isn't his purpose to force harridans like Mrs. Telcor to accept us?"

Catherine started to object, for Laura did not understand the gravity of their position, but William interrupted.

"We can do both," he said, smiling. "Saturday's play is scheduled for two o'clock to allow people to attend the assembly."

She stared. William was so intent on fostering a match with Laura that he had forgotten the scandal. They could not attend the assembly. Granted, it was open to anyone with the price of admission, but appearing would force everyone to choose sides on her reputation, making it harder to change their minds in the future. And what would happen when they arrived? Even an earl lacked sufficient power to control tempers. There was bound to be enough unpleasantness to ruin the evening for everyone.

But Mary prevented a protest. "Can we?" she demanded, sounding more excited than she'd been in weeks. She rarely left the estate, so an outing would be good for her. "What a wonderful brother you are, William. I've wanted to see *Mysteries of the Black Tower* this age and more."

Catherine bit her lip. Maybe it would work if she stayed behind. Rockhurst's credit might defray doubts about her family.

She watched as he took advantage of the informal setting to draw everyone into the conversation, quizzing William about the recent harvest and asking Mary about the book she was reading. It was so good to see Mary talking that Catherine nearly protested when Laura interrupted with another plea for London *on-dits,* then launched a monologue that included descriptions of a ball Tessa had attended, the most recent tales about the Regent, a local confrontation between Squire Pott and his prize pig that had left the squire stuck in a mud wallow, and a contretemps in London during which Lord Blackthorn had supposedly disowned his heir—which was probably false, judging by Rockhurst's expression.

Catherine frowned. Laura had been the area's diamond before Jasper's rumors put them all under suspicion, but tonight she had abandoned moderation, adopting the frenzied gaiety that had already cost her two suitors. As soon as they were alone, they must review proper manners.

Blake finished his blancmange, then sighed in relief as the ladies left the room. The food had been excellent, but this dinner had seemed even longer than his last meal with the Regent. Laura had talked constantly—brightly, vivaciously, flirtatiously, but incessantly. Mary had rarely spoken except in response to questions, though he suspected that this was in self-defense. Laura corrected much of what she said, often sharply.

He had managed to start William talking about the estate at one point, but then the man had abruptly fallen silent. Had he recalled his reason for issuing this invitation, or had Laura kicked him under the table? Blake couldn't tell. Nor could he think. His ears rang from endless chatter.

Catherine had offered occasional relief, conducting

intelligent conversation on a variety of topics, but he'd soon realized that she intervened whenever he was too irritated with Laura to bear her prattle a moment longer. Each time, Laura had been more subdued when she reclaimed his attention, though it never lasted.

By the end of the meal, he had acquitted Mary of conspiring against him, but he had yet to decide on the others. William was as bad as any London match-maker, extolling Laura's virtues and drawing attention to her blonde hair and blue eyes. Catherine remained an enigma. He could not tell whether her efforts to deflect his attention were based on a hostess's desire to set a guest at ease or a matchmaker's determination to show her protégée in the best light.

He had no doubts about Laura. She posed a serious danger. Desperation lurked beneath her forced con-viviality and bright chatter. Why was she unwed at the advanced age of twenty? She was pretty enough to attract offers despite her reduced circumstances, so he had to suspect a serious flaw. Girls who knew they would never see London chose the best of their local suitors. But whatever her former reasons, Jasper's at-tacks promised her a bleak future. With scandal swirl-ing about the family, he represented her only option.

Hours of icy responses and lengthy silences must have warned her that he had no intention of offering. She was too like the girls he saw in London every Season. A wife who never stopped talking would make his home intolerable. Mary would be better suited, though he had no interest in her, either. Again the image of Cousin Jacob surfaced. Perhaps he should introduce them.

William drained the last of his port, then led him to the drawing room.

Blake suggested that Laura demonstrate her mas-tery of Beethoven's latest offering. Then he engaged William in a spirited discussion of agricultural reform.

Two sonatas later, Seabrook left on the flimsy ex-cuse of speaking with Rob. Blake suggested that Laura

entertain them with Mozart, then detached Mary from
her book to ask about Catherine's work in the parish
and how the rumors were affecting it.

He slipped away before Laura finished the coda, not
trusting her to perform another piece. At least she
was talented. He would be listening to a lot of music
in the days ahead.

Chapter Five

When Blake entered the library the next morning, he was not happy. Sleep had been a long time coming. He wanted to blame the lumpy bed, but he'd slept quite soundly on worse. The real culprit was his mind.

He had lain awake half the night as his thoughts spun in unproductive circles. If his encounter with Catherine had not muddled his thinking, he would have realized Seabrook had ulterior motives for this invitation. Men did not ask virtual strangers to investigate members of their family.

She had a most unsettling effect on him. He still couldn't believe he had lost his temper and promised more than he could deliver. Yet that was not his only mistake. In Exeter, the black-haired woman and bright-eyed girl had occupied his thoughts even after he believed she was immoral. Why else had he failed to ask Mrs. Telcor or Mrs. Crumleigh about William's family? It would have prepared him for the surprises he'd encountered at the manor.

Regrets were useless, of course. The past would never change, no matter how much he might wish it. He'd wasted more than a week on pointless invective after his father's death, but he could not afford to make that mistake this time. Allowing his mind to drift, even pleasantly, would expose him to danger from Laura.

Spending time with Catherine posed a different problem. To redeem her reputation, he must learn as much as possible about her, Jasper, and the other victims. Yet lengthy discussions would feed the very gossip he sought to repress. Even keeping their meetings open would not help, for servants shared information about their masters. Some gossips would assume that he was her latest paramour. Others might recognize the truth, but that, too, was dangerous. He did not want Jasper to learn of his interest as yet.

Both William and Catherine had described Jasper as society's darling. Thus people would refuse to cooperate if they thought he was seeking evidence against the man. Even worse, Jasper would consider him a threat and seek to discredit him. Both actions would make it much harder to fulfill his vow. So he must keep his purpose secret.

But hiding his association with Catherine would leave the impression that he was courting Laura, thus raising expectations—few would expect Mary to attract his attention. Even if Laura swore they were mutually disinterested, her credit would suffer if he left without making an offer.

Claiming long friendship with Seabrook—which was an exaggeration at best—would not eliminate expectations, for he had never called before. And anyone who had visited London would know that Seabrook was nothing like his other friends. In fact, anyone who had been in London recently would assume that he was using a tenuous connection to Seabrook to sample the favors of the delectable Catherine.

He swore. His reputation could easily ruin any chance of helping her. But there was nothing he could do about it. Cursing the past never worked. All he could do was address the present and take steps to see that problems did not recur in the future.

One of those problems was Catherine. When he had finally fallen asleep—only four hours ago—she had invaded his dreams, inviting him to share her passion and calling him twenty sorts of fool when he held back.

Temptation personified, he'd decided on awakening. He had been drawn to her since his first glimpse in

Exeter, but he was not interested in a well-bred mistress encumbered with a child. Nor did he need a dream to remind him that avoiding intimacy was the only way to prevent mistakes that would destroy them both.

Now he closed the library door and joined her near the fire, welcoming its warmth. Charlie's predicted storm had arrived at dawn, raising the damp chill typical of winter.

"I trust Sarah slept well and that Annie's ankle is no worse," he said, forgoing a formal greeting.

Her eyes widened, but she followed his lead. "Quite. The ankle is much improved, allowing her to resume her duties."

"Then we can discuss Jasper's revenges. You mentioned that he punished any insult. I need details if I am to help."

"I actually know very little." She stared into the fire. "My husband considered him venal, though he never explained why. It wasn't until after his death that I began hearing tales firsthand. The villagers often ask my advice. Others seek a friendly ear when they are troubled, some from as far away as Exeter."

"So I understand." Mary had described her activities.

Her hands twisted, drawing attention to her slender fingers. "Jenkins was the first case I discovered in detail. He has a tailor's shop in Exeter. Jasper ordered a complete wardrobe from him—a little surprising, for he usually patronizes a tailor in Bath and occasionally sends his valet to London. Jenkins welcomed the business, of course. His customers are mostly merchants and gentry, so it puffed his consequence to dress a viscount's heir."

"I am sure it did. And I suppose purchase of fabric and thread put him in debt."

"Exactly. He postponed other commissions so he could complete the order before Jasper returned from a house party."

"Then Jasper refused to pay."

But she was shaking her head. "Nothing so blatant. That would have tarnished his own image—he pretends to be the area's benefactor, a gentleman whose honor is inviolable and whose magnanimity exceeds expectations. Of course he would pay—as soon as he was satisfied. But he no sooner took delivery than he had to send a jacket back because a sleeve hung poorly. Then there was the crooked seam on a waistcoat, too much shoulder padding, insufficient thigh padding—"

Blake shook his head. "What did he expect of a country tailor?"

"Exactly that," she assured him. "As days turned to weeks and then months, Jasper kept up his complaints, postponing payment because he was not yet satisfied. Repairs left Jenkins no time to serve his other customers. Without income, he could not pay his creditors."

"Diabolical," he murmured.

She nodded. "Inevitably one of them complained to the magistrate, sending Jenkins to debtors' prison. It took his family eight months to raise enough to free him."

"The magistrate did not demand that Jasper pay his own debt?"

"Of course not. The magistrate is Lord Rankin. Why should he force his son to pay for inferior goods? Not that the request arose. He refused to allow Jasper's name into a dispute between a tailor and a silk merchant. Though he has ignored his son since birth, he won't hear a word against his heir, particularly from a tradesman."

"Hardly unusual. But I have to question your basic assumptions. Many young men make the mistake of ordering clothes from an inferior tailor, then go through the frustrating process of trying to make them fit. I can recall half a dozen cases among my own friends, including a particularly hideous coat I ordered myself. So why do you think this situation was intentional?"

"Several reasons. First, Jasper had rarely purchased

more than an occasional neckcloth from Jenkins in the past. Second, he has publicly worn none of the clothes Jenkins made. Not one item, though he has had them for more than a year."

"Not one?" He raised a brow.

She shook her head. "Yet Jenkins is a good tailor. You can scoff about country tradesmen, but Sir Richard proclaims him the equal of all save Weston. Perhaps he exaggerates, but he is quite particular about his wardrobe." She shifted a fire screen to shield her face. "Third, Jenkins is known for sober styles and quality seams. His customers are tradesmen, clergy, solicitors, and the like. His coats have a quiet elegance that appeals to men like Sir Richard, but Jasper is a dandy enamored of bright colors, extreme styles, and flamboyant decoration."

"I noticed," he murmured, recalling the towering shirt points, oversize buttons, and excessive fobs favored by the man who had accosted Catherine in town. Such a man would not patronize a tailor who dressed vicars and barristers.

"Then there is character," she continued. "Jasper contradicts many of Jenkins's claims, yet I know Jenkins to be honest. He swears that Jasper plotted against him. I believe him."

"Why?"

"Because he is honest." Her hand gripped the chair arm.

He laid his atop it to calm her, then cursed as heat sizzled into his palm. "I meant why was Jasper trying to ruin him?" he explained, releasing her hand before he turned the friendly gesture into a caress. "What had Jenkins done?"

"Nothing. Jasper needed a scapegoat." Despite the screen, her cheeks were red. Blake forced his eyes to the fire. Perhaps she also needed space, for she retreated to the window and stared out. "A month earlier, Jasper had ordered a waistcoat from Jenkins, specifying in great detail what he wanted—a friend's letter had mentioned seeing such a garment in London, but Jasper didn't have time to commission it from his usual tailor before leaving for a house party."

"Was the waistcoat unsatisfactory?"

"That depends on your perspective. It was made exactly as Jasper had ordained, though Jenkins had tried to talk him into several changes. Jasper was delighted—until one of his friends disparaged his taste the first time he wore it."

"What was wrong with it?"

"From Jenkins's description, I would call it gaudy and wholly unsuitable for a formal occasion. Since Jasper has never accepted blame for anything in his life, he decided Jenkins had deliberately turned him into a laughingstock. By the time he returned home, he had convinced himself that Jenkins had twisted his suggestions, changing an elegant evening waistcoat into a costume suited only to a jester."

"Petty. And disturbing if he actually believes it."

"He does. One reason he deludes people so easily is that he first deludes himself, so he always sounds sincere." Shivering from the chill near the window, she resumed her chair. "He is also sly. Last spring he seduced the chandler's daughter, leaving her with child."

"What had she done?" He folded his hands in his lap to prevent further touching.

"Nothing. His real target was the chandler himself. Amy's ruin hurt Carruthers worse than if he'd lost his business. Once he discovered who was responsible, he was even more distraught, for he knew he had no recourse. Complaining would merely draw worse. He knows Jasper's ways too well, for he has long watched him destroy others. He and Harold often discussed ways to manage him."

"Is that why Jasper attacked?"

She shook her head. "They were always careful that no one overheard them—or so Carruthers swears. But he sometimes warns others of their peril. Someone probably heard him issue such a warning to the innkeeper at the Golden Stag. Dougan was furious after

Jasper threw a platter at a serving maid, breaking her arm—the girl was his daughter. If Carruthers hadn't talked Dougan out of it, he would have complained."

"What did Carruthers say?"

"He reminded Dougan that Jasper could easily burn down the inn if he caused trouble." Fury flashed across her face. "Neither man reported their talk to others, but it is possible that a servant overheard them. They were behind the taproom at the time."

"But that makes no sense," he insisted. "No one in his right mind would strike out over something so petty. Jasper should be grateful that Carruthers saved him some trouble. Attacking the man would make it more likely that the earlier tale would become public."

"You are assuming that Jasper is in his right mind. I have long suspected that he is not. There's hardly an inn in the district that hasn't sustained damage from one of his tantrums."

"Yet no one in society knows of his deeds?"

"How many society figures talk to innkeepers beyond demanding and paying for service?" She glared until he acknowledged that truth with a nod. "Carruthers's crime was not calming Dougan's fury but understanding Jasper's ways. Beyond that, he discussed Jasper's misdeeds with others. Jasper is attacking me for the same reason. Turning down his advances would have drawn a reprisal, but it is my knowledge of his other attacks that drove him to destroy me."

"He fears exposure." It fit with his own thoughts, though the apparent depth of that fear still surprised him.

"It is not fear so much as annoyance. Carruthers could never undermine his credit—he is merely a tradesman, so who would believe him? But Jasper would have to spend time refuting the charges."

"How awful," he said with a sarcastic snort. "It would divert him from worthy endeavors like seducing girls and damaging property."

She laughed, but quickly sobered. "You forget that understanding him destroys respect." Her head shook.

"Another attack occurred just before harvest. Jasper
and several friends destroyed a tenant's grain fields in
a reckless midnight race. Jones had complained to
Lord Rankin's steward after another of Jasper's rides
disrupted the planting last spring."

"Yet he waited several months."

"If he had retaliated immediately, Jones could have
repaired the damage and realized a reasonable profit
from the crop. By waiting, he inflicted severe losses
that will cause distress for at least a year."

"I cannot believe anyone would be that devious."
Nor did he believe that a man would do so much harm
for so little cause—and so little personal gain. The
long wait eliminated anger as a factor.

"That was my first reaction when I heard the earlier
stories," she admitted. "But the pattern of abuse is
clear. Take Jones. Four fields were destroyed, though
the plots were widely scattered. Yet no other tenant
suffered the least bit of damage."

"None?"

"Not one, though the smallest of Jones's plots is
surrounded by other fields and can be reached only
by a narrow path. High-spirited riders indulging in a
cross-country race would hardly enter and leave in a
single line along the same trail."

"Persuasive evidence, so why would others believe
it was an accident?"

"Jasper claims he sobered up enough to realize
what they were doing, so he forced his companions to
leave in an orderly fashion. He has been praised for
his concern and swift action."

Blake shook his head. The gossips of Exeter must
lack reason.

Catherine continued. "Another fact is that every
victim provoked him, though few did so wittingly. If
he was merely careless or subject to high spirits, that
would not be the case."

"And this has been going on for years."

"Two or three instances a year that I know of.
Sometimes more. It may have been more when he was

younger. Since the lower classes rarely travel—some
of our villagers have never even seen Exeter, though
it is barely four miles away—it would have taken time
for word to spread. Now the lower classes for miles
around are so cowed they avoid him, reducing the
potential for irritation. But there is nothing you can
do to stop him. I doubt even his father could control
him anymore. Jasper believes the man is an old fool
whose best contribution to the world would be to die.''

"I can see why the task is so formidable," Blake
said, frowning. Though he had peppered her with
skeptical questions, he believed her. Yet few would.
And others would applaud Jasper's ability to control
the lower classes. Fear of the French contagion perme-
ated society. French émigrés were always at hand, a
perpetual reminder of what could happen when people forgot their place.

He shook his head, taking a turn about the room
while he digested her information. Despite her misgivings, he must try to stop Jasper. But it would be difficult. The man ruled by fear, forcing people into
servility. By mimicking the heedless behavior of arrogant lordlings, he masked his purpose, protecting himself even when society knew what he'd done. Who
could look into a man's mind? Negligence and spite
differed only in intent. Since no rational man would
take serious offense from these slights, few connected
them to later tragedies.

Like the tailor's complaint. Who would believe the
man had spent eight months in debtors' prison because Jasper's friend poked fun at his waistcoat? It
was hardly an earthshaking insult. People poked fun
at society figures every day. Caricaturists made careers
of the practice, publishing illustrations ridiculing the
Regent, Brummell, and a host of other figures. He'd
featured in one himself when Rowlandson had depicted him as a decrepit old man feasting on a table
of young beauties. Granted, he had been twenty-eight
at the time, a little old to be cutting a swath through
the muslin company with all the abandon of a lad just

down from school, but he had been too busy to visit London earlier. Only after he paid his father's last debt had he been free to pursue the pastimes his friends had enjoyed for years. His behavior may have bordered on wild at first, but a gentleman was expected to bring a certain level of expertise to his marriage bed. How else was he to acquire it?

He stifled a grin at such a ridiculous justification of a period he would rather forget, then forced his attention back to the business at hand.

"Is there anyone in society who believes that Rankin is short a sheet?" he asked, resuming his chair.

She shook her head. "The lower classes are too concerned with avoiding his wrath to ponder his mental state. The upper classes ignore his wildness out of respect for his position as heir to a viscount, though a few consider him recklessly high-spirited. But even if they knew the full extent of his plots, they would turn a blind eye because his victims are commoners."

"But you are not from the lower classes," he reminded her again.

"I am a woman, which makes it easy to believe the worst of me."

True, he agreed silently. Society held men and women to different standards.

"No one will look beneath the surface to detect his manipulations, let alone examine his motives. He charms the hostesses, hangs on every word of the gossips, disarms the older gentlemen by listening attentively to their advice—"

"I've met men like that," he admitted. "Their toadeating makes one ill as they admire pets, children, and hunters with such insincerity one wonders if they can tell them apart."

"But the ploy is effective," she reminded him. "The gossips chuckle as they shake their heads over his scrapes, treating him like a favored nephew. Especially Mrs. Telcor. The slightest hint of criticism has her snarling like a mother bear protecting her cub."

"Yet they turn on you, though your position is nearly as high."

"Thus speaks ignorance. Mrs. Telcor is the most powerful gossip in Exeter, so few argue with her. My birth may be high, but my position is not. I married down, reducing my consequence even before this began. My work in the parish raises distrust. One lady claims I've become a Methodist because I champion the poor instead of chastising them for complaining about their betters."

"Ridiculous." He ignored her bitter tone, though he knew exactly how she felt. He'd been taunted on the same ground as far back as the Easley affair.

"But true. The rumors justify every suspicion. And you must remember that Jasper's name is not connected. No one in society knows he is involved."

"Then how did he start them? He must have told someone." The fire was burning down, so he added coal, not wanting to interrupt the discussion while a servant performed the chore.

A comment on his unconventional manners hovered on her lips, but she bit it back. "They begin as innuendo. He asks the listener's help in refuting a wildly improbable tale, then casually drops an insinuation at the end."

"I am not sure I understand."

"If he decided to punish you for sticking your nose into his business, he might say, *Lord Gossip swears that Lord Rockhurst sneaked out of Lady Purity's rooms at midnight last night, stark naked. Ridiculous, of course. Rockhurst cannot have been the culprit, for I saw him myself at White's barely half an hour earlier, in deep play with Lord Gamingwhiz. I wonder how much he lost this time.*"

He glared, though the point was clear. "Diabolical. The last comment would imply that I was prone to heavy losses and that everyone knows it. Admitting ignorance would prove the listener was not *au courant*. Thus most people would accept the insinuation as fact."

"Exactly. No one suspects Jasper made the tale up on the spot or that his purpose was to destroy a reputation."

"I must talk to the other victims," he said, shaking his head. "Will they discuss this, or are they too cowed by their experiences to take a chance?"

"They will talk if I introduce you."

"No. People must not see us together. It would add new rumors about you and tell Jasper that I am investigating him. He thinks that I despise you—I passed him after attacking you in Exeter, so he undoubtedly overheard us. Let us keep that impression intact."

"Dear Lord!" She paled.

"This is good," he insisted. "As long as he believes your reputation is in shambles, he has no incentive to blacken it further. Do not disabuse him that notion, for it protects you."

"True." She sighed. "I will visit Exeter today—it is not raining hard enough to close the road, and there are people I need to see. In the course of my errands, I will call on Carruthers and Jenkins. They will expect you tomorrow."

"Weather permitting. Thank you. In the meantime, I must speak with Sarah. My apology will not improve by keeping."

Nodding, she led him to the nursery.

Chapter Six

Catherine introduced Rockhurst to a wary Sarah, then remained long enough to see that he did not further upset the girl. But she need not have fretted. Unlike most gentlemen, he did not treat Sarah with condescension, instead addressing her as an equal. After admitting that his behavior in Exeter had been wrong, he apologized, explaining that even adults sometimes forgot their manners.

"Honorable people make amends for their errors," he added. "But it is better to avoid making mistakes in the first place, for nothing can erase the memory."

"That's what Papa used to say." Sarah smiled.

"Your father was a wise man." He joined her at the schoolroom table, asking questions about her studies.

Catherine slipped out. He was as honorable as Harold, despite his high station. Most men claimed honor but applied the gentleman's code only when it was convenient, choosing behavior expedient to the moment the rest of the time. The result was an arrogant selfishness that ignored anything bothersome—except for Jasper, who punished anything bothersome. But Rockhurst would atone for mistakes, uphold his vows, and protect anyone he cared for. Laura would be fortunate to catch his eye.

She shivered, then frowned. The hall was no colder than any other room this day, so her sudden chill must come from the fears that had surfaced last night. What would happen when he realized why William had invited him? Rockhurst was not one to accept treachery lightly, and inviting him here under false pretenses would seem treacherous. So would eliciting a vow he could not keep. Not only would he despise failure, but he would believe that she had schemed to tie him here so Laura could pressure him. Treachery, indeed. Having vowed his help, he could not honorably leave.

In that light, Laura's behavior last night appeared more obnoxious than she had feared. Laura was a prattler in the best of times, but she had surpassed herself at dinner. Even William, who usually delighted in her gaiety, had been cringing by the time the meal ended.

She had tried to convince Laura to relax and behave normally, going to her room after Sarah fell asleep to chide her. The fact that Rockhurst had retired early was an ominous sign, but Laura had refused to listen.

"You are imagining things," she'd claimed, brushing her carefully lightened hair. "A London gentleman is accustomed to dinner conversation and would think us wholly backward if we ate in silence."

"I was not suggesting silence, Laura. But conversation requires two participants. You talked with hardly a pause to eat, giving him no opportunity to say a word."

"He did not try. I suspect he is the silent sort who saves his breath for making pontifical remarks at his clubs."

Catherine had nearly choked, for the description bore no resemblance to Rockhurst. While she could hardly claim to know him, the passionate man who had accosted her in Exeter could never be pontifical. Yet she could understand the misconception. Laura had not recognized the irritation beneath his brusque responses.

"If you think him cold, then ignore him," she'd suggested. "There is no need to attract a man you cannot like."

"But there is. William is right. Life has played me a dastardly trick, so I may never have this chance again. Rockhurst is titled, wealthy, and quite good-looking. His reputation as a caring man means he will treat his wife decently. And his lack of emotion will give me free rein to run the house as I choose. Where else can I find such a paragon?"

"He may be caring, but he was also irritated by your loquacity and may wish us all to Hades for tricking him into this visit."

"Fustian! He is fascinated with me. And he loves music. He asked me to play, then listened raptly to piece after piece. The interest was not feigned, for he recognized every selection, one of which is not well known."

Laura had continued extolling his instant infatuation for nearly an hour, ignoring all caveats. She had not even recognized the ploy that had ensconced her at the pianoforte so he could escape her attentions. Even William had understood that motive.

Catherine sighed. Laura would make Rockhurst a perfect wife, but he would never recognize it if she presented herself as an aggressive fortune hunter instead of the sweet, accomplished lady she really was. He was not the sort to enjoy pressure. When she returned from Exeter, she must speak to Laura again. William was out with the steward, or she would ask him to do it now.

She ducked into the suite that had once been her mother's. William had given it to her when she'd returned home after Harold's death. Placing her here had subtly increased her authority, widening the gulf marriage had already placed between her and the girls.

She would soon lose these rooms, though. William was actively seeking a wife. Even if his courtship of Miss Wyath failed, he would find another candidate. Thus her position in the household would change again, stripping her of much of her current authority and relegating her to the role of poor relation. And her head approved. It was time William looked to his own future, and she had often pressed him to do so. But her heart knew she would be biting her tongue often in the years ahead. And how would Sarah enjoy sharing the nursery with cousins whose importance exceeded her own?

One benefit of Jasper's rumors had been Miss Wyath's sudden coolness. Catherine had approved the courtship in the beginning, for Alicia had seemed sweet and well trained. Only after several meetings did she suspect that the girl's parents were pushing the connection to improve their own consequence—though the Wyaths were respectable, their aristocratic connections were remote. But if Alicia did not truly want William, then she would care little for Laura and Mary.

She had shared her concerns with William several months ago, but he'd refused to listen, swearing that Alicia had made no attempt to force an offer. Nor had she tried to catch his eye in the beginning. Catherine didn't believe it, but when he'd accused her of opposing the match so she could retain her position in the household, she'd dropped the matter.

Yesterday, Alicia had sent a polite note canceling his weekly call. William had accepted her claim of a headache, but Catherine recognized the ploy as a way to distance herself from the Seabrooks until she could determine the effect of the current scandal.

But William's courtship was not today's concern. She had interviews to arrange. Donning her cloak and bonnet, she headed for the stable.

Blake left the nursery floor when Mary arrived to start the day's lessons. Sarah was an enchanting angel, quite precocious for her seven years. None of his cousins had been likable at that age. In truth, few were likable at any age, having been spoiled by inept nurses and indolent parents. Whenever he declined their demands, they erupted with tantrums and destructive pranks. He'd finally banned two from the Abbey and informed a third that she was welcome only if she left her children at home.

Few of his relatives were pleasant. His father's inability to turn down requests for money was responsible for most of his financial losses, a fact the family refused to accept. The most importunate of the cousins had denied that the money was actually gone. When he'd declined to pay their debts, they'd retaliated by publicly calling him a miser. The unpleasantness had created rifts that still remained. Their children perpetuated the myth, viewing him as an ogre bent on making them miserable.

But Sarah was a delight. He smiled, recalling her descriptions. She'd been amusing herself by painting portraits when he'd arrived.

"Aunt Laura is silly," she claimed, showing him a watercolor that vaguely resembled Seabrook's sister. "She's always putting lemon juice on her hair to make it lighter, and she giggles every time a man comes near her, though Mama says that is quite all right." She shook her head, not yet understanding the game of flirtation she would embrace when she was older. "Uncle William says she reads far too many Minerva romances and should stop dreaming and accept one of her suitors instead of turning them all down."

Laura would be horrified to hear Sarah's chatter, he decided as the girl continued with a witty recitation of the stratagems Laura used to avoid the nursery. Children recognized insincerity. Though Laura played the role of doting aunt in company, she did not like Sarah, whose sweetness made her occasional waspishness more obvious and whose good sense made her seem frivolous.

Mary was quite different. "She's a great gun," proclaimed Sarah, pointing to a better picture. "She tells the most wonderful stories about birds and animals and flowers."

"You do your lessons with her, I believe."

"Some of them. She teaches me about places where people wear odd clothes and do strange things. They sound exciting, though she says I wouldn't enjoy an actual visit. It's like ghosts. They are funny in stories, but when Mr. Farley actually saw one last year, he nearly died of fright."

She had chattered for over an hour, delighting him with her observations. By the time he left, he had a clearer understanding of the household. Mary was a bluestocking and quite painfully shy. Though already eighteen, she attracted none of the gentlemen who called on Laura. Few even noted her presence long enough to greet her. Catherine devoted her life to helping others, becoming almost despondent when faced with a problem she couldn't fix. William hadn't changed much since school. He focused on the estate, spending little time in the nursery, though he'd taught Sarah how to ride.

Her observations were not confined to family. The area was populated by a host of people she described as giggly, grumpy, kind, or cruel. Miss Wyath was grumpy, ignoring Sarah unless William was with her— he was courting the lady. Then she cooed in feigned delight. Miss Hawkins was even sillier than Laura, making sheep's eyes at Jasper whenever they met. But Sarah's harshest words were for Jasper. He was a bad man, who hated children and punished anyone who bothered him. Her papa had said that those who hurt others also hurt themselves, but she didn't see that Jasper was hurting.

"Isn't it a beautiful morning, my lord?" asked Laura, appearing as he reached the foot of the stairs. Again, she moved a step too close.

He backed a pace. "If you enjoy rain."

Uncertainty flashed in her eyes, though his response did not dim her enthusiasm. She was again over-dressed, in a walking gown suitable for the fashionable hour in Hyde Park. "You have not yet seen the house, my lord. It has a distinguished history. The Seabrooks have even entertained royalty."

Not recently, he decided uncharitably, then evaded her attempt to take his arm. "Mrs. Parrish gave me a tour this morning." He saw no need to mention that it had covered only the rooms between the library and the nursery. "If you will excuse me, I have an errand in town."

"How delightful. So do I. We can share a carriage."
Her expression seemed guileless until he looked into
her eyes.

He let ice into his voice. "Sharing a carriage would
be most improper, Miss Seabrook. Where is your
decorum?"

"I would take my maid, sir." But her face reddened.

"Insufficient. Have you forgotten why I am here?
The rumors have tarnished the entire household. Setting foot in Exeter will attract cuts, even if you go
without me. What you suggest is hoydenish enough
to ruin you. If you wish to emerge from this scandal
unscathed, you cannot raise even minor questions
about your propriety."

"But—"

"Truth is less important than appearance, Miss Seabrook. And even appearance can be twisted. I've no
doubt you are a lady, but I will have no part in confirming suspicions for those who wish you ill. Now, if
you will excuse me, I must be away before the roads
deteriorate."

Nodding curtly, he escaped to his room. Perhaps his
scold would keep her at a distance, but he doubted it.
She was too self-centered to understand that rumor
could turn people against her in a trice. If he had
interpreted Sarah's chatter correctly, Laura had turned
down several offers because the gentlemen did not
offer the adventure and romance embraced by the heroes in her favorite novels—which made his own position precarious. The moment reality crashed through
her self-absorption, desperation would rule. Eyes
clouded by fantasy often twisted events to fit desire.
She had already dismissed last night's rebuffs and
would likely twist this scold into concern for her reputation. From there, it was a short step to convincing
herself that he wanted her, justifying any action to
bring them together.

He grimaced. Had Jasper used Laura's flirtations as
the basis of his campaign against Catherine? He might
make a case that Catherine was corrupting her. Even

though Catherine had married when Laura was twelve, she had lived nearby and often tutored her sisters.

It was a thought to consider, for Laura's flirting was visible to all. But his immediate problem was to escape further confrontations. He could not visit Exeter until Catherine set up the promised interviews, but he could talk to the villagers.

Donning his greatcoat and hat, he headed for the stables. A cold drizzle continued to fall, making the path slippery and chilling him to the bone. It changed his mind about riding. He would take his carriage for this short journey.

"Will the roads hold up in this weather?" he asked as his groom harnessed the team.

"Charlie says they will." Ted nodded toward the Seabrook groom. "He has a uncanny knack for knowin' the weather. And for knowin' people," he added in an undertone. "Talk is Miss Laura has her cap set for you."

"I know."

Ted ignored his oppressive tone. "Charlie calls her a romantic, though she's refused half a dozen gentlemen—too old, too cold, too brutal . . ."

"If she is particular, then I've nothing to fear."

"Maybe. But you are an earl, beggin' your pardon. And she knows she'll never see London."

Blake nodded.

"One of the lads claims she feels stifled at Seabrook."

The information corroborated his impressions. A yearning for excitement. A longing to escape. The realization that no one in the area could provide either, and that the rumors promised worse to come. And Laura was not the only threat. William must be nearly as desperate to see her off his hands.

"You might mention that my sole reason for calling is to conduct business with Seabrook—but not personal business," he murmured as Ted finished buckling the harness.

The village was too close, he decided, climbing into the carriage. She might follow him there. He could talk to the locals another day. Instead, he would learn more about the countryside.

Half an hour later, he regretted his decision. Though the rain remained light, only one reasonable road ran through this part of Devonshire. The lanes that branched from it were narrow, poorly maintained, and very slick. And the temperature continued to fall. It wasn't fair to subject his horses and coachman to these conditions merely to escape one forward lady. Overgrown hedgerows made this lane nearly impassable. It was time to turn around and head back—if turning was possible.

He'd raised his hand to rap on the roof when the near hedge ended, providing a view of a gorse-studded hillside dotted with sheep. A boy of about nine was poking a stick into the ditch. Signaling the coachman to stop, he opened the window.

"Did you lose something, lad?"

"Nah, sir." Guilt flashed across his face. The boy was undoubtedly supposed to be working.

"Then perhaps you can tell me whether this road leads to Lord Rankin's estate."

"Sorta, but you don't want to take no fancy carriage that way. 'Tis better to take t' main road to town. But not today. He ain't home. Went down to Plymouth last week to visit his lady friend. You can talk with t' heir if it's urgentlike—he lives at t' old Wilkins place—but I don't advise it, sir. He's a bad one, he is. Like to put your head on a pike, he would, if you disturb him."

Blake stifled a grin, imagining his coachman's face at this bit of impertinence. "So I understand. What has he done to you, lad?"

"Nuttin, but he sure made trouble for Jemmy. Told his pa Jemmy'd throwed rocks at his carriage, but I swear he didn't. Jemmy wouldn't do nuttin that bad. He minds his manners better'n that."

"I'm sure he does, but he must have done something to prompt such a plumper."

"Well . . ." He dug one toe into the mud. "Jemmy did peep into his carriage, but he didn't touch nuttin. Just wanted to see what it were like 'cause his sister Carrie'd been bragging about riding home in a fancy carriage, and he didn't believe her tales."

"So he satisfied his curiosity but called down Rankin's wrath for his pains."

"I don't know why. What's t' harm in looking? He kept his hands behind his back and didn't leave even a speck of dust."

"But some folks care less for the effect than for the offense," Blake reminded him. "What was his punishment?"

"Double chores." He sighed. "I never see him no more."

"Patience, lad. He won't be busy forever. In the meantime, stay away from young Rankin."

Guilt bloomed in the boy's eyes, confirming that he'd been entertaining himself with plots for revenge.

Blake smiled. "Don't play tricks on the man, or you'll find yourself in worse trouble than Jemmy. I've a bone to pick with him myself, and I'll add yours to my list."

"You're going after Master Jasper?" His eyes widened into white globes.

"That's our secret for now," he cautioned.

"I won't tell a soul." Excitement lit his face. "Can I help?"

"Perhaps. I don't know how yet, but I will keep your offer in mind. Where can I reach you?"

He gestured to a cottage in the distance. "Harry Fields, sir, at your service."

"The Earl of Rockhurst. Are you one of Rankin's tenants?"

"Lord Seabrook's, my lord."

"I am his guest."

"Jemmy's pa works Rankin land," said Harry, frowning.

"Then Jemmy is fortunate his punishment is no worse. His father would have no choice but to follow Jasper's orders even if he believed Jemmy innocent."

"That don't seem right."

"It is not." He met Harry's eyes, man to man. "But sometimes life is unfair. No one can fix all wrongs, though I will do my best to address this one. In the meantime, stay away from Jasper and don't ask questions about him. He will hear, and be just as displeased as if you'd poked around his carriage."

Bidding the lad farewell, he turned back toward the stables, content with the day's outing. With luck, he could slip back to his room before Laura realized he had returned.

Chapter Seven

Catherine bit back an oath. This errand was proving far more difficult than she had expected. When Rockhurst had asked to speak with the other victims, she'd thought they would welcome his help. But they didn't.

"I don't know," said Carruthers, keeping his eyes on the door. His fears were obvious. The last time someone had overheard him discussing Jasper, his daughter had suffered. She was now staying with a distant cousin in Somerset and would probably never return home.

"No one will know unless you tell them," she insisted. "Rockhurst will keep your story secret, but he cannot stop Jasper from preying on others unless he understands his methods."

"Can't stop him anyways," muttered the chandler. "He does whatever he wants. Lord Rankin don't care. Jasper knows his pa won't admit he's guilty of wrongdoing, for that would besmirch the family name. It is easier to turn on anyone who complains."

"Jasper might hurt you or Jenkins, but he can do nothing to Rockhurst. This is our chance for justice."

"But Rockhurst won't stay 'round Exeter. His seat is far away." He waved vaguely toward London. "Don't let him bedazzle you, Mrs. Parrish. He might owe Lord Seabrook a favor, but he cares nothing about us. Once he leaves, we'll never see him again—which the Rankins know quite well. Lord Rankin will pretend shock when he hears of his son's antics, but his interest will fade before Rockhurst is out of sight.

And Jasper will retaliate against us for putting him through such embarrassment."

"He won't know that you said anything," she insisted again. "Rockhurst will only demand redress for Jasper's attack on me." This wasn't strictly true, for she did not believe he would file formal charges of any kind. His investigation would prove what she already knew—there was no way to show intent, so Jasper had broken no laws. Without a crime, there could be no punishment. But she could honestly promise that the tradesmen would not suffer.

Carruthers frowned. "If he needs my evidence before he can believe you, then how can he file charges without it?"

The man was sharp-witted, she admitted. But she dared not agree with him. How was she to explain that she wanted him to bare a painful episode in his life so that a pointless investigation would keep Rockhurst at Seabrook long enough to form an attachment to Laura? It was an unworthy goal, but she thrust down her self-loathing. This was Laura's best chance to find a husband.

"Please, Mr. Carruthers," she begged, touching his arm. "Talk to him. You can trust him to do what is right. He is an honorable man who would never harm you or your daughter."

Carruthers hesitated, but finally nodded.

"Thank you." She placed another order for wax candles—with Rockhurst in the house, they would need even more than usual—and took her leave.

Carruthers was not the only one who was reluctant to speak with Rockhurst. Everyone feared what Jasper would do if they revealed their experiences, and the fear ran even deeper than she had expected. Were there worse crimes than she knew? Her mind whirled at the possibility that Jasper had caused serious harm. But how could she tell when the victims remained silent?

Misfortune was part of life, rarely arising from more than a moment's carelessness or blind fate. Harold

had often bemoaned life's cruelty—Mrs. Smith's long
illness, Ned Thomas's death at age two, the fire that
had destroyed the Hunt cottage, Mr. Barlow's broken leg . . .

Jasper had caused none of those problems. Ned had
been sickly from birth. The fire had clearly been an
accident, witnessed by three people. And Mr. Barlow's
horse had thrown him when a buck burst out of a
copse practically in its face.

But Harold had known more than he'd shared with
her. He'd often warned her to stay away from Jasper
and to keep Sarah well away. And there were many
misfortunes that might be more than bad luck. Like
Squire Pott's daughter, who had found herself with
child two years ago. Threats had not elicited the father's name. Nor had beatings. Speculation ranged
from her father's steward to a married lover to an
escapee from Dartmoor Prison. No one had suggested
Jasper, but now she had to wonder. Daisy had often
made cutting remarks about him. Perhaps her antago-
nism had hidden an affair, or maybe had he repaid
her disrespect by forcing her. But it was too late to
ask. Her father had sent her to a spinster aunt, where
she had died in childbirth five months later.

Then there was the blacksmith's son, who had run
into a press gang. Bad luck or Jasper? It was impossible to tell. Though less prevalent since Trafalgar had
reduced the threat of a French invasion, press gangs
still worked the area.

And what about the night Tom Daily had drowned?
No one had considered it aught but an accident, for
he'd imbibed freely in the taproom before falling into
the river. But he'd never liked Jasper.

That was the problem with Jasper. His victims knew
better than to cross him by complaining about his
crimes. The rest remained ignorant of his nature.
What had Harold known? She searched her memory,
trying to recall a look or gesture that might have
hinted that Jasper had been responsible for a particu-

lar misfortune. But she could recall nothing. Harold had protected her too well.

Blake remained in the stable for over an hour, rubbing down his horses and talking to his groom. He had never enjoyed a similar camaraderie with his coachman, but Ted had taught him to ride and drive, and it had been Ted who had told him about his father's death in a riding accident. Everyone else had glossed over the details, but Ted had known that he needed the unvarnished truth. His father had been arrogantly stupid, paying for drunken carelessness with his life.

"I need information about Jasper Rankin," he said now, having made certain that they could not be overheard. "I know about his status as heir to Lord Rankin, and I know that the local gossips dote on him. That is his public side. What I want are his secrets. Who has he hurt and why? And is there anyone who has annoyed him lately?"

"That won't be easy. People don't share secrets with strangers."

"Then make some friends. Seabrook expects me to rescue his sister's reputation from Rankin's lies. I can't do it without information. But be careful. If he discovers your interest, he will find a way to hurt you."

"How?"

"He would start with lies, hoping I would turn you off. When that failed, he might attack directly."

Ted nodded.

Satisfied, Blake returned to the house, where he helped himself to several biscuits to explain why he'd entered through the kitchen. Savoring their tart sweetness, he took the servants' stairs toward his room. Midway up the last flight he found the narrow steps blocked.

"Good afternoon, sir," said Sarah politely, then giggled when she spotted the biscuits in his hand and the crumbs on his greatcoat. "Look, Aunt Mary. Even earls sneak treats."

He smiled. "Indeed, we do. What is the point of having a title if I cannot break a rule now and then?"

"But only now and then," put in Mary firmly. "And decorum is very important for those of us who lack titles."

"But an occasional lark does no harm—within reason," he pointed out.

"Like the time Aunt Mary spent half the night watching the barn owls hatch?" asked Sarah.

Mary blushed, but kept her voice firm. "And that visit to the dairy last week when you should have been practicing your stitchery."

"As I said, within reason," he repeated. "There are rules for breaking the rules—it can only be done occasionally, and it must never cause harm." A smile tugged at his lips. He was hardly in a position to condemn mischief after perpetrating so much of it himself.

Sarah tugged Mary's hand. "Can he come with us?" she asked before turning to Blake. "We are having a history lesson in the gallery."

Mary tried to shush her. "I don't think—"

But Blake nodded. "I would be delighted to accompany you, Miss Parrish. I will even share my spoils." He handed her a pilfered biscuit, then popped the last one into his mouth and led the way back to the gallery floor.

"You can call me Sarah," she said, nibbling happily.

"Thank you. I will cherish the privilege." He had little interest in a seven-year-old's history lesson, but it would keep him occupied for the next hour. As he reached for the door handle, he glanced back at Mary. "Sarah says that you teach her about other countries. Is one of them Russia? I had a delightful conversation with the Russian ambassador not long ago. He claims that they build a ceremonial palace for the tsar each winter, entirely of ice."

"You are back!" exclaimed Laura as he emerged from the stairway. But her smile collapsed when she beheld Sarah's hand clasped in his.

He cursed his luck. Of all the stairs in the house, why had she been lurking near this one?

"An ice palace?" Mary said as she followed them. "Fascinating. Are the furnishings also made of ic- Oh!" Laura's piercing glare cut off her words.

"There is no need to waste time on these children," said Laura, laying a hand on his arm and attempting to slide between him and Sarah. "You will prefer a glass of wine in the library. And Cook has just finished a batch of cakes."

"I am the best judge of my preferences, Miss Seabrook," he said stonily, sidestepping. His hand kept a firm hold on Sarah's. "If you will excuse us—or would you care to join us for a history lesson?"

"Hardly." He could have sworn she sniffed, though no sound emerged. Turning on her heel, she stalked away.

He filled the uncomfortable silence by answering Mary's truncated question. "I didn't think to ask about furnishings, though I doubt ice would be particularly useful. The ambassador claims that state functions are actually held there." He then turned to Sarah, forestalling any comment on Laura's lack of manners. "What sort of history are you studying today? Family or English?"

"Both." Her voice had lost its laughter.

"One complements the other," explained Mary, "for our family is quite ancient. But we've only held a few lessons on the subject."

"Old families are the best sort to have," he told Sarah. "I learned many of my own lessons in just that way. So who have you talked about?" They entered the gallery.

Sarah's free hand waved at the walls. "These men are all my grandfathers, and the ladies are all grandmothers, except for her." She pointed to a dour-faced woman in republic black. "She's an aunt." Her voice was back to normal as Laura's unpleasantness faded into the past.

"Cousin," said Mary.

"A nasty cousin," added Sarah, then giggled at Mary's frown. "Uncle William said so."

"Every family has a few of those," said Blake with a smile. "My own great-great-grandfather was as big a scoundrel as you can find. If he hadn't been an earl, no one would have spoken to him."

"No need to exaggerate," murmured Mary.

"I'm not," he murmured back. "He very nearly lost his head."

Sarah ignored the byplay, leading him to a gentleman clad in Tudor dress. "This was the first baron. He won the title for helping Henry solve the monsters."

"*Dis*-solve the *monasteries*," said Mary, her face pink with embarrassment. "It was the eighth Henry who founded the Church of England—the same church your father served so well. Edmund Seabrook rendered great assistance to his king."

Blake looked into the eyes of a dyspeptic old man and could easily imagine him looting and pillaging— not out of religious fervor or even because of Henry's orders, but for the sheer joy of it.

"Dissolve the monasteries," repeated Sarah dutifully, but he could tell that her mind was not on the lesson. Her own version was more fun. She skipped ahead to a later portrait. "Grandfather Christopher was too old and sick to fight against Cromwell, so he stayed home when his grandson joined the king. But Christopher didn't die until Charles came back, so we didn't lose anything."

Mary choked.

Blake grinned. Those families who had survived war, Parliament, and the Restoration with fortune and title intact had every right to be grateful. Sarah would learn to gloat less as she aged. But it was important for children to know how their families had fared in England's various upheavals. It was part of their heritage.

Mary led Sarah to a more recent portrait. "This is my great-grandfather, Edwin Seabrook—your great-great-grandfather, Sarah. You may call him Grandfather Edwin. He was the luckiest man to ever break a leg."

She explained that Edwin had been determined to join Bonnie Prince Charlie in the last Jacobite rebellion. But as he rode north to raise his standard beside the false prince, his horse stepped in a hole, throwing him against a wall and breaking his leg. Thus he was confined to bed in great pain when Charles and his supporters met their end at the Battle of Culloden. And he had escaped losing his head for treason when the surviving Jacobite lords were executed.

The Seabrooks had mellowed since the first baron, Blake decided, but they were still fighters—William had campaigned against a particularly vicious tutor at Eton. Had Catherine inherited their feistiness? She would need it to vanquish Jasper Rankin.

Sarah was caught up in the tale of the Jacobite Seabrook's exploits, so he quietly wandered off to study the other portraits. None were by the hand of a master, but most were quite good. Catherine's features appeared on several faces and her coloring on others, though most lacked her intensity. Then there was the tilt of her chin, the slender neck, the tapered fingers . . .

Lust stirred deep in his groin, snapping his attention back to business. No purpose was served by thinking about her charms. He was here to redeem her reputation, not ruin it. His immediate goal was to avoid Laura until their inevitable meeting at dinner.

Glancing quickly at the remaining portraits, he moved to a window. The rain had stopped, leaving the park fresh. Sheep dotted a nearby hillside, shearing its grass into emerald velvet. A rainbow flashed as the sun found a hole in the clouds. Beauty, and the promise of peace.

He had no idea how long he remained lost in the sight before Sarah tugged on his hand.

"Will you take tea in the nursery today, sir?" she asked, only the tiniest tremor in her voice revealing that she understood the temerity of her question.

"I would be delighted."

Sarah's smile lit her face in the same way the rainbow had lit the park. She was a beautiful child—and a more entertaining companion than many of his friends. Perhaps it was the fresh enthusiasm she brought to each day, which contrasted so strongly with the ennui that was currently the mode. Or maybe it was because she was the first female in years—of any age—who was neither flirting with him nor making demands. All he knew was that he had not been this relaxed in months.

"What are you doing here?" demanded Catherine, then snapped her mouth shut, appalled at the rudeness of her question.

She had just returned from town. As usual, her first stop had been the nursery—not that she distrusted Annie, but she was accustomed to passing a portion of her day with her daughter. The last person she had expected to find there was Rockhurst.

"Enjoying the best lemon biscuits I've tasted in years," he said calmly. Then he winked at her.

"But—"

"He's an earl, Mama. He can break the rules whenever he wants to."

"But only the small ones, and only occasionally," he said sternly. "Like begging biscuits in the kitchen on a rainy day or taking my tea where I choose."

"I fear you are undermining discipline, sir." But she could not help smiling. He looked perfectly at home with his legs stretched under the low table.

"I don't doubt it." He grinned. "My nurse always swore I'd be the death of her."

Everyone laughed.

She handed her cloak and gloves to Annie. "Since Mary is also here, perhaps I should join you."

"Wonderful, Mama. A real party!"

Rockhurst nudged the teapot toward Sarah as Annie produced another cup. "As hostess, it is your duty to pour."

Catherine held her breath as Sarah lifted the heavy pot, but she managed by using both hands. *She is growing up so fast.*

She said little as Rockhurst resumed a tale about a boyhood expedition to track down a badger that had ended with him and a friend stuck in a hedgerow. He was remarkably attentive, with no pretense tarnishing his demeanor. Sarah was blossoming before her eyes, showing more animation than she had since Harold's death.

The realization sliced her heart. Harold had doted on Sarah and had spent time with her every day, unlike other men, who rarely exchanged more than a few words with their daughters. But since moving to Seabrook, there had been no men in her life. William had been too busy taking control of his inheritance to bother with his niece. If Laura could catch Rockhurst, she would be truly blessed.

Laura!

She nearly groaned. Laura had planned an elaborate tea today so she could show off her skills as a hostess. She would not be pleased that Sarah had stolen her guest.

But she wasn't about to scold the girl. This impromptu party was too beneficial.

Yet watching Rockhurst amuse Sarah revived some of her earlier doubts. Had William asked him to spy on her? Courting favor with Sarah might be a way to gather information. Sarah was not shy about showing off her knowledge.

Sharp pain accompanied the suspicion, for she did not want it to be true. Sarah would be badly hurt if she learned that his attention was feigned.

So would she.

"I spoke with Carruthers and Jenkins," she told him half an hour later as he escorted her downstairs. "Also the blacksmith—he suffered a rash of broken tools after shoeing Jasper's horse; the beast was so jumpy, it took longer than usual. They are reluctant to discuss the situation, but all eventually agreed to talk to you in private, provided you not repeat their tales to others."

"I will adhere to their wishes. But perhaps I can learn something that will make it easier to deal with Jasper. I must understand how his mind works."

"So I told them. But they fear your influence will fade once you return home. Jasper will again be the most powerful man around, free to exercise that power as he pleases—and more brutal than ever if he has suffered embarrassment."

He nodded. "I spoke with one of your tenants today—Harry Fields. He disclosed an incident involving his friend Jemmy. Jasper lied to the boy's father, claiming he threw rocks at his carriage when he'd merely peeped through the door to see if it was as elegantly appointed as rumor claimed. Jasper did not appreciate the liberty."

She sighed. Another victim, though there was nothing anyone could do. If people refused to believe her, why would they listen to a child? "Do you really expect to prevail?" she asked.

"It will be difficult," he admitted. "But I cannot allow him to misuse his position. Lords should look after their dependents, not prey on them. His actions reflect poorly on all of us." He paused outside the door to her bedchamber. "Do not look too far ahead," he said quietly. "First I must gather information, being careful not to draw Jasper's attention. Only then can I decide how best to use that information. In the meantime, hold your head high and go about your business. Acting guilty plays into Jasper's hands."

Chapter Eight

As he emerged from the tailor's shop, Blake spotted Mrs. Telcor and invited her to tea. Perhaps he could deflect her attention from Catherine. At the very least, he hoped to reduce speculation about his intentions toward Laura, though her avid gaze as he seated her in the confectioner's shop made that unlikely.

But she surprised him. "I was shocked to learn that a man of your credit would associate with Mrs. Parrish," she said, her hand hovering over the sugar bowl as if debating whether to add a third lump to her cup. Her eyes gleamed in anticipation. He suspected her purpose was to confirm the notorious widow's misdeeds.

"Seabrook swears the rumors lie, though I wouldn't know," he countered mildly. "I've seen nothing improper, but the ladies only join us at dinner."

She raised a brow, clearly suspicious. Laura's flirtations must be common knowledge.

He leaned closer as if sharing confidences. "I am trying to convince Seabrook to take his seat in Parliament. The progressive leadership needs support from the younger lords if they hope to pass reforms."

"Politics!" She snorted. "I've not heard your name mentioned in that context."

"I prefer to work behind the scenes." He was stretching the truth, though he voted on measures he cared strongly about or on those whose outcome was in doubt. While he favored reform, the time was not right for a determined push for change. The opposition was firmly entrenched, and he harbored no illusions about his credit. Even without his recent excesses, he lacked the power to sway the Tory leadership. Now that Prinny had abandoned the Whigs, they had no choice but to exercise patience.

Prinny's change of heart had raised questions in many minds. Had his long support been a way for the government to keep an eye on the opposition? Or maybe Prinny had only embraced Whig ideals because strong-minded friends like Fox and Sheridan had convinced him to. Now that they were gone, he was being led by determined Tories. It was not a comfortable thought. Many problems would grow worse if the Regent bent with every wind.

Their cakes arrived, interrupting him—and just as well. He had more urgent problems just now than the fate of the reformists. He had only raised the subject to explain his visit to Seabrook. Selecting two small cakes, he smiled.

"Seabrook is not the only lord I wish to see." He kept his voice conspiratorial. "What can you tell me of Jasper Rankin? I hear his father's health is failing, so he will soon step into the title."

"Hah!" Mrs. Telcor's cup rattled as she set it down. "Rankin has imagined himself at death's door for thirty years. I've not seen anyone so convinced he is going to die. That man has drunk enough healing waters to fill a lake and tried nostrums from every village witch in England. When he is not at a spa, he remains in bed, summoning a host of London physicians. Even Miss Mott, who has suffered megrims and spells for sixty years, consults healers less often."

He hid his surprise, for he had invented the failing health on the spot, taking a page from Jasper's book. "Is he well enough to receive callers?"

"He is in Bath just now, taking the waters, though he should return shortly. But don't expect him to receive you. His megrims make him short-tempered, and his complaints drive everyone to teeth gnashing, sleeplessness, and drink. Poor Jasper had to move out in the end."

"Because his father is ill?" He was comparing her claims with Harry's assertion that Rankin was visiting a mistress in Plymouth.

Mrs. Telcor shook her head. "There is not a thing wrong with Rankin beyond a wish to command attention, and Jasper knows it. When he refused to treat his father as an invalid, the man threw him out. He doesn't want a son, but a slave who will fetch and carry and obey even the pettiest orders without question. But Jasper has other responsibilities."

"Surely you exaggerate," suggested Blake. "Most parents draw comfort from their children's company."

"Not Rankin. He hates Jasper. 'Tis a miracle the boy grew into a sensible, caring man." When the confectioner frowned, she lowered her voice. "I doubt Jasper has heard anything but demands and complaints from his father since the day he was born. His mother died when he was five, leaving the boy to a series of brutal, incompetent tutors."

Blake pretended commiseration, though he had to question her understanding. Most boys considered their tutors brutal—at least until they reached school. It was a rare student who did not long for home. Only later did they understand that discipline was necessary to prepare them for future responsibilities. "It is the price we all pay for the privilege of our positions."

"For some the price is too high." She wiped a crumb from her chin. "Did your parents ignore your very existence? Did they enjoy snubbing you?"

"No," he admitted. His father had been no more aloof than any other lord. His mother had been warmer, but only because she needed someone to lean on. Since his father was away so often, she'd depended on her son from the time he was six.

"Jasper's did. He has run tame in my house since he was a child, so I know how Rankin's rejection hurt. The servants followed Rankin's lead. It was only my intervention that rescued him from the brutality of two of his tutors. But he is blessed with a great deal of sense and has become a credit to his class. A kinder, more thoughtful lad would be hard to find."

Blake nearly bit his tongue trying to remain silent. The woman's credulity defied description.

She poured more tea, helping herself to another scone. "Not everyone understands him, of course. Some cause trouble for him because they are jealous of his position. Only last month, Justin Hawkins claimed that Jasper had seduced his sister. I can't believe he thought such fantasy would work. Helen has been throwing herself at Jasper for months, hoping to marry up. When he refused to smile her way, she concocted this scheme, but she failed. He was in Bath at the time, as I know full well, for he brought me a charming china bird when he returned. It is all the crack in London." She described it in glowing terms.

"Thoughtful," he managed, though the bird sounded like one of the cheap trinkets peddled to the merchant classes.

"And generous to a fault," she added. "He uses most of his allowance to aid tenants and villagers. Like the Hadleys. Their barn burned down last year. Jasper helped them rebuild, and they aren't even Rankin tenants. I would like to think that he learned such kindness from me—he often passes afternoons with me, and I have contributed to many of his causes—but I expect he was born kind. If only his mother had lived. She was a dear woman who should never have wed so uncaring a man. After her death, I tried to offer Jasper the same guidance, but nothing can replace a mother's love."

"You are to be commended for seeing after him." The words were sincere, though it was a pity she had not bestowed her mothering on a more worthy child. Jasper had been manipulating her for most of his life. Her support protected him from suspicion, allowing him to take increasingly daring chances. And he'd probably been milking her for funds nearly as long.

"Someone had to do it." She shook her head, falling

into murmured reminiscences. They proved that everyone who tried to exert authority over the boy—servants, tutors, even a vicar—was banished, often with Mrs. Telcor's unwitting help. Rankin had probably found it easier to replace employees than to withstand her lectures.

His image of Jasper Rankin was clearer. Something had created a rift between father and son. Jasper's willfulness might originally have been a bid for his father's attention. When that failed, he'd lashed out against underlings to elicit the fear he confused with respect. Each victory had increased his arrogance.

School must have been a shock. Jasper would have met boys whose precedence exceeded his own—not pleasant for someone accustomed to being the most important person around. No wonder he had eschewed time in London. Only at home could he wield power. Jenkins claimed that Jasper had returned more arrogant than ever, despite being sent down in disgrace.

Since then, Mrs. Telcor had expanded her role as confidante and substitute mother by burnishing his reputation in the upper classes, cutting anyone who criticized him, and dismissing his public excesses as youthful high spirits.

Like she was doing now, in response to his question about the destruction of Jones's crops.

"That was unfortunate, and I scolded him for thoughtlessness," she said through a bite of cake. "Not that my lecture was necessary. He was appalled at the damage. He and his friends had gone riding after an evening in the Plate and Bottle's taproom. A race got out of hand." She shrugged. "He made generous reparation, of course. I would expect no less."

He held his tongue, though the minuscule damage payment had been an insult in itself. Jasper had made it clear what would happen if Jones complained. Catherine knew the details only because she had been with Mrs. Jones when the woman collapsed in tears, terrified about how they would survive.

"I trust he has compensated every victim of his high spirits," he said, hoping to discover other cases.

"Of course, and he has sobered with age. Only once did he truly lose control of a situation, and you can be sure I took him firmly to task for it."

"What happened?"

Her mouth tightened in a grim line, and for a moment he feared she would turn the subject. "When some friends damaged the parlor at the White Hart Inn, he did little to stop them. There was no excuse for such laxity, and so I told him. I don't care what they were celebrating. But he learned a valuable lesson that day and terminated his friendship with the lad who started the fight."

"Quite proper," he murmured, again refusing to challenge her. "He will be a charming addition to Parliament when the time comes."

Having barely managed to keep the sarcasm from his voice, he turned the topic to other gossip while they finished their tea, then bade her farewell and headed for the White Hart. He must risk exposing his investigation if he was to discover the details of this latest story.

The innkeeper smiled when he arrived. "Lord Rockhurst! Will you be needing rooms again this evening?"

"Not today, Falconer, but I am looking for information if you can spare me a few minutes."

"Of course, my lord." He gestured to a parlor, then sent a servant for ale.

"I am investigating a complaint against Jasper Rankin," said Blake when they were alone. "I would prefer to keep it quiet until I discover whether it has merit, you understand—no cause to start rumors if this proves groundless. So far, there is little evidence either for or against the charge."

"You will find nothing you can use," said Falconer stiffly. "Rankin is an exemplary man."

"So I've been told, but someone mentioned an incident that destroyed this room." He had already spotted the damage. It would take years before the new paneling matched beams darkened by centuries of smoke, and he would stake his favorite team of horses that the cracked flagstone and chipped fireplace dated to the fight.

" 'Twasn't the first fight at the White Hart. Nor will it be the last."

"What happened?"

" 'Twas a boxing match that day out toward Topsham—Barlow versus Gates. Not as important as the Cribb-Molineaux fights, but it drew a good crowd." He shrugged. "Rankin and several friends met here before driving out to watch, then returned afterward. A fair amount of money had changed hands, as expected, but they was a jovial bunch. The trouble only started after they'd emptied a few bottles."

"Who started it?"

Falconer shook his head. "Two of the lads were demonstrating what Gates could have done in the final round to win—he'd lost. One struck harder than intended. The other retaliated. Tempers snapped, and before you could say Jack-a-dandy, they was all involved." He shrugged. "Rankin blamed young Collinsworth, not that it matters. Collinsworth has never returned. Rankin paid for the damage and a bit over. These things happen."

Blake drained his ale slowly. Falconer had not suffered from the incident, so either he was not the intended victim, or it had truly been a case of high spirits. "Was anyone injured?"

"Richard Umber, though not badly, and several lads sported black eyes. Collinsworth took the brunt of it. Rankin called him a fool for losing his temper, and he cut the connection for hurting Umber."

"Trouble happens when too many bottles go dry, so why end their friendship?"

Falconer drained his own ale. "Collinsworth had been looking for a fight all day—insulting the Davies boy's horses, flirting with another lad's companion, arguing with anyone who bet against Gates. As they left for the mill, I heard him question Davies's intelligence for backing Barlow. When Gates lost, Collinsworth turned surly. Maybe he'd wagered more than he could afford, or maybe meanness was in his nature."

"So he started a fight. Which boxer did Jasper support?"

"Barlow. He has a good eye for horses and fighters. I doubt you'll find evidence against him. He's no saint, but he does right by anyone what's hurt, even if he was not at fault. That's more'n I can say for many lords."

"So it would seem." He rose. "By the way, how badly was Collinsworth injured?"

"Broken nose, cracked ribs, and he lost an eye. I hear he stays on his estate these days."

Blake nodded and took his leave. The description had jogged his memory, recalling a scrap of conversation at White's. Collinsworth did more than stay in the country. He'd cut all contact with others, becoming so reclusive that men were already calling him a hermit, though he was barely five-and-twenty. Another victim of Jasper's spite. He had probably disparaged Jasper's eye when they placed their bets. So he'd lost one of his own.

Pondering Jasper's nature, he hardly noticed the countryside as he rode back to Seabrook. Not until he reached the stables did he take in his surroundings. Catherine was waiting for him.

"Is there a problem?" he asked, turning his horse over to Ted.

"I don't know. Harry Fields turned up an hour ago. He demands speech with you but refuses to say why."

He could see Harry lording it over Catherine. "Where is he?"

"The kitchen." Curiosity blazed in her eyes, tempered with hurt at being snubbed by a tenant child. After everything else she'd suffered, this was the last straw.

"He meant no disrespect," he murmured, offering his arm. Heat flowed from her touch, so fierce he nearly cursed. "He must have heard something about Jasper. I'd asked him to keep my interest secret."

She relaxed.

"You will join us, of course, for this concerns you," he added. "Where should we talk?"

"The folly, I think. It is cold enough that even the gardeners are remaining inside."

He stopped at the corner of the house, covering her hand with his own. It slid past her glove before he could stop himself. "Then it would be better if you and Harry joined me there. And perhaps you can come up with an innocuous reason why he would seek me out—for the benefit of your staff," he added.

"Right." But anger glowed in her eyes.

"Catherine, I know any deception must grate, considering Jasper's rumors, but the longer I can hide my interest in his affairs, the easier it will be to learn the facts I need to defeat him."

"I know." She managed a tremulous smile. "We will meet you in the folly." Relinquishing his arm, she headed for the kitchen.

Catherine's hand tingled. But at least he had mistaken her fury at her unwarranted reaction for distress over the situation. She had no right to find him attractive. Quivering in delight every time they touched would bring nothing but trouble. From now on, she must remain as far from him as possible and hide any hint of silliness.

Harry was sitting at the table, devouring a plate of lemon biscuits. Foam clung to his upper lip from a cup of new milk, but he scrambled to his feet when she appeared. "Mrs. Parrish. Is he here?"

Conscious of Cook's sharp ears and two hovering maids, she ignored the question. "Come with me, Harry."

He complied, then frowned when she led him outside. "I have to see Lord Rockhurst," he insisted.

"And so you shall. But he prefers to meet in private, particularly if you wish to discuss his secrets."

He nodded but did not relax until he spotted Rockhurst in the folly. Then he sprinted up the steps.

"I understand you wish to see me," said Rockhurst when Harry skidded to a stop in front of him.

Harry glanced her way, frowning.

"She knows everything," Rockhurst assured the boy. "Rankin is telling lies about her, just like he did about Jemmy. But I need information if I am to prove it and prevent him from doing so again."

Harry cocked his head at her, sending the strangest sensation through her chest. Never had she encountered anyone who was so obviously judging her. Her face heated.

"I 'spect you're right," said Harry at last. "Georgie over at t' smithy claims she's a great gun, and even Pa was glad for t' help she give him last winter when Ma was so sick."

"How is Jemmy?" asked Rockhurst, recalling him to the subject.

"Snappish. He don't mind his usual chores or even being punished for something he done, but this is different."

"No one enjoys paying for someone's lies," he agreed. "Now what did you wish to tell me?"

Catherine took a seat out of Harry's sight so she would be less distracting. She didn't expect Rockhurst to succeed, but she had to admit that enlisting a child to search for evidence was an interesting approach. Children went everywhere and were often overlooked by adults. Few people expected them to understand what they heard or saw. Of course, a child's word would not outweigh Jasper's denials. Nor would it prevent him from retaliating once Rockhurst was gone.

"I don't know if this means anything," Harry began diffidently. "My brother Bob had to fetch some nails from t' smithy yesterday and took me with him." He grinned. "Bob flirts with t' smith's girl, but he don't want Pa to know. He blames me for not being at hand when he's ready to leave to explain why t' errands take so long. In return, he does some of my chores so's I can check on Jemmy.''

"I presume he encourages you to run off for a good long time," said Rockhurst.

"Right. Anyway, Georgie and me went downstream, looking for mushrooms. When we got to that copse just past t' village, we heard Master Jasper shouting on t' other side of a hedge."

"Who was he with?" asked Rockhurst.

"Farmer Lansbury."

"He owns a farm near Exeter," Catherine clarified when Rockhurst glanced her way.

"I take it Jasper was unhappy?" Rockhurst said.

Harry nodded. "We didn't dare creep close enough to see. If he'da heard us, we'd be doing double chores for a month or more. But I think Lansbury's cart was blocking t' road. Or maybe he was moving slower'n Master Jasper wanted to drive. The road pinches there, with high hedges both sides so's two wagons can't pass. Master Jasper went on and on about inconveniencing one's betters. Then he swore Lansbury would be sorry."

"But he made no specific threat?"

"No. But he'll do something. He said it t' same way he told Jemmy he'd be sorry he poked his head in that carriage."

"Thank you." Rockhurst laid a companionable hand on the boy's shoulder. "I can't promise to protect Lansbury, because I don't know what Jasper has in mind. But I will do what I can to keep him from harm. Have you heard whether Lord Rankin is back yet?"

"Last night. Happy as a lark for now. It'll be a week afore he gets that—" He glanced over his shoulder and snapped his mouth shut.

Catherine felt her face heat.

"Just so." Laughter bubbled under Rockhurst's voice. "You'd best be heading home before your father sees you're gone. Let me know if you hear anything else, but don't ask questions. And stay away from Jasper."

"Yes, sir." Harry skipped happily away.

"You know there is no way to protect Lansbury," she said softly.

"Who is he?"

She shrugged. "A yeoman farmer, who works his land, pays his taxes, and leaves others alone. He and Edna have no children, but he brought in a nephew to help with the farm. Everyone assumes Brad will inherit. And soon. Lansbury's health is not good."

"Harvest is complete, so he won't suffer like Jones. Does he raise animals?"

"A few, but only for his own use."

"Can his wife be seduced?"

"Never!" Picturing Edna making eyes at another was ludicrous. "She dotes on him, dividing her time between running the house and helping with parish work. Harold found her invaluable, as have I."

"And Brad? How old is he?"

"Eighteen."

He grimaced. "An age ripe for trouble—or an explanation for trouble once it finds him. My groom will keep an eye on him to keep Rankin from tempting him into deep gaming or some other excess."

Chapter Nine

"Look at the geese," exclaimed Sarah, bouncing with excitement as she pointed out the carriage window. "I thought they were all gone." Her face suddenly twisted into a frown. "I hope they don't freeze. Mary says they have to leave in the winter because it is too cold here."

Blake turned until he could see where she was pointing. She was right. A dozen geese flew in a ragged vee headed south. "It *is* rather late," he agreed. "But the weather has been quite mild, so they are fine. Animals sense how severe a season will be."

"Maybe they are snow geese," she suggested. "Mary says that snow geese can live in very cold places."

"I don't know about that, for I've never seen a snow goose, but I suspect that these are common gray geese."

"We had gray geese by the lake last month. Uncle William was pleased."

Because they made such good eating. But he said nothing lest he dampen Sarah's spirits.

Inviting her to Exeter had been a good idea. She had a unique way of looking at the world that made the journey seem shorter. When they'd passed a farm, she had not mentioned the men repairing a fence or the maid beating a carpet or even the toddler rolling on the grass with two puppies. "Look at the haystack," she'd said, giggling. "It looks just like Grandmother Ernestine's hair!" Which was true, he reflected, recalling his visit to the gallery. One of the ladies had sported the towering hairstyle popular during the previous century.

He'd also discovered that she knew more about birds than about the estate animals.

"Mary tells me about them," she had explained. "She loves birds. Laura teases her and says we must find a man who looks like a bird if we ever expect her to wed."

"There are a few who come to mind," he'd answered without thought, making her laugh. Then he'd had to describe the tulips who strutted about London. Lord Wigby's spindly legs and long nose demanded comparison to a stork, though his gaudy waistcoats would have been frowned upon by that black-and-white bird. Jeremy Grant's elaborate plumage rivaled descriptions of the fabled bird of paradise. And Lord Edward's excessive padding and towering cravats threw his chest out like a pouter pigeon's. But none were suitable mates for an intelligent lady, particularly an educated one. Grant restricted his thoughts to clothes, hoping to replace Brummell as an arbiter of fashion; Wigby cared only for horses; and Lord Edward considered that dedicated rake Devereaux his mentor.

"Did you remember the bread?" Sarah asked when a tree blocked her view of the geese. "We always feed the cathedral squirrels when we visit Exeter."

"Right there." He pointed to the bundle on the opposite seat. Catherine had explained the ritual when he requested permission for Sarah to accompany him. Though feeding the squirrels was not among his usual pastimes, he had agreed. He suspected she'd been trying to discourage this jaunt—which showed how much she feared Jasper.

With justification, he admitted, while a portion of his mind responded to Sarah's chatter. He risked raising questions by appearing in public with a child, even a precocious charmer. It was not the action of a man seeking political support. Nor did it fit a gentleman's visit to an old friend. He would have to make a show of seeking Sarah's help to buy a gift for one of his cousins—Camilla's youngest was almost tolerable— and hope the explanation would quiet people's tongues.

In truth, he had invited Sarah to deflect another of Laura's plots. This time, she had announced that she and her maid would also be in town today, and wouldn't it be fun to meet for tea at the Golden Stag before returning to Seabrook. The idea of sharing a private parlor with Laura and a maid who could become blind and deaf—assuming she remained in the room at all—curdled his blood, but Laura had dropped the idea when he mentioned Sarah.

Be careful about using an innocent, warned his conscience, raising a twinge of guilt.

He stifled it. Yes, he was using her, but he really did enjoy her company, and she would come to no harm. He would protect her from Jasper and give her a pleasant outing. Soliciting her advice would explain her presence and preserve the story he'd told Mrs. Telcor. And no one would realize that his primary motive was escaping a determined flirt.

Avoiding Laura grew harder every day, for she was even more forward than he'd feared. She had abandoned her routine, turning up wherever he went— except the nursery, which had become his refuge. The servants must be helping her, for she managed to follow him everywhere.

Like yesterday. He had walked to the village to gather additional information about Jasper. To avoid Laura, he'd told no one of his intentions—which made the trip pointless, he admitted now. Since Catherine had not arranged interviews, the people had seemed sullen and uncooperative. Blake had no way of knowing whether their wariness reflected fear of Jasper, distrust of strangers, or awe of his rank. Not that it mattered. The effect was the same.

As he'd returned to Seabrook, he'd heard a branch snap up ahead. Instinct drove him behind a tree. Thus he'd been hidden when Laura hurried past, sans maid, headed for the village. Cursing her persistence, he'd waited until she was out of sight before fleeing. At least he'd been in the woods, wearing a greatcoat that faded into the shadows.

But something had to be done. Unfortunately, proper manners forbade complaints to William, nor could he confront her directly. Just as Jasper excused blatant attacks as youthful high spirits, Laura could claim that she was merely being a good hostess to her brother's guest. And he still had no idea whether Catherine and William were actively helping her. Even fate was conspiring against him. Like last night.

When he and William reached the drawing room after dinner, Catherine had just left to settle a dispute in the kitchen. Almost immediately, William was summoned to the stable, where one of the horses had kicked a lad in the head. Thus Blake had been left alone with Laura and Mary. He had pulled Mary from her book, demanding that she join the conversation. And he had escaped to his room the moment he could do so without insult, but it had been another unpleasant evening. Laura had again twisted his departure into concern for her reputation. Her willingness to overlook his patent disinterest bothered him more each day.

His investigation was taking longer than he'd expected, for he kept running into walls. The village had not been his only failure. Ted had learned nothing. The other grooms refused to discuss Jasper, making signs against evil whenever his name was mentioned. It was beginning to look like Jasper was worse than even Catherine knew.

The carriage clattered onto Exeter's cobbled streets. His original pretext for bringing Sarah was a geography lesson. They would visit the stationer to study the latest map of the world—Mary used rough sketches to illustrate the various countries. And it would allow him to decide whether Cavendish was deliberately defrauding his customers or was unwittingly selling another man's fakes.

"What is Vicar Sanders doing here?" Sarah's surprise pulled him away from his thoughts.

"He seems to be arguing over a horse. Who is the man with him?"

"Squire Pott." The two men were gesticulating wildly as they examined a mare. "Papa would be angry to find him here. He said a vicar's first duty is to his parishioners, so he helped people every day."

"Your mother does the same." He distracted her as the vicar landed a blow to the squire's belly, making the horse's ears prick to attention. "And I've heard that you assist her. Your father would be proud."

"I wish I could do more," she said with a sigh that belied her tender years. "She won't let me distribute remedies to the sick, but I got to talk to Mr. Matthews. He came back from the army with only one leg. We found him a position as a clerk."

"Very good, Sarah. Injured soldiers deserve our help." His upraised hand stopped another protest that she wanted to do more. "*Your* first duty is to learn the lessons Mary and your mother assign."

"I suppose, but it's more fun to help others." The carriage turned into High Street, drawing her eyes back to the window. "Look! There is Mrs. Telcor." She pointed toward the gossip.

"Manners prohibit pointing," he reminded her.

Mrs. Telcor frowned when she caught sight of Sarah, probably expecting Catherine to be with them.

"Mama says it's bad manners to say nasty things about people, too, but Mrs. Telcor does it all the time," Sarah confided.

"Not everyone follows the rules. And most rules have exceptions. Sometimes people need to know bad things." Like warning young men about suspected cheats and warning young ladies about predators like Dornbras.

"Then why does no one talk about the bad things Mr. Rankin does?" This time her sigh expressed a seven-year-old's perplexity.

"If no one talks, how do you know he does anything bad?"

"Papa called him a bad man. Besides, I saw him. He cut the harness on Mr. Howard's carriage, then claimed Billy Wyath did it. Billy tried to protest, but Mr. Rankin pinched him to make him be quiet. When I told Mama, she just said to stay away from Mr. Rankin and never talk about him."

"Did you see what Billy did to annoy Rankin?"

She shook her head. "But it must have been bad. They sent him away to school the next day."

"Not as a punishment," he said firmly. "Most boys go away to school. It would have been arranged long before."

"Maybe." She didn't believe him.

"Trust me, Sarah. I started school at age eight, as did most of my friends." He squeezed her hand as the carriage drew to a halt. "I will take care of Mr. Rankin, but your mother is right. He is powerful and can hurt your whole family, so stay away from him."

He mulled her words while they examined the map Cavendish spread on a table for them. He was amazed at how many people knew Rankin for the tyrant he was. Children, tenants, tradesmen. Yet all were so far beneath his consequence, they could never fight back. How many others hugged the pain to themselves, unaware that they were not alone?

Catherine had fretted all day about letting Rockhurst take Sarah to Exeter. It wasn't a matter of trust—she knew so proper a man would do nothing to harm Sarah—but appearing together would link him to her. What would Jasper do?

The most innocuous response would claim that Rockhurst was her latest lover. Jasper might already have done so, for he must know Rockhurst was staying at the manor. Or Jasper might know about Rockhurst's investigation and try to discredit him. She didn't want William's plan to hurt the earl. But her greatest fear was that Jasper would take advantage of Sarah's public appearance to injure her.

By sunset, she was frantic. When Rockhurst's carriage headed straight for the stable instead of dropping its passengers at the door, fear sent her flying after it. She needed every bit of control she could muster to greet them normally when they emerged unscathed.

"Mama!" shouted Sarah. "Mr. Cavendish has a huge map that shows every place in the world, and Rockhurst taught me how to read it. Then we fed the squirrels, and had cake and chocolate, and Miss Ander's dog escaped and rolled in the mud, and—"

"Slow down, sweetheart." She glanced apologetically at Rockhurst. "I hope she was not too demanding." She should have sent Annie with them. Few gentlemen cared to have sole charge of children.

"She is a delight. And the dog made quite an impression, sharing its mud coat with a dozen observers, including Mrs. Telcor."

"Heavens. We will be hearing about this for months."

"Years." He chuckled. "She was wearing a new ermine-trimmed cloak, which is now plastered with mud. It will never be the same."

It was a delicious image, for the woman was her most scathing detractor.

Sarah was still dancing with excitement. "Vicar Sanders was in town, wasting a whole afternoon arguing with Squire Pott about a horse. Papa would have called him a lazy scoundrel for ignoring his duty."

"It is not your place to judge him, Sarah." Embarrassment heated her cheeks.

"Papa would," Sarah insisted. Clearly the excitement of the day had tired her. "Just as he would have said Mr. Cavendish was sly. He whisked a pile of maps out of sight the moment he saw Rockhurst at the door."

"Sarah—"

"It's true," confirmed Rockhurst, interrupting. His

eyes forbade her to pursue the subject. "We conducted our lesson, then visited some shops—"

"He bought the most beautiful doll for his cousin, Mama, with real hair even lighter than mine." That Sarah dared interrupt him proved she had forgotten her manners entirely, but Rockhurst merely smiled. "And we stopped at the confectioner's for chocolate. And there was a new squirrel today, so dark he almost looks black. He hung back at first, as if he didn't trust us, but Rockhurst convinced him to take bread right out of his fingers."

"Quite a talent," agreed Catherine lightly. Rockhurst's amusement eased her embarrassment. "So I presume you are too full to want dinner after such a day."

"I only had three cakes and two cups of chocolate. I'm starving."

"As is Horace," said Rockhurst, producing a carrot. "Ted has him unharnessed now, so you can reward him for his fine service."

Catherine watched Sarah skip off to feed the horse. Hopeless longing cracked her heart. Rockhurst was perfect—perfect gentleman, perfect father, perfect friend. He would make a perfect husband for Laura, but she finally admitted that she wanted him for herself.

Yet that was impossible, she reminded herself, ignoring the muscles rippling across his shoulders as he absently patted his other horse while issuing instructions to his groom. She lacked Laura's beauty. Harold had been her only suitor eight years ago, and she now carried the additional baggage of age, a child, and a reputation that would bar her from every drawing room in London. Even if Rockhurst vanquished Jasper, her reputation would remain suspect. No lord would risk tarnishing his image with such uncertainty, particularly a paragon like Rockhurst. People would look askance at his children, wondering if his blood truly flowed in their veins.

Besides, Laura needed a husband, and they had all

agreed that she could try to attach him. Laura had formed a *tendre* for the dashing earl. His intentions remained unknown—he was avoiding any hint of impropriety lest it worsen the rumors—but Laura was so obviously suited to be a countess, he must be considering her.

So Catherine could never admit her own interest. Not only had she already claimed one husband while Laura remained single, but Laura would see such an alliance as a betrayal.

Laura was not as carefree as she seemed. Fate had handed her several failures, each eroding her confidence further. After their mother's death ten years ago, Catherine had stepped up to supervise her younger siblings and oversee their flighty governess. Once she'd wed Harold, Laura had tried to take over that job, but at twelve, she had failed. She'd tried again when the governess left four years later, with nominal success. But when tragedy thrust William into the title, he had placed the house and his sisters in Catherine's hands. Only later did she realize that Laura had seen this demotion as another failure. At an age when her friends had been setting up their nurseries, she'd been thrust back into the schoolroom.

By the time Catherine recognized what was happening, the patterns had been set. Laura flirted outrageously, hoping marriage would restore control over her life. Yet her unrealistic expectations again set her up for failure. She sought a heroic man who would provide excitement and who would love her enough that he would never thrust her aside.

But fictional heroes did not exist. While several gentlemen had made offers, the men Laura sighed over had not. Lately Laura had begun to fear that she could never find happiness. People praised her, but in the end she never satisfied them. Now she had new expectations over Rockhurst. Losing him to her widowed, notorious sister would cause irreparable damage to their relationship.

Goose! she admonished herself firmly. *What makes*

*you think you have any chance of stealing him from
under Laura's nose?* Just because he had been appearing in increasingly lascivious dreams did not mean
he actually cared for her. Or that he ever could. No
earl would saddle himself with her shortcomings, for
it would reduce his credit and raise doubts about his
judgment.

She briefly considered luring him into an affair, but
that would eliminate Laura's chances. No man of
honor would wed a lady after bedding her sister. Besides, an affair would ruin her in truth. Sarah did not
deserve that handicap. She would face plenty of others, considering the length of country memories.

"I discovered another of Rankin's revenges," he
said, interrupting her fruitless thoughts. The groom
had joined Sarah and was letting her feed the second horse.

"What now?"

"Sarah told me about Billy Wyath and Mr. Howard's harness."

She flushed. "I had forgotten that one. I am not
even sure Jasper was responsible. The talk died immediately, for Billy left for school the next day."

"I think we can trust Sarah's word on this. She saw
him cut the harness and heard him charge Billy with
the crime."

Berating herself for not listening, she nodded. She
should not have put Sarah off that day, but the rumors
had just begun, and she had been terrified that Jasper
would turn on Sarah if he heard her talking about him.

"You might ask her if she knows of any other incidents," he said quietly. "I did not wish to press her
in public, but children usually see far more than we
think they do."

"I know," she agreed, backing away lest his near-
ness prompt her to do something stupid. Desire
warmed her until she feared her face was cherry red.
"Thank you for suggesting this outing. She enjoys visiting town."

She fled, so discomfited that she almost left Sarah behind.

Blake shook his head over Catherine's abrupt departure, then headed for the folly, where he could think without having to look over his shoulder every minute. Laura was reportedly practicing a new Beethoven sonata.

Catherine's sudden skittishness disturbed him. It was possible that Sarah's chatter had embarrassed her. Custom demanded that children utter only polite responses to simple questions. But her uneasiness had grown worse after Sarah had left them.

Thus he had to question his own behavior. He had meant to discuss Cavendish's forgeries with her, but somehow he must have revealed how much he ached to hold her. More than ached, he admitted, running his fingers through his hair. It was a gnawing hunger raised by the countless times she had prowled his dreams since he'd spotted her in Exeter. Even before he'd learned her name, she'd plagued him.

Now it was worse. He saw her a dozen times a day. Every time her eyes warmed, flames raced through his body, even as he reminded himself that she felt only gratitude for his promise. When she'd appeared unexpectedly in the stable just now, his knees had gone weak.

He had thought he was controlling his face, but she must have realized where his thoughts had drifted. Embarrassed, she had fled. If he did not find evidence against Rankin soon, he would do something regretful. Making unwanted advances to any widow was wrong, but seducing Catherine would create an impossible tangle. Not only would she think he believed Jasper's lies, but word would leak out, further eroding her reputation.

He couldn't do it.

Yet he also couldn't sleep for wanting her, and not just in his bed. She was a delightful lady, intelligent, caring, delectably sensual . . .

She is also encouraging Laura to pursue you.

The reminder doused most of his ardor, for it was undeniably true. She had avoided him whenever possible, leaving him to Laura and making her own lack of interest clear. If he pursued his attraction, he would be no better than the conniving Laura.

Thrusting aside the nebulous idea that Catherine would make an interesting countess, he turned his attention to business.

He had collected the Seabrook mail while in Exeter, including two letters addressed to him. The first was from a former schoolmate who lived near Plymouth.

I know little about Mr. Rankin, Robert wrote, *for he rarely enters Plymouth society. But my mother distrusts him—something about his eyes. I do not wholly understand her reasons, but she has an uncommon knack for identifying rogues and other undesirable persons.*

Blake swore. The information fit his impressions, but a woman's instinct did not constitute evidence. He opened the second missive.

Charles had not seen Jasper in ten years, but he remembered him from Harrow. *Disliked by students and tutors alike,* he confirmed. *I avoided him whenever possible, for his arrogance far surpassed his station. He was constantly in trouble with the tutors and was sent down at least once a year. Just after we started at Cambridge, he was sent down for good, though I never heard why. Few people cared enough to discuss him.*

That was the unkindest cut he'd ever heard, decided Blake. And how it must have chafed Jasper. No wonder he eschewed London. Only at home could he attract notice.

Catherine left Sarah in the nursery, then headed for the drawing room to talk to Laura. There was just enough time before they must dress for dinner. Discussing Laura's courtship would remind her unruly passions of the facts.

"Beautiful," she said a few minutes later, having

paused in the doorway while Laura finished playing. "That piece reminds me of rippling water."

Laura's eyes glowed. "It's called *Für Elise*. Perhaps I will play it this evening. Rockhurst appreciates good music."

"As do we all." She paused, but there was no easy way to issue her warning. "You should be less aggressive this evening. I heard he was avoiding you last night."

"Nonsense. He is head over heels for me."

Catherine ignored the pain cracking her heart. It was no more than she had expected. Yet she had to be sure. "Then why has he grown so cool? He hardly spoke to you at dinner, and he slipped away from the drawing room after only a quarter hour."

"To protect my reputation, of course. He has said so more than once. Jasper's rumors make me more susceptible to suspicion than most girls, so he must keep his distance. But you need only watch his eyes to know he cares. He can't keep them away from me. I rarely glance his direction without meeting his gaze. He is perfect."

Catherine bit her tongue, letting Laura's words batter and bruise. Even Jasper's rumors had not drawn this much pain. But now she knew. Her impression of irritation was a fantasy created by her own unworthy dreams. Laura had too much experience with infatuated suitors to doubt her reading of Rockhurst's intentions.

"You will be quite well suited," she agreed when Laura paused for breath. "But if he is truly enamored, then there is no reason to pursue him so doggedly. Demonstrate decorum this evening. Prove that your behavior is all that is proper for a countess."

Doubt flashed through Laura's eyes. Or anger, decided Catherine in correction. "He loves me as I am," snapped Laura. "Why should I raise suspicion by changing?"

She stalked away before Catherine could respond.

Chapter Ten

Catherine glared at Rockhurst as he stalked across the library. She had avoided him since leaving the stable yesterday, even eating dinner with Sarah on the pretext of listening to the girl's adventures in Exeter. Revealing her foolish heart would drive him away—no gentleman wanted a wife whose sister lusted after him. Laura already carried enough baggage in the form of an impecunious brother, minimal dowry, and notorious sister whose sordid reputation would never completely die.

She needed time to subdue her unruly desires, and Laura's flirting made the process harder. But Rockhurst made avoidance difficult. Not only had he tracked her down, he was demanding that she accompany the family to Exeter's monthly assembly.

"You have to attend," he repeated. "Staying away admits that you are unfit for society."

"That is the most absurd piece of nonsense I've ever heard," she snapped. Granted, she would rather avoid the inevitable cuts, but that wasn't why she was staying home. "I rarely attend assemblies, so no one would expect to see me."

"You chaperon your sisters whenever they attend," he reminded her. "Mrs. Telcor will take note if you do not."

"That was before Jasper began maligning me. People would be appalled if I chaperoned them now. Public association with Laura and Mary will tarnish their reputations. William must assume the job."

"Nonsense. I warned you not to change your behavior. It is your duty to look after your sisters. Abjuring that duty is cowardly and lends credence to Jasper's claims. Follow your usual routine. Ignore any cuts. Hold your head high and look people in the eye. You are an exemplary chaperon and a pattern card of propriety. Demonstrating decorum will raise doubts about the stories, whereas skulking at home will add fuel to the fires."

She began to pace the library, searching for an argument that might sway him. He was right, which made it difficult. But she could hardly discuss her real reasons.

Attending the assembly would throw down a gauntlet for Jasper, forcing him to invent new charges because she was not yet vanquished. Rockhurst's escort would trumpet his support, making further investigation difficult and shocking the gossips. He would spend the entire evening deflecting cuts and planting doubts. And he would have to guard against Jasper's inevitable counterattack.

Could she hide her attraction for Rockhurst amidst all of that? Revealing it would hurt Laura, disgust Rockhurst, and confirm her reputation as a wanton.

Then there was Laura. Having to battle Jasper and the gossips would leave Rockhurst no time for courtship—time Laura counted on to bring him up to scratch. And the cuts and insults would prove how badly these rumors were affecting them all. Earls chose their wives with their heads, not their hearts. It wouldn't do to remind him that Laura might erode his credit and tarnish his image. Without scandal to distract him, a day of theater, dinner, and an assembly would focus his attention entirely on Laura. So she must act in Laura's best interests and stay home.

"No one will question my decision to remain here," she said firmly, returning to his side. "Annie's ankle remains weak, so I must look after Sarah and conduct today's lessons. I cannot expect Mary to give up this trip to the theater."

"Unless Annie reinjured her ankle in the last hour, she is fine. And you know very well that Sarah does not do formal lessons on Saturdays—I cannot believe she would lie to me."

Damn! She was running out of excuses.

"Are you afraid to face the world?" he asked, stepping in front of her. One finger turned up her chin, forcing her to look at him.

"Of course not!" She whirled away to stare out the window. Her knees wobbled from his touch. She prayed he hadn't noticed.

"You will accompany us to town," he ordered. "I vowed to redeem your reputation. The task is difficult enough without creating new hurdles."

"Attending is a mistake," she repeated. He had not moved, so she turned to face him. The sun pouring through the window would turn her into a silhouette, hiding her expression. "It will reveal your purpose, inciting Jasper to new lies."

"That is less onerous than confirming his older ones. Either we all go, or none of us goes. I will not be a party to making the problem worse."

"Very well." She shut her mouth before she could add, *We'll stay.* The day would be a disaster, but Rockhurst was adamant. Laura would never forgive her for canceling the outing. Nor would Mary. Even William would be upset, and not just on Laura's account. He hoped to revive his courtship of Alicia Wyath. The only one not doomed to disappointment was Mary.

As she headed upstairs to change, she pondered Rockhurst's stubbornness. He was exaggerating the damage that staying home might cause, but at the same time he was dismissing the trouble Jasper would raise when he discovered this investigation. Such muddled thinking hinted at impatience—or temper. She could not forget what temper had done to him in Exeter that day. If he felt he had to fulfill his vow before offering for Laura, he might act hastily to force the issue.

Or there might be a darker motive behind his insistence, she realized as she pulled out her best gown. She hadn't forgotten her earlier fears. Had William convinced Rockhurst to spy on her? She was innocent, of course, but perhaps he thought attending the assembly might cause a partner to reveal guilt.

Impatient suitor or scheming investigator? Either way, she was condemned to a painful day.

Blake scanned the assembly room as he ushered Catherine inside. He would rather be anywhere but here. She was right that Jasper would initiate another round of rumors. Yet leaving her home would have put Laura on his arm, raising expectations he could never fulfill.

The admission increased his guilt.

Catherine's arguments had been sound, though he still believed that holding her head high was the best course. But he had selfishly twisted facts and exaggerated consequences to force her to accompany him. He'd been desperate, though that was a poor excuse. Manners demanded that he participate in the entertainments provided by his host, but he expected William to disappear once they reached town, leaving him with only Laura and Mary. It would have placed him in the untenable position of damaging Laura's reputation when he failed to offer. Even the tale he'd spun to Mrs. Telcor wouldn't protect her if William wandered off.

So he'd forced Catherine into a painful evening. He would do what he could to minimize the agony, but hovering nearby would make the rumors worse by hinting that she was under his protection.

He had to spread his attentions equally among William and the three ladies. So far, he had maneuvered to sit with Mary at the theater. Laura had grabbed the seat on his other side, but he had exchanged comments only with Mary during the play, then procured refreshments along during the intervals.

At dinner, he had engaged William in a lively discussion of the play, comparing this company to productions they both recalled from school. He had not allowed William to change the subject or leave the parlor. Laura had glared daggers at him more than once, raising his hopes that she finally understood he wasn't interested.

Now he faced a more challenging test. There was no play to divert attention, and they were no longer in a private parlor. Every word and gesture would be analyzed by the gossips. Catherine was on his arm because she was the eldest, but he kept his expression dutiful.

When a matron cut Catherine, he recoiled as if the cut was directed at him, then cut the woman in return—not that he expected the ploy to work. It would not be long before the gossips knew he was taking Catherine's side against them. He only hoped Jasper would not attend the assembly. It would be a long enough evening as it was.

"I told you I should have stayed home," Catherine murmured as Mrs. Telcor added her own cut.

"Nonsense. You have as much right to be here as they. More, for your breeding is better."

"Reputation surpasses breeding. Leave me before you tarnish your own. Dance with Laura."

"No. I will lead you out." He could not dance with Laura first, but he could dance with each of his host's sisters in turn.

Or so he hoped. In truth, he had ached to touch Catherine since succumbing to temptation in the library that morning. His finger tingled whenever he recalled that brief contact.

It was the situation, he assured himself. Once his task was finished, these feelings would fade. The only reason he was turning into a maudlin fool was because his vow forced him to think of her day and night, yet spending time together would hurt her. No wonder she invaded his dreams to suggest ways he could brush against her as they moved through the patterns of a country dance.

Don't feed the gossip, warned his conscience.

It was right. He must be careful. Too much contact would suggest that she was his mistress. Too little would condemn her as wanton, for his supposed friendship with William had led several people to assume he shared William's priggishness—which had raised more than one private chuckle.

She shrugged and accompanied him to the nearest set. William led out Laura. Mary slipped into a corner, where she happily greeted an elderly gentleman. When the words "green woodpecker" penetrated a lull in the conversation, Blake relaxed. Mary had found another bird lover.

He had his baser instincts firmly under control by the time the music started, though it was hard to ignore the bosom peeping above Catherine's decorous neckline. His conscience kept up a running commentary as he executed the steps: *No one will notice if you grip her hand too firmly, but don't brush her shoulder or hip; hold her gaze only when together; don't peer down her bodice on the passes; think depressing thoughts so your desire doesn't show; don't brush against her, you idiot!*

As the dance advanced them up the set, he watched the gossips whispering in the corners. Mrs. Telcor glared as though he'd betrayed her. Her closest friends sported expressions ranging from disapproval to appalled fury. Several men seemed envious. One conveyed pity, making him wonder if the man knew Jasper was behind the rumors. But two ladies surprised him by ignoring Catherine to shake their heads at Mrs. Telcor. Perhaps he could use that animosity later.

"I told you I shouldn't have come," repeated Catherine when they reached the top of the set and stood out for a pattern. "I don't know which is worse—the men's leers or the ladies' cuts."

"Both will admit the truth in the end." He tried to sound reassuring even as he projected polite ennui for the benefit of their audience.

"Being here reminds everyone of the scandal," she continued, ignoring his words. "Did you see Alicia cut William when we arrived?"

"The girl in the green silk gown?" She had reminded him of every encroaching mushroom he'd ever met. A heavy necklace more suited to a dowager circled her neck. At least three strands of oversized pearls threaded her hair. And her gown was cut scandalously low.

She nodded. "He has been courting her for months and planned to speak with her father before the rumors started. Now his hopes are shattered."

"Is that a tragedy?" he asked, glancing toward the next set, where Alicia danced with a young dandy. The look in her eye was familiar. Miss Wyath might enjoy flirting, but William was not wealthy enough to satisfy her ambitions. "She does not strike me as a welcome addition to the household. William will soon rejoice at his lucky escape."

Catherine's smile raised his temperature. "You are right, of course. I had hoped marriage would settle her, but I have wondered about the effect she would have on my sisters."

"And on Sarah," he murmured as the next pattern began, drawing them back into the dance. As always with country dances, they had no chance to exchange more than an occasional comment as they worked their way back down the set. He kept his expression polite and his eyes on the crowd, but he could not help gripping her hand tighter than was necessary whenever the steps drew them together.

He led Laura out for the next set. This time he had no trouble producing the expected ennui, though he soon had to hide disgust. Her desperation was obvious this evening. Perhaps the cuts brought home the extent of Jasper's schemes, or maybe she was frustrated over his lack of interest. Whatever the cause, she grew more brazen with each repetition of the pattern. By the time they ducked under the third couple's upraised arms, she was plastered so close to his side, she was wrinkling his coat. Her proprietary manner froze his blood.

His temper finally exploded. He let disapproval show on his face and maintained as much distance as possible. It made her seem crassly forward, but calling censure onto her shoulders was better than facing her at an altar. And he was ready to strangle her for adding credence to the rumors. How could he convince people that Catherine was proper when Laura put on such a vulgar display? Had Laura no thought beyond her own ambitions? Surely she could see the damage she was doing to her family. He would have abandoned her on the dance floor if it would not have hurt Catherine even more. But the experience cleared his thinking.

"To the devil with convention," he muttered when he finally escaped her company. He would speak to William in the morning and make it clear that he had no interest in the girl.

In the meantime, he approached Mary.

"Your turn," he said, smiling easily, for he genuinely liked her. "Will you join me for the next set?"

"But—"

"Nonsense, child," said her companion, cutting off her protest. "Don't waste time on an old codger like me when you have a chance to dance with a handsome lord."

She blushed. "I rarely dance."

"Then it is time you did." Blake reached for her hand. "You are long out of the schoolroom, Mary."

"I suppose I am," she admitted, rising. "But I find conversation more interesting than parading about with boring peacocks."

Blake laughed. "I have been firmly set in my place," he told the old man.

"I didn't mean you," she gasped, blushing.

"Manners, child," chided her friend.

Her blush deepened. "Oh! My lord, this is Mr. Fester, who shares my interest in birds. The Earl of Rockhurst."

Blake acknowledged the introduction, then led Mary away. "I won't bite," he promised as they took their places in the set.

"I know." She sighed. "Please forgive me for sound-

ing rude. I can never say the right thing in public. My
mind empties of all rational thought."

"Because you try too hard. You talk easily to
Fester."

"But that is about birds."

"A topic you know and love, so you don't heed the
impression you might be making. You know much
about many fascinating topics. Mention one and you
might discover other gentlemen who share your
interests."

"Why do you care?"

"You are far too young to interest me personally,"
he said, emphasizing the "far" in hopes that it would
put Laura in the same category. "But you are charming, intelligent, and very likable. Unless you intend to
spend the rest of your life teaching girls like Sarah,
you need to consider what will happen when William weds."

The faintest frown creased her forehead, disappearing when the music started.

"Alicia will never accept him," she murmured when
the dance brought them together.

"True." He backed into place. "But he is looking
and is bound to find someone who will," he reminded
her when they came together again.

She let the next two meetings pass with only a social
smile before responding. "I have avoided thinking
about the future."

He nodded, but did not answer until they reached
the head of the set. "Is the idea of marriage so
terrible?"

"I hate the sprigs who scramble to attract Laura's
attention. They are such silly fribbles."

"But not everyone is like that," he reminded her.
Losing her governess at age fourteen had not helped
her social education. "Many men enjoy serious pur-
suits. Some even enjoy serious ladies. My closest
friend's new wife has read thousands of books and
knows more about estate management than he does.
He welcomes her knowledge. And he is not alone,

though it is unfashionable to admit that one prefers an intelligent woman."

"Are you implying that men hide their interests in public?"

"Of course. So do most women. Every occasion has its rules. Society gatherings are for light conversation and flirtation. But that does not mean that no one is capable of thinking. While some men consider blue-stockings unladylike, that usually hides their own lack of understanding. Ask questions, and you will eventually find someone who shares your interests."

"Like Mr. Fester?"

"Exactly. People do not wait until old age to develop serious interests. Ask him how long he has studied birds."

The dance drew them back, preventing further conversation. He wondered how one family could produce three such different women—caring, sensible Catherine; flirtatious, self-absorbed Laura; shy, intellectual Mary, though her shyness was produced in part by Laura's vivacity. Having a beautiful sister could not have been easy. To avoid competition, she had withdrawn into books and teaching. But a baron's sister deserved more than serving as governess to a sequence of nieces and nephews.

He returned Mary to Fester's corner, then slipped away before Laura could accost him. Empty space surrounded Catherine, but she was holding her head high. William had stepped outside, so he followed.

"Good evening, ladies," he said as the two women he'd spotted earlier emerged from an antechamber.

"My lord." The taller one pursed her lips in disapproval as she examined him from head to toe. "I must say I am shocked that a man of your standing would flaunt that woman in decent company."

"Clara!" gasped her companion.

"I refuse to ignore what is before my eyes, Hortense," Clara snapped.

"You are referring to Mrs. Parrish, I presume?" he asked.

"Who else?"

"I know Mrs. Telcor condemns her, for she told me so herself, but I prefer to form my own opinions." He smiled at Clara. "I have known William Seabrook for sixteen years. Not once have I heard him lie, even when doing so might save him grief. So when he swears his sister is innocent, I must take heed."

"What does he know?" demanded Clara with a snort. "He's such a prude he'd have to throw her out if he admitted the truth. Then he'd have to look after those girls himself."

"I agree that men are often blind," he said soothingly. "But Seabrook is hardly a fool. Nor would his priggishness allow him to leave his sisters in the care of a wanton."

Hortense frowned.

"Judge for yourselves. Mrs. Telcor undoubtedly claims that Mrs. Parrish slips away while Seabrook is occupied on the estate." Clara was nodding. "I would counter with my own observations. Since my arrival, Mrs. Parrish has spent the better part of every day teaching in the schoolroom. Sarah considers this normal. Mrs. Parrish spends at least an hour each morning with the cook and housekeeper. They consider this normal. She eats breakfast with her brother and dinner with the entire family, then spends her evenings in the drawing room. Again, this is a daily habit that no one questions. Thus I must ask how a woman could carry out frequent assignations when those closest to her remain ignorant of her activities and can account for all of her time."

"He has a point," said Hortense. "I've seen her feeding the squirrels with Sarah. They have a remarkable bond."

"But rumors do not grow themselves," said Clara.

"Not without malicious help," he suggested. "But I've no doubt you can discover the truth. No one guilty of such excess can escape notice by astute ladies such as yourselves. If you have seen nothing untoward all these years, then perhaps there was nothing to see."

"Hmph." Clara snorted, but Hortense seemed thoughtful.

"Observation might also reveal who is starting these tales," he added before bidding them farewell. Perhaps they would ask questions that would make people more receptive to admitting Jasper's guilt.

Or perhaps not. Some people had no interest in logic. The discussion wafting out of the ladies' retiring room proved that self-interest often reigned supreme.

"Shocking!" Miss Wyath exclaimed. Her voice had a piercing quality that made it unforgettable—and quite irritating. "I cannot believe she had the nerve to come here. A harlot has no place in genteel company."

"I cannot understand why your mother allowed you to remain, my dear," said another woman. "I sent my Harriet home to protect her sensibilities."

"And not only from Mrs. Parrish," put in a third. "Her sister is just as bad. I've never witnessed such a shocking flirt. Did you see how she wrapped herself around the earl? Shameless!"

Blake grimaced. Not that the words surprised him. Had Laura realized how badly she had tarnished her own reputation? And in front of a hundred witnesses. When she did, she would become even more desperate.

But he could not linger in the hallway. He knew why Miss Wyath had not left. Her eyes had followed him all evening, greed glittering in their amber depths. He'd learned that her mother was better-born than Mr. Wyath and dreamed of regaining her social position by arranging a splendid match for Alicia. Alicia seemed eager to comply. Her unseemly neckline and excessive jewelry were intended to draw his eye.

Stepping outside, he pulled the door closed, then ducked around the corner.

William was leaning against the wall, staring at nothing.

"Trouble?" asked Blake, joining him.

He shrugged.

"She is not worth such melancholy," he said daringly, for it was not the thing to interfere in a gentleman's courtship, even if the man was a close friend.

"That is not the problem. Alicia must follow her parents' lead, and they are understandably cautious about the rumors. But I had not realized how bad those had become. Bringing Catherine was a mistake. We should leave before the situation grows worse."

"She is here on my orders. Hiding from her detractors makes her seem ashamed. And now that we are here, leaving would cause even more harm." He paused to make sure William understood. "As to Miss Wyath, while I am sure she is a dutiful daughter, I doubt she disagrees with her parents on this point. I have met many girls like her in London. Their sole ambition is to attach the greatest fortune and highest title available. She would never consider yours without first testing her charms on a wider market."

"You wrong her." His fists clenched, driving off every trace of low spirits. "Her parents may have hopes, but Alicia is sweet and kind."

"Perhaps, though my own impressions are otherwise. Her eyes reveal the sort of calculation I've seen before—on Miss Edgerton, for example. She made her bows in London two Seasons ago, flirting lightly and smiling sweetly. Not until accepting a wealthy earl did she reveal her true nature. One of my friends owns the adjacent estate. He reports that she makes constant demands for jewels and clothes and trips to London. And she despises her husband's sisters and two aunts, who live with them."

"Alicia would never hurt my family." But his protest lacked force.

"Three observations, Seabrook." He kept his tone friendly. "First, she not only cut Catherine, but referred to her as a harlot barely five minutes ago in the retiring room. Second, it is my experience that girls usually become much like their mothers after marriage; from what I've heard, Mrs. Wyath is not a comfortable wife. And third, she has been trying to catch my eye all evening."

Seabrook's own eyes seemed troubled. "She *did* express surprise when I mentioned that I've no interest in London society, but she never raised the subject again."

"It is my guess that she has been practicing her flirtation skills on you. If you offered, she would refuse, but she would prefer to keep you at hand in case she fails to find a better match. You *do* have a title."

"Perhaps." He sighed. "No, there is no *perhaps* about it. You are right. She deflected an offer last summer. I thought it was because I had not yet spoken to her father."

"You should return." Blake nodded toward the ballroom. "Implying that either Miss Wyath or the cuts drove you away will do no good."

"Of course," William acknowledged. "I should not have left Catherine to face people alone."

Pasting on a smile, he headed back to the assembly.

Blake waited several minutes before following, not wanting to suggest that he had fetched the baron. But one glance from the doorway had him cursing under his breath. Laura had joined Mary and Fester in the corner, her tremulous smile hinting that she was close to tears. Mrs. Telcor was reading William a scold, judging from his expression. And three men had backed Catherine against a wall, their leers making it clear that dancing was not on their minds. One of them was three sheets to the wind.

Grinding his teeth, Blake shoved his way through the crowd. "My set, I believe," he said when he reached her side.

"Wait your turn," suggested the drunk. "We was here first."

"Do you wish to postpone our dance?" he asked Catherine, shifting so he stood between her and the men.

"Of course not, my lord." She emphasized the address, making one of the men blink.

"The lady has chosen." He put steel in his tone, his look promising trouble if they persisted.

The drunk raised a fist to protest, but one of his friends grabbed his arm. "Let's go, Jake. This ain't your lucky night, after all."

They headed for the door.

"Thank you." Catherine managed a smile as they joined a set. "Now you understand why I wished to stay home."

"Forgive me," he begged. "I should not have stepped out."

She moved into the first figure, relaxing now that the danger was past.

His own mind was less sanguine. The men had not been in the room when he'd left, so they must have come solely to find the harlot—which meant news of Catherine's attendance was spreading. That was hardly a surprise, given that at least one girl had been ordered home to avoid her.

But the potential of outside trouble was not as important as the damage they had done inside. Expressions had hardened, putting glares on faces that earlier had seemed neutral.

"I met two ladies named Clara and Hortense," he said when they came together. "Who are they?"

"The Peters sisters."

Blake raised his brows in silent question as they separated.

"Spinsters who live in that cottage just outside of town," she explained at their next meeting.

"With the roses over the door?"

She nodded.

Two patterns later, they reached the bottom of the set.

Blake waited a moment to catch his breath—the lead fiddler was picking up speed, making this dance unusually energetic. "I suspect that Hortense does not like Mrs. Telcor."

"Nor does Clara, though she is less obvious about it. They grew up together and have long been rivals.

Mrs. Telcor feels superior for having landed a husband, however short-lived, while the Peters sisters did not."

"Her husband died young?"

"After barely six months of marriage. She miscarried a month later."

No wonder she had turned her maternal urges on Jasper.

"Their most recent tiff is over Jasper," Catherine continued as if reading his mind. "The Peters sisters dismissed his explanation of the Jones incident, informing Mrs. Telcor that he was too old for heedless destruction and juvenile pranks. She tolerates criticism of herself, but never of Jasper."

"Perhaps we can use that rift," he murmured as the dance reclaimed them. And just as well, for he had no real ideas how he could use them beyond what he'd already done.

When the set ended, he left Catherine with William, then turned toward Mary's corner. But Mrs. Telcor pounced. "You haven't met Miss Wyath, my lord." She performed the introductions. "Her mother is granddaughter to Lord Seaton and cousin to the Duke of Everleigh."

Tenth cousin, at best, he decided as he greeted her in a very bored tone. He doubted if either lord knew the Wyaths. Miss Wyath's long nose and amber eyes reminded him of a hawk.

How had she wangled this introduction? Mrs. Telcor might be smiling now, but she'd been furious with him for escorting the Seabrooks. But perhaps she was also unhappy with Alicia. This might be her way of repaying both of them.

The hairs on his neck stiffened under his cravat. Alicia had reportedly made a bid for Jasper's hand before turning to William, but Mrs. Telcor would never approve such a low connection for her favorite.

"I've always admired men who are active in politics," Miss Wyath said, fluttering her lashes. "You must tell me about your plans for reform."

"I doubt you would understand rotten boroughs or the rules of taxation," he said untruthfully.

"Nonsense. My father often debates such matters with me." She laid a hand on his arm.

"Lead the girl out," suggested Mrs. Telcor. "You can talk during this cotillion."

"Another time, perhaps," he said, stepping back. "I promised this set to Miss Mary. Mrs. Telcor, Miss Wyath." Bowing, he fled.

The last thing he wanted was to dance a cotillion with a fortune hunter. It was the one dance that would keep her at his side for most of the set. He had hoped to share it with Catherine, but that trio of drunkards had forced them into the country dance. Fortunately, Mary was free. And dancing a second time with these two should force Laura to recognize his disinterest.

An hour later, he wished that none of them had come. The crowd remained cool, though Catherine was the only one being actively shunned. William had danced every set since their talk, forcing a gaiety he did not feel. Blake hoped the gossips would attribute his strain to Catherine rather than dashed dreams. Laura was flirting with every man in the room. He'd refused to stand up with her a second time, even to avoid Miss Wyath, who was clearly stalking him. So far, he'd evaded her by asking strangers to dance, but he wasn't sure how long he could escape her clutches.

Yet when deliverance finally came, it made Alicia's stratagems seem benign.

Jasper arrived.

Blake held his breath, for Catherine and William were standing just inside the entrance. Even from across the room he could see the fire in William's eyes. If Jasper cut Catherine or greeted her with the false familiarity he'd used in Exeter, William would attack.

The outcome hung in the balance for a long moment while Jasper examined Catherine from head to toe with an ornate quizzing glass. Then he greeted her civilly.

Blake cursed under his breath. He should have

known Jasper would employ cunning. A brawl would terminate the evening and would allow Catherine to claim that Jasper was behind the rumors. She might also reveal his other crimes. To maintain his own façade, he provided no excuse to accuse him. Not that he accepted her—his demeanor announced that he was overlooking her reputation to protect the other guests from William's violence.

Clever like a fox, admitted Blake reluctantly, though he cringed at Jasper's taste. His clothes would have made even a London tulip flinch—a yellow wasp-waisted coat with enormous buttons, blue pantaloons, and a red-striped waistcoat embroidered with lavender flowers. The fact that his friends hadn't told him how ridiculous he looked indicated that they knew him well. It also proved that the infamous waistcoat must have been truly awful.

Five minutes later Blake pricked to attention, cold clutching his stomach. A new rumor was spreading as knots of gossips formed and reformed. Voices rose in agitation. "Scandalous . . . Landsbury affair . . . Parrish . . . they don't even try to hide . . ."

"Lies! All lies!" shouted a man into the rising furor. "There's not a word of truth to any of it."

Blake couldn't see the speaker through the shifting crowd, but it had to be Lansbury.

Catherine rushed up to clutch his arm, panic filling her eyes. "We have to leave."

He covered her hand. "No. Leaving now will make it worse."

"Tarradiddles, every one, I tell you!" shouted Lansbury, his face purple as he shook a fist at a matron. "Plumpers and clankers of the first order!"

Blake cursed. "His protests make him seem guilty." Already the crowd was condemning Lansbury for ignoring indisputable evidence, though no one seemed to know what the evidence was.

"Poor man. We should get him away before his wife returns," Catherine murmured. "She is in the retiring room."

"Try to warn her—"

But it was too late. A screech drowned the music, pulling every eye to the door. Mrs. Lansbury clutched her heart, cried out once more, then collapsed on the floor.

"Fool!" Mrs. Telcor shook a fist in Lansbury's face. "What were you thinking of to hurt that dear lady? You should be transported."

"I did nothing!" he protested, but a dozen others shouted him down.

"You should have turned that whore off months ago," yelled a youth in the opposite corner.

"Don't you dare insult my family," snarled William in reply.

Damn! Blake jerked his head around in time to see William land a facer on a young dandy he suspected was Lansbury's nephew.

"My God!" gasped Catherine as several men jumped into the fray. Two ladies shouted for hartshorn as another swooned. Furniture cracked when William bore his opponent to the floor.

Blake grabbed Catherine's hand and headed for the fight, dodging people who were trying to escape.

"See what you've done!" cried a lady, shaking a fist as she blocked their path.

Clara Peters shoved her aside to spit in Catherine's face. "And to think I've entertained you in my own drawing room!"

Blake slipped Catherine behind him. "She has done nothing wrong," he swore. "Nor has Lansbury. Will you allow Mrs. Telcor to dictate your every thought? You are capable of thinking for yourself."

"Hmph! I have eyes and ears and decent morals besides." Clara glared at Catherine. "Stay away from Exeter. We don't need your sort disrupting our lives and seducing decent men." She stalked away to add her smelling salts to those already waving under Mrs. Lansbury's nose.

"Steady," Blake murmured to Catherine, sensing her fury. He offered a handkerchief. "Hysterics will play into Jasper's hands. William's temper is bad enough."

"You expect me to do nothing after that?" she demanded.

"I expect you to control yourself. You are a dignified widow who is above these childish lies and above this low behavior." He wanted to comfort her, but this was neither the time nor the place. "Hold your head high and remain calm."

"Do you know what you are asking?" Yet she straightened her spine and unclenched her fists like the warrior she was.

"Yes, but you cannot succumb to fury just now. Find Laura and Mary. They were in the corner with Fester when Jasper arrived. I will fetch William."

"Harlot!" Mrs. Lansbury screamed, overriding Catherine's response. She was propped in a chair, glaring through a break in the surging crowd. "Jezebel! Fiend!" She tried to rise, but her knees wouldn't support her, so she increased her invective.

Lansbury formed a counterpoint to his wife's accusations as he accosted lady after lady to proclaim his innocence, making himself seem guiltier with each repetition.

Mothers hustled their daughters out of the room, some clamping hands over their darlings' ears to block the increasingly graphic charges. Most cut Catherine as they left.

"Fetch the girls and meet me back here," Blake ordered, nodding toward Fester's corner. The thinning crowd revealed Laura in tears. Mary was trying to calm her. "I must keep William from hurting anyone."

Catherine nodded.

The fight now involved a score of men. Blake doubted most knew whom they were hitting, though they seemed to be quarreling over Lansbury's guilt. But the confusion made it all the more dangerous. He waded in, ducking fists and sidestepping feet until he finally spotted William and Brad Lansbury on the floor. A tangle of chairs separated them from the others.

"Stop this!" he demanded, deflecting William's blow before it could land on Brad's ear. "I mean it!" He rolled William off and pulled Brad to his feet, pinning the boy's arms to his side when he tried to escape.

"Fighting will only make things worse." He stepped on William's arm, then shook Brad to get his attention. "The stories are lies from start to finish. You would be better served to get your uncle out of here before he makes enemies that will plague him for years. No one is in a mood to listen just now."

The sound of breaking crockery cut through the noise. Someone was peppering Lansbury with plates and bottles. Wine soaked his coat, drawing new protestations of innocence. Jasper stood nearby, sheltering Mrs. Telcor from flying debris.

Brad broke away, shoving men aside as he rushed across the room. Mrs. Lansbury's wails had progressed to full hysterics.

"Get up and control yourself," Blake told William.

"He called Catherine—"

"I don't care what he said. I've heard worse. But fighting will accomplish nothing. Now pull yourself together. You are a baron, not a brawler. Start acting like it."

Brad's efforts to calm Lansbury distracted men from the fight.

Blake grimaced. Now that tempers were cooling, Jasper stepped forward, making a great show of separating combatants. Satisfaction blazed in Jasper's eyes.

Catherine was struggling to control her sisters. She had one hand clamped around Laura's wrist and the other on Mary's skirt. Laura was wailing at the top of her lungs. Mary must have seen Jasper's triumph, for she was dragging the others in his direction, fists raised in fury.

Alicia stormed across the room. "Stop this cater-wauling at once," she snapped, slapping Laura in the face. "If you insist on living with a harlot, people will shun you."

The blow penetrated Laura's distress. "Hussy!" she screamed, slapping her back. "How dare you judge me when you are no better than a vulgar bawd?"

"Who are you calling vulgar?" Alicia landed a blow to Laura's shoulder.

"We all saw you stalking Rockhurst." Laura shook off Catherine's hand, grabbed a hank of Alicia's hair, and pulled. Strings snapped, scattering pearls across the floor.

"Alicia shrieked, then waded in, both fists flying. A new melee erupted as people scrambled to recover the pearls.

Blake groaned. "Do something," he ordered William. "Catherine can't control both of them." By now she had her hands full trying to prevent shy, docile Mary from attacking Mrs. Telcor, who was praising Jasper for his masterly action in quelling the first riot and urging him to stop this new fracas.

"We should have stayed home," moaned William.

"Save the regrets," Blake snapped. "Fetch the girls and meet me by the window. And no more fighting, no matter what the provocation."

"Right."

Blake didn't completely trust him, but he had to do what he could to minimize the damage. He pushed through the crowd until he found Hortense. "The timing of this revelation is quite interesting," he said, so only she could hear. "It began only moments after Jasper Rankin arrived. Three days ago, two boys overheard him threaten revenge on Lansbury for having the audacity to drive his wagon along a narrow lane at the precise moment Rankin wanted to use it."

Hortense frowned, but she made no comment. He held her eyes a moment, then slipped away, hoping she would remember his suggestion once the dust settled.

William had routed Alicia and was dragging his sisters away. But the melee was growing. Three merchants' wives were hacking up the floor, looking for pearls that had rolled down a knothole. Chairs flew as others scrambled into corners. This assembly would be remembered for generations.

William finally escaped the crowd. And just in time. Mr. Wyath arrived, fire in his eyes. Alicia burst into tears at his greeting.

When Blake reached the window, Catherine's eyes glittered with unshed tears. "Now we know how Jasper will ruin Lansbury," she murmured. "I should have considered his wife. Edna clings to him. Suspecting him of infidelity will destroy her, and seeing her pain might well kill him."

"If she truly cares, she will let him explain. A lifetime of trust cannot be undone by one venal rumor." He sighed. "Tempers are too high to do anything more tonight. We must concede this round to Jasper, but I am more determined than ever to defeat him."

"Impossible."

"We must leave," William said, holding Laura and Mary so tightly that Laura could not throw herself against Blake's chest.

Blake checked the room. More than half the guests were gone. The musicians had fled. So had the servants. Someone was probably fetching the constable.

"Very well." He let William lead the way, then whispered to Catherine, "Go with them and make sure William does not respond to taunts as he leaves. His temper is still precarious. I will join you shortly."

"What are you doing?"

"Fulfilling that promise I made to Harry. Now go."

She nodded, but she glanced back several times as she headed for the door.

Edna Lansbury had finally lapsed into silence. When everyone turned to watch the Seabrooks' exit, Blake whispered in her ear. "The story is a lie concocted by Jasper Rankin to hurt your husband, though he did nothing to deserve such spite. Don't let Jasper destroy your trust."

Before she could respond, he slipped into the night.

Chapter Eleven

Something halted Blake just outside the library. Maybe it was a sound or the slightly ajar door. Or perhaps it was merely instinct. But once he had glanced through the crack, he fled.

Damnation! More explicit curses followed. Never had he been so furious.

He'd been set up. Thank heavens he'd been heading for the breakfast room when he'd received the summons. He'd arrived before Laura had finished arranging the scene. Was William positioned to jump out and cry compromise the moment he entered the room?

A new stream of invective tripped off his tongue. He should have expected this after the fiasco at the assembly last night. For the first time, Laura had experienced the same ostracism Catherine had suffered for weeks, and his disinterest must have finally penetrated her conceit. So she had taken matters into her own hands.

As soon as he found William indisputably alone, he would denounce them both, then move back to the White Hart. Leaving Seabrook would make it more difficult to fulfill his vow, but that was a price he must pay.

In the meantime, he would check on his horses. They, at least, offered undemanding company.

He was rounding the corner of the manor when he nearly ran William down. "Cad!" he snapped, unable to hold his temper. "I hadn't believed you would stoop so low, though I should have expected it when I realized you brought me here under false pretenses.

I should call you out—and would if it would not harm Catherine beyond repair."

William recoiled. "What?"

He ignored the overdone shock. "This would have been bad enough if I weren't your guest, but abusing your hospitality after tying me to the estate makes it worse. I will never—"

"What the devil are you talking about?" demanded Seabrook, interrupting. "If you have a complaint, we will discuss it, but let's at least go inside instead of sharing it with the staff." He gestured toward a pair of gardeners clipping hedges in the distance.

"You won't set me up a second time. I'll see—"

"Stop!"

William's voice cut through Blake's protest. Snapping his mouth closed, he stared at his host, then applied curbs to his temper when he spotted the confusion simmering in the man's eyes.

William let out a deep breath. "I have always considered you a fair man, Rockhurst. If you feel wronged, I must respect that, but I have no idea what you are talking about. Your summons said only to meet you in the library."

"Summons?" Blake glared. "I sent no summons."

"No su—" William frowned. "Bill told me that you wished to see me in the library as soon as possible. Since he'd chased me down in the stable to deliver the message, I presumed the matter was urgent."

"How interesting." Blake cupped his chin. "Rob met me outside the breakfast room. According to him, you needed me in the library immediately. He was so anxious that I postponed eating."

"But—"

"The only occupant of the library is Laura. When I peeped around the door, she was pulling the pins from her hair."

"She wouldn't!" William's horror finally convinced Blake that Laura had concocted this plot on her own.

"She is. If you join her, she will weep and wail over my supposed attack. I won't stand for it, Seabrook. I

meant to speak with you this morning anyway, for her
antics have become more than irritating. I must lock
my door at night to keep her from crawling into my
bed. She has the entire staff spying on me. I cannot
sit down for a moment without her appearing. Her
constant prattle gives me headaches. But this is too
much. I have no interest in the chit. Any lies she de-
vises will ruin her, for I will never offer. I would leave
the country first, for I despise schemers."

William's shoulders sagged. "I cannot believe that
she is this desperate. She has turned down four offers
that I know of, and I've no idea how many others she
dissuaded from speaking with me."

"None were from gentlemen who would whisk her
away to a life of adventure," Blake reminded him gently. "Now she finds herself with no suitors and a questionable reputation, so she has abandoned her dreams
to claim the nearest male. What she refuses to admit
is that she would be as unhappy with me as you would
have been with Miss Wyath. She wants adventure, society, and fawning adoration. I prefer the Abbey to
London. When I go to town, it will be for Parliament
and not for an endless round of boring parties. Our
ambitions are too disparate."

"She isn't as selfish as you claim. She's—"

"Don't." Blake put as much ice in his tone as possible. "Nothing you say will make a difference. I know
she is your sister, but to outside eyes she is a self-
absorbed, greedy fortune hunter who ignores even obvious truths if they contradict her fantasies. Right now
her goal is to escape Devonshire. She will do anything
to achieve it."

William turned away, staring into the distance as his
fists clenched and unclenched. He finally turned back
to meet Blake's gaze. "I owe you a great deal for
opening my eyes to Alicia's faults. When I saw her
pursuing you last evening, her avaricious nature became clear. And her attack on Laura was inexcusably
vulgar. She would have made an abominable wife."

"You can pay the debt by passing the lesson on to

your sister. She will destroy her reputation if she persists with this plot. And her blindness is appalling.
Even if she had succeeded in wresting an offer from
me, word would have leaked out about her methods.
It would have destroyed the rest of you by confirming
the rumors of gross indiscretions."

"I am not looking forward to the conversation,"
William admitted.

"I would be surprised if you were. You might mention that I see little difference between her and Miss
Wyath, especially after her performance at the assembly. Both flirt with anyone at hand while they scheme
to trap a man who will elevate them. Both are selfish,
caring little about how their actions affect others. And
both are stupid, ignoring the inevitable result of their
schemes. Husbands have no duty to their wives beyond providing food, clothing, and shelter. A loaf of
bread, a tattered robe, and space in the dungeon
would be sufficient."

"True. I will see that she behaves in future."

It wasn't enough, decided Blake. Laura might ignore William's orders. "If I cannot concentrate on
countering Jasper's plots, I must return to town."

William grimaced. Leaving Seabrook would inten-
sify the gossip, raising new charges against the entire
family. "That won't be necessary. I'll lock her up before I'll let her bother you again." He paused. "I am
curious, though. Might you have considered Laura if
she had not been so brazen?"

"No. She exhibits none of the traits I demand in a
wife. Besides, I have my eye on someone else," he
added in patent untruth.

"Well . . . that's that, then." William squared his
shoulders. "I will see her now. Please accept my apologies, Rockhurst. This should never have happened.
I cannot condone force, no matter what the goal."

Blake watched him leave. He would never blame
William for entertaining hopes. The man had two sisters to settle, a task made difficult by straitened cir-

cumstances and Laura's air dreaming even before Jasper's attacks began.

Abandoning his plans to visit the stable, he headed for the formal garden. But William's question teased his mind. His answer had sought to deflate even the tiniest hope that Laura could bring him up to stretch, but now he wondered if it had contained a grain of truth. He envied Max's luck in finding a wife who complemented him so perfectly. The two shared a link felt by few aristocratic couples.

Catherine is very like her, whispered his conscience.

Perhaps. And it was true that she elicited some of the same reactions Max had described. But he could not afford to consider the possibility of Catherine as his wife just yet. Unless he kept their relationship firmly focused on business, he would make the situation worse.

Business meant identifying Jasper's closest friends. They were the ones most likely to know his motives. The fact that they rarely teased him proved that they understood his reactions. Ted could discover their names. So could Catherine, of course. But asking her required going indoors. Until William had dealt with Laura, he couldn't risk it.

Again he turned toward the stable, but Sarah shouted a greeting and beckoned him to join her near the folly. Within minutes he found himself tramping through the woods, diligently matching fallen leaves to the trees that had produced them.

William paused in the library doorway. He'd been hoping that Rockhurst had misinterpreted what he'd seen. Though he knew the assembly had shocked Laura into hysterics, he hadn't thought she would employ dishonor. So he'd made excuses and invented other explanations—perhaps Rob had summoned both men to the library, but Bill had garbled the message; maybe Laura had taken advantage of an empty room to repair a slipping hairstyle; Rockhurst might be lying . . .

But even imagination could find no reason for

Rockhurst to lie. He was too honorable—which made Laura's dishonor even worse.

Now he glared at her as his last hope died. She was standing by the window, her hair in artistic disarray. A torn shoulder drooped from her gown as she clutched a drape to her bosom. The moment he entered, she burst into sobs. "He attacked me," she cried, flinging herself into his arms. "He c-claimed he c-couldn't live another d-day without me. I tried to fight—"

"I am appalled," he snapped, shoving her away. He clasped his hands behind his back to keep from shaking her. "I never believed a Seabrook could play so dastardly a trick."

"Me? Rockhurst assaulted me!"

"Stop this, Laura." He backed away from the stranger inhabiting his sister's body. "You demean yourself more with every word. You arranged this dishabille yourself, as a witness will attest."

"You can't believe—"

"I just left Rockhurst," he continued, ignoring her. "How interesting that each of us received a summons supposedly from the other. Who do you suppose gave those messages to Rob and Bill? I will ask them if I must. Neither of them will lie to me, for doing so would cost them their positions." Her recoil was all the confirmation he needed. "That was not well done of you. I am ashamed that such a schemer shares my roof and name."

She collapsed onto the couch, crying in earnest. "B-but how else am I to attach him? I've never met anyone so slow to respond to me."

"Beware of arrogance," he warned, pulling a chair around to face her. "I warned you not to press him, Laura. Like most wealthy lords, he is plagued by fortune hunters. They throw themselves at his title in droves—just as you have been doing. He pulled no punches when describing you. One of his less vulgar comments compared you to Alicia Wyath, who did everything but tear her clothes off trying to draw his attention last night. But even Alicia did not stoop to trickery."

She flinched. "I never meant—"

"Intentions no longer matter. Whether he might have formed an attachment if you had met under different circumstances is moot." He frowned. "I think he seeks something quite specific in a wife, though he did not say what. But whatever that is, he considers you an irritating, unscrupulous fortune hunter."

"But I don't care about his fortune."

"It makes no difference. Look at yourself. If you were a man, would you want ties to such a woman? Would you wish to live with her, have children with her, or accede to a single one of her wishes?"

"Dear Lord!" She hugged herself, shaking.

"It is over, Laura. He wants nothing to do with you, and I don't blame him. I promised that you would leave him alone for the remainder of his stay—which he was ready to terminate immediately. If you make the slightest overture, he will leave. After last night, you should understand what that would mean to Catherine."

"And all of us," she managed. Panic filled her eyes.

"Now you see your peril. Your future depends on exposing Jasper's lies. As does mine and Mary's. I have tried to pretend it does not, but even turning Catherine off would not save us. We have become pariahs in the public eye. Rockhurst is our best hope of recovering."

She reached out to touch his arm. "Does losing Miss Wyath hurt?"

"I am angrier at myself than at her," he admitted. "Jasper's rumors kept me from making a serious mistake. She has been using me to hone her flirting skills while she waits for a man worth trapping. And she was hoping to keep me in reserve in case she failed to do better—you can imagine how she would have behaved in that event. While I do have a title, I lack the fortune and social connections she seeks."

"She would be furious."

"Exactly. Having already failed to attach Jasper, she is heading for Bath and then London. If she had been forced to settle for me, she would have made endless demands for money, clothes, Seasons . . ." He let his voice fade as he shook his head. "She would have been very unhappy when I refused. I would have had to live with an increasingly waspish wife. And think of what that would have meant to Catherine and Sarah."

"Or Mary and me," she agreed, shuddering.

"Don't make the same mistake," he urged her. "Trapping a man who does not want you will bring you nothing but grief. It would be better to remain here than to wed a man who resents you. I would have survived marriage to Alicia because in the end, I have the power to control my wife. You lack that power. A husband can dictate where and how his wife lives, whom she sees, and what she does. No one will stop him from enforcing his rules however he sees fit. No one will condemn him if his discipline causes pain, or even injury. So make sure that you find a man who will treat you well."

"I am so ashamed," she murmured, biting her lip as new tears slid down her face. "And appalled at my behavior. I cannot imagine why I thought something this despicable could work." She shook her head. "In truth, I did not think ahead, ignoring his discouragement and imbuing him with interests he does not have. He even warned me that he prefers a quiet country life."

"While you prefer excitement. You should have taken the hint. He claims his interests are fixed elsewhere, and he is not a man whose head can be turned by a pretty face." At least not permanently, he amended silently. There wasn't a man alive who didn't admire a lovely view. But that was irrelevant. Straightening, he produced a brisk tone. "You owe him an apology, Laura. Today. Then you will avoid him for the remainder of his stay. I want nothing to distract him from his vow to help us."

Laura sighed. "You were right, William. I have

grown arrogant, assuming that every man who calls will fall instantly at my feet. I even discounted Catherine's good advice because I resented her efforts to control me."

He paused, but this was an opportunity he could not ignore. "Are you sure it was not disdain that she had attracted fewer beaux than you?"

"That's ridi—" She pulled herself up short and blushed. "Perhaps I am more arrogant than I thought. She and Harold were so well suited, it hardly mattered that no puppies dangled after her. I've treated her abominably since her return."

"Do not exaggerate your faults, Laura," he warned, fearful that she would slide into despair. "You are intelligent, with a strong capacity for caring. Yes, you've made mistakes, but nothing that will ruin you." *As long as Rockhurst keeps quiet,* he added under his breath. "Take advantage of your isolation in the coming days. Think about how you behave toward others. If there is a problem, then fix it. The right man will eventually appear. You will want to be ready."

Catherine finished the linen inventory. It was a chore that could easily have waited until spring, but she needed to keep busy and away from Rockhurst.

She should have stayed home yesterday. Jasper would not have attended the assembly unless someone had informed him of her temerity. If she'd remained away, the gossips would not have hardened their hearts, William would not be blamed for starting a brawl, and Laura would not have spent the night in tears.

Fustian! snorted her conscience. *Jasper would have gone anyway.*

She smoothed the last pile of sheets, pulling herself from the mire of regret that had trapped her since leaving the assembly rooms. It was true. His attack had not been aimed at her. He'd merely grazed her in passing—not that he cared. Nor did he care that he was destroying her family. William had been seething and Laura hysterical. Mary had huddled in the corner of the carriage as if trying to escape notice. The journey home had been the worst of her life. She couldn't blame Rockhurst for riding on the box.

But it wasn't Jasper's latest attack that had kept her sleepless. Every time her eyes had closed, she'd relived her two sets with Rockhurst—which was ridiculous. Both sets had been simple country dances performed with others more than with him. Yet her fingers still tingled where he had gripped them. Warmth radiated from her upper arm where his hand had touched above her glove.

She blushed.

She was not a green miss to be seduced by the prescribed patterns of a dance. It was dangerous to imagine his hands expanding those innocuous touches into the intimacy she had allowed no one but Harold.

Swearing under her breath, she slammed the linen room door and headed for the garden. Her imagination had run completely amok if it was conjuring images of Rockhurst in bed. And it would get worse. Somehow she had lost all control over her fantasies.

The only solution was to release him from his vow. Jasper had proved himself invincible. He did whatever he pleased with impunity. Rockhurst would never force him to recant, for Jasper knew that no one who mattered would turn on him. Thus Rockhurst should return home before she embarrassed them both.

Laura will be furious.

True, but not as furious as if he stayed. It was only a matter of time before he realized how much she wanted him. Even a saint would accept such an invitation. Laura would have to attach him from a distance.

But he was the stubborn sort who would keep his promises or die trying, she admitted as she slipped down the servants' stairs. So what argument would convince him to abandon this one and leave?

Fulfilling his vow was so important to his honor that he would twist facts to make winning seem possible. Like their confrontation over the assembly yesterday.

Her arguments had been valid, yet he'd ignored every one—and look where it had gotten them. Publicly supporting her had eliminated his ability to learn anything useful. Opinion had hardened against her, making Jasper's position more secure than ever. And her family now shared her disgrace. That brawl was already being laid at William's door. Laura's attack on Alicia hadn't helped.

Grabbing her gardening cloak, she slipped out the kitchen door past two maids shelling peas. A gardener clipped a nearby hedge. Another raked the path to the stables.

She needed privacy to organize her thoughts, marshal her arguments, and bring her unruly passions under control. Other groundskeepers toiled in the formal garden. A flash of blue showed that Mary and Sarah were in the folly, so she headed for the walled rose garden.

It proved to be a bad choice. Rockhurst emerged from the arbor as she shut the gate behind her.

"Who are Rankin's closest friends?" he asked abruptly.

"Tom Potter and Jack Henshaw. Why?" She remained near the gate, fighting to calm herself. Seeing him so unexpectedly made it difficult to breathe.

"The people who know him best might know his motives."

"Don't waste your time. Even if Jasper told them— which is unlikely—they would never discuss his business with you." This was the ideal time to terminate his visit. "I appreciate your efforts on my behalf, but last night proved that the situation is hopeless. Continuing the fight can only harm others."

"So thank you and farewell?" Sunlight turned his hair gold as he moved closer.

"It is for the best. William should never have asked you to interfere. But I accept full blame. If I had told him everything, he would have understood Jasper's determination earlier. We could have retired from society until the furor died down."

He snorted. "If you'd told him everything, he would have met Jasper at dawn. Even if he'd survived—he is a terrible marksman—the resulting scandal would have been worse."

"Arguing might-have-beens serves no purpose," she said, shivering at his words, for they voiced the biggest reason she'd remained silent. She put a rosebush between them, on the pretext of examining a lingering bloom. "My situation is beyond recall, but if I retire from public scrutiny, my family will survive."

"Your situation has already improved," he insisted.

"How can you say that? You were there last night. Jasper's lies carry more weight than the Magna Carta and the Bible combined. Virtue is hard enough to prove in the best of times. Now it is impossible."

"Never." He followed her around the bush. "It merely requires the right evidence. Don't turn cowardly now. If last night proved anything, it is that retreat will no longer protect your family—if it ever could. And retreat will not satisfy Jasper. With or without your help, I will continue this crusade, for he will attack at will until he's stopped. I cannot allow an unscrupulous fool to ruin five lives."

"Seven," she said, correcting him before she realized that doing so added two new reasons to continue. His brow quirked in a question. "We have other brothers. Andrew is with Wellington in Portugal. Thomas is away at school, thank heavens. His temper is unpredictable. He would retaliate against Jasper if he knew what was going on."

"So we must resolve things soon. Winter break starts next month." He combed his hair with his fingers. The separated strands snapped into curls, making her hands itch to test their softness.

Her reaction made it imperative that he leave, she realized, clutching her skirt so she didn't reach for him. "You misunderstood the cuts last night. People were upset that my family allowed me to attend. If I disappear, their reputations will survive. Persisting will hurt them further, so thank you for your efforts, but

it is time to face the truth. You will never find the
evidence you seek. Jasper is too cunning to act with
obvious malice and too careful to confide even in close
friends, for they might one day turn against him. Retiring from society will pose no hardship, for society
does not appeal to me. Once William marries, I can
fade into the background and be forgotten."

"That could be a very long time, for he will never
offer for Miss Wyath."

"True, and to be honest, I am glad he came to his
senses. But he is looking for a wife. Someone is bound
to catch his eye."

"And in the meantime, who will chaperon Laura
and Mary?" Only mild curiosity showed in his tone.

"William, of course." She relaxed, congratulating
herself on finding an argument he could accept. But
the thought had barely formed when his face snapped
into a glare so fierce, she recoiled, backing into a
rosebush.

"I hadn't considered you a quitter, Catherine," he
growled, following her retreat. "I realize you are
smarting from last night's cuts, but you cannot stop
now. It would validate every falsehood, including
those directed at William, Laura, and Mary." She must
have gasped, for he nodded. "Quitting would give credence to the charges against Lansbury and risk new
attacks on anyone who has confided in you. Jasper
would be free to launch a reign of terror. Is that what
you want?"

"That's not—"

"That is exactly what you are proposing," he said,
reading her mind. "You are crawling off to lick your
wounds, handing Jasper a victory by default. He will
censure you openly. People will laud him as an honest
man protecting society from a disreputable woman.
And they will believe the other rumors, too—like the
one claiming that William beat a prostitute to death
in Plymouth last month."

She gasped, biting the back of her hand to keep
from crying out.

"You hadn't heard that one, had you?" He loomed over her, his harsh voice and flashing eyes hinting that he could be as dangerous as Jasper when in a temper. "That's not the worst tale I've encountered. Some were circulating before I arrived, but most appeared more recently. And not just about William. There are tales about Laura and innuendo about Mary. I even heard one condemning your servants."

"I haven't heard a word." The enormity of the charges made her reel.

"Of course not. By the time these stories arose, no one was speaking to you. But I doubt you would have heard them anyway. William only knows the mildest of your supposed exploits. No one would dare tell him the worst tales, for his temper is well known."

"Yet they threw those very tales in my face."

But he was already shaking his head. "Not the worst ones, Catherine. You don't want to know some of the things I've heard against you. You don't," he repeated when she opened her mouth. "And it no longer matters. Jasper stopped maligning you as soon as he realized that you were less concerned with society's opinion than he is. To protect himself in case you reveal his crimes, he keeps the old tales alive, and he willingly used you to damage Lansbury. But he does not count that toward your punishment. Instead, he will destroy your family, for he knows that will hurt you far more than ostracism."

"My God." She had to escape. He stood between her and the gate, so she fled in the other direction, even knowing there was no way out. The garden walls imprisoned her as surely as Jasper's spite. "I can't stay here," she gasped, pushing against the stones when he cornered her. "I have to leave."

"And go where?" he demanded, pulling her around to face him. "Stop reacting and think," he added, shaking her. His touch burned into her shoulders. "You lack any means for support. No one would hire you as a governess or even as a companion with this cloud hanging over your head. Do you want to prove

Jasper's claims by setting up as a courtesan? What would that do to Sarah?''

Each word struck like a stone, battering her against the wall. Why had they asked his help? Jasper must have known of his investigation from his first talk with Ms. Telcor. No wonder he had broadened the attack. William's plot to find Laura a husband would destroy them all.

"It is too late to hide," he continued relentlessly. "Only by exposing Jasper as a tyrant can you reclaim your life."

"And that is impossible." As her temper shattered, she shoved his hands aside. "Admit it. Your thinking is as clouded as you claim mine is. Your damned honor is so tied to fulfilling every last vow, you refuse to admit that this one is impossible. It should never have been made, so I am releasing you from it."

"You can't."

"I can, and I will. Forcing me to lead my family into danger is dishonorable, and thinking you can win is pure fantasy. Pull your head out of the sky. No one will believe me innocent without proof of Jasper's motives. That proof doesn't exist."

"But it does," he insisted. "Even if he told no one his schemes, the pattern is clear to anyone who cares to look—which they will do as soon as doubt begins to grow. I sowed the first seeds last night. Jasper made a huge mistake in destroying your family. His charges cover a host of crimes, most of them unspeakable. But this time his cunning failed."

"Are you deaf and blind? It succeeded all too well. Laura cried half the night."

"She will recover. Think, Catherine. He is attacking a lord, a man whose precedence exceeds his own until the day he actually steps into his father's shoes. Not only that, he is attacking three ladies and an entire staff whose only offense is defending you."

"I am aware of his actions," she snapped.

"You are missing the point." Again he grabbed her shoulders, scrambling her thoughts. "It is too much.

In his zeal, he has set you up as emissaries of the
devil, delighting in every excess known to man. But
no one has seen a single example of evil. All they see
are your continuing efforts to make life easier for
those less fortunate than you. What self-respecting
gossip can admit that she lived in the midst of such
unbridled debauchery without once suspecting its
presence? When the initial pique over your supposed
trickery subsides, they will ask questions. These tales
are an insult to their intelligence and powers of
observation."

"But it will change nothing," she insisted. "You forget that no one else knows Jasper is behind the rumors. At the first sign of doubt, he will take a public
stand against us. That will kill any further discussion.
Those few who suspect I might be innocent will never
admit it aloud, for fear of jeopardizing their own reputations. In the end, everyone will accept his version of
events. You do not understand how much power he
wields. Forget his current precedence, for William has
never traded on his position and doing so now will
further erode his credit. So stop this farce before Jasper ruins you, too."

"He can't hurt me."

"Yes, he can. You care about people. How will your
conscience react to renewed attacks on Carruthers,
Jones, and anyone else you have interviewed? He saw
you whisper to Edna Lansbury last night. If she
doesn't turn on her husband, Jasper will know why."

"He will have other problems by then. I've only
begun to attack."

"Devil take you! Why can't you pay attention?" She
pushed against his chest, trying to escape his looming
presence. "It is over. If you don't accept that, I will
stand on the altar in Exeter cathedral and announce
to the world that every tale is true."

"And build a legacy of lies for Sarah?" His eyes
blazed as he captured her hand to prevent further assault. "I won't let you capitulate. You are the most
honorable woman I've ever met. I cannot allow him

to destroy you. Nor can I abandon Sarah to an untenable future."

She began a new argument, but he cut off her words, crushing his mouth against hers, pulling her into his arms, and kissing her with an intensity that shocked her to her toes. Excitement streaked along every nerve, more intense than any dream. Pressing closer, she kissed him back. It had been so long since she'd enjoyed a masculine embrace, but even Harold's arms had never felt this good.

She tried to believe that her reaction was caused only by her long loneliness, but the argument seemed spurious even before his tongue stroked hers into new excitement. When his hand reached inside her cloak to brush the tip of her breast, all thought ceased. Passion exploded.

His hair was softer than she had imagined, softer even than Sarah's. But his body was hard. And hot. Frantically, she pressed closer, reveling in every well-developed muscle. This was not a man who needed to pad his coats or pantaloons. Laura often laughed over the lengths some cubs went to improve an inadequate physique. Like that coxcomb—

Laura!

She stiffened, shoving frantically against his chest. What the devil was she doing? This was precisely why he had to leave.

He dropped his arms and stepped back. "Forgive me." His voice was hoarse, the words barely audible as he gasped for breath. 'I should not have done that."

"Nor should I." She fought down hysteria as desire battled honor. Her own breathing was far too fast. "Temper sometimes provokes regrettable behavior." Already her body was longing for the warmth of his, but she stifled its demands. She could not inflict her reputation on a man of virtue. Nor could she betray her sister. "We will forget this incident, my lord."

He nodded, as though he did not trust his voice. She knew what his forebearance was costing him, for she had felt evidence of his passion. But he was too honorable to allow a moment's diversion to lead him astray. And she would never be more than a momentary diversion.

"You will not withdraw from the battle, Mrs. Parrish," he said, returning to their argument. "I *will* expose Jasper's schemes. Last night's victory assures an even harder fall. The rumbling has already begun. If you think of anyone I should interview, let me know."

Turning on his heel, he left.

She staggered to a bench, dropping her head into her hands. What had possessed her? After all her care and all her warnings, she had fallen into his arms without protest. She should have fled from his first touch. Instead, she had remained, welcoming the warmth flowing from his hands, even as her arguments tried to send him away. Her ambivalence must have invited that kiss. Why else would he have abandoned his own scruples?

She had always wondered how women could be seduced. It implied a loss of control she had never understood. While she had enjoyed that part of her marriage, the pleasure would not have tempted her to risk her reputation before they had wed. And she knew that many women found it an unpleasant duty.

But they had never been kissed by the Earl of Rockhurst.

Guilt washed over her, for she had wanted that kiss and longed to repeat it. And more. Excitement still burned, tightening her nipples and building the craving for his body she'd been trying to ignore. She would welcome an affair with him in a minute, should he offer.

And there lay her gravest danger, she admitted, succumbing to tears. He was too stubborn to leave, so she must avoid him. Pursuing the attraction would ruin her and betray Laura. She couldn't let this happen again. She would take all meals in her room for the remainder of his stay.

Chapter Twelve

Blake fled the rose garden, furious with himself for succumbing to temptation. Why the devil had he kissed her?

Because you knew how good it would be.

He cursed. That was not an acceptable excuse. He'd vowed that he would not explore this attraction until after he'd vanquished Jasper. Doing so sooner would complicate everything. How could he redeem her reputation if he was enjoying her favors himself? It wasn't something they could hide. With the number of servants scattered about the grounds today, he was lucky no one had caught him devouring her.

Again he cursed.

He had been so careful to keep every meeting focused on business. He'd allowed no assignations, no casual conversations, not even an exchange of warm glances. She had rarely remained in the drawing room after dinner. The closest they had come to social intercourse was at the assembly, but even those dances had been business. So how had he lost control so thoroughly?

You panicked, taunted his conscience.

"Absurd," he muttered, resuming his thrice-interrupted trip to the stables. Her insistence that he abandon his vow had annoyed him, but that was hardly cause for panic. He would not give up the fight, whatever her fears. And she was entitled to an attack of nerves after last night. In the end she would stand firm, for she shared his devotion to justice and fair play.

But she was trying to send you away.

Nerves, he insisted, though he had recognized panic in her eyes. It had increased with each new argument in favor of quitting—almost as if she feared to keep him near those she loved.

"Dear God!" His fists clenched. How could he have missed so obvious an explanation? She must have stumbled across the scene in the library—which would explain why she'd looked so distressed when she'd entered the garden. Laura's description of his supposed attack would produce exactly this reaction. And kissing her would reinforce those impressions. Catherine would be even more determined to drive him away now. How else could she protect her family? She might even bar him from the nursery.

He stifled a cry at the thought of not seeing Sarah again.

William would set her straight about Laura's plot, but nothing could erase her own experience. He had grabbed her without warning, giving her no time to protest. The first touch of her lips had shredded his control, releasing such a jumble of sensations that he had no real recollection of his actions.

He groaned as the image of grinding her against his groin flashed through his brain. No wonder she'd panicked. If she hadn't stiffened and pushed him away, he would have taken her on the spot. He'd never felt such desire.

So did she, taunted the voice of temptation. *She didn't fight back like she did with Jasper.*

He thrust it away. He'd given her no opportunity to refuse, pulling her so close that her knees had been caught in her cloak. And the fact that she'd returned his kiss meant nothing. Only moments earlier, she'd threatened to tell the world that she was guilty of all charges. Perhaps she'd been trying to demonstrate that guilt.

That was what had led to the kiss, he admitted with a sigh. He'd had the misguided notion of proving she was no wanton. Instead, he'd proved himself a weak-willed rakehell for whom honor meant nothing when placed against desire, more than confirming his reputation. If she'd heard even a whisper of it, she would now think him degenerate.

He owed her a larger apology than he'd offered. He must make it clear that she was safe. He would never assault her again. Nor would he touch her sisters. But he could not leave yet. Jasper would use his departure against her, destroying any progress they had made last night.

Are you sure, or is desire still interfering with your judgment?

He ignored the voice. His judgment was sound. Staying was the only rational choice.

"My lord!" Harry Fields raced out of the stable yard as Blake approached, skidding to a halt barely a foot away. "I found it!"

"Keep your voice down," he advised. "What did you find?"

"T' proof against Master Jasper," he whispered, his eyes glowing with excitement.

Blake glanced around. A groom lounged against a post, overseeing two stableboys as they raked droppings into a pile. Groundskeepers continued clipping. Catherine was nowhere in sight, but she might still be in the rose garden. Mary and Sarah remained in the folly. "This way, Harry." He gestured toward the drive.

Harry was bursting with impatience, but Blake kept their pace casual as they strolled along the drive. Not until they reached the woods and lost sight of the house did he speak. "Tell me about your proof."

"Bob and me visited t' smith again. Georgie was making a delivery, but Peter was there."

"Who is Peter?" Blake leaned against a tree, crossing his arms as he weighed each word.

"Peter Ballard. His pa makes saddles and harness and such. Mr. Ballard was talking to t' smith, and Bob was flirting, so Peter and me went down to t' river."

"And?" asked Blake. Relief lit Harry's face that he

hadn't asked what the boys had been doing. Up to mischief, no doubt, but that wasn't his problem.

"We seen Master Jasper cross t' bridge into town. I said as how I wished I knew something really bad about him, 'cause I was still angry over how he lied about Jemmy. So Peter tells me Jasper killed a man."

Blake jumped. Killed? He inhaled deeply, ignoring the excitement that tingled along his nerves. This would come to nothing. Even if it were true, it would turn out to be a duel. Though dueling had long been illegal, few condemned the practice.

"Who died?" he asked instead.

"I don't know."

"Peter didn't say?"

"He don't know, either. But he don't lie," he added when Blake sighed.

"I'm sure he is as honest as you, but how could he hear a story without knowing the details?"

"He lives on t' edge of Exeter. His pa keeps him busy learning t' trade, but whenever he can get away, he stops at t' White Hart to feed apples to Miss Wilson's chestnut what she keeps stabled there."

Blake nodded. He had no idea who Miss Wilson was or why the saddler's son had permission to feed her horse, but it didn't matter.

"About a week ago, Peter was in with t' chestnut, when Master Jasper and George—he's one of t' inn's grooms—come by. Master Jasper was leaving his horse for t' day, and he was rattling on and on about what to do and how to handle t' beast. When he finally left, George grumbled about how he'd been caring for horses since before Jasper was born and why'd he act like he knew more'n anyone else."

"Understandable," said Blake, having indulged in similar muttering when his father had treated him like an ignorant child even after he'd reached Oxford.

"George hadn't seen Peter, and Peter didn't want his pa finding out he'd snuck off for t' day, so he sat down and waited for George to leave—Miss Wilson's chestnut has one of t' loose boxes, so it's easy to stay out of sight. George grumbled louder and louder as he unsaddled Master Jasper's horse—real het up, he was. Most of it didn't make much sense, but a couple of his complaints you can maybe use."

"What?"

Harry paused, seeming uncertain for the first time. "One sounded like, *Won't be no trouble today 'cause he don't want Ajax kept ready.*"

Blake's heart thudded. Did Jasper behave differently before causing trouble? Evidence of planning would override the claims of high spirits and happenstance. "And the other?"

"He was talking to Ajax, asking how he liked serving a fool. *But you and me know t' real Jasper Rankin,* he muttered—least that's what Peter recollects. *We know he killed*—Peter couldn't catch t' next words, so he don't know who died. Then George says, *'Twas no accident, was it, boy? But telling's no good. He'd see me turned off in a trice and take a whip to you.*"

"He would," confirmed Blake. "And he'd do the same to you and Peter. Did George actually see the killing?"

Harry shrugged. "Peter didn't hear no more. Another groom called George away to change out t' mail coach, and Peter left."

Blake nodded, even as he cursed under his breath. They were so close!

But Harry knew nothing more. Nobody had died recently except old Mr. Parkins, who'd passed on peacefully in his sleep after a long illness. The incident, if it had happened at all, must predate Harry's memory. Thus only George could supply the information.

He should send Ted to talk to the fellow. Another groom might learn more than he could himself. Yet impatience clawed at his mind, along with the desire to escape Seabrook for a few hours. By the time he returned, William should have Laura under control.

As he rode toward Exeter, he kept a firm hand on his rising excitement. The tale might not be true.

Though he was sure Harry had reported it accurately, he knew nothing about Peter. Even gentlemen sometimes twisted or exaggerated news, and the boy might not have heard George correctly. And even if the story was perfect, George might refuse to talk. He had every reason to fear Jasper. Beyond that, the death might have been the accident George hadn't believed it was.

But it was difficult to remain calm. His instincts shouted that this was what he needed. Jasper was a man who avenged any insult. Since his retaliations always surpassed the original irritations, it would be surprising indeed if an occasional plot did not run amok.

He found George in the White Hart's stable. Business was slow this late in the year. The other grooms were busy out back, leaving only George to watch for new customers.

Blake relaxed. They had met when he'd stayed at the White Hart, and George remembered both him and his horse. Perhaps that would work in his favor.

Mindful of Peter's eavesdropping technique, he glanced into each of the stalls edging the stable yard as he joined George in the far corner. Picking out Miss Wilson's chestnut was easy. He occupied the loose box nearest the arched yard entrance, which made it easy for Peter to slip in unseen.

"I am investigating Jasper Rankin," he said quietly, turning a gold coin through the fingers of one hand. Its value was more than a groom might make in a year. The surface winked each time it caught the sunlight, drawing George's eyes.

Yet George was already shaking his head. "Best stand clear of that, my lord. No good can come of it."

"I understand, George." The coin winked. "He's a bad one to cross. Yet I have no choice, for he is hurting people even as we speak. I vowed to stop him, but I need information."

"What you'll get is trouble. T'ain't no information that can harm him."

"Maybe. Maybe not. I'll tell no one that you

helped." He stepped away from the eaves so the coin caught more sun. "But I cannot let him destroy my friends."

George seemed mesmerized by the glinting gold. "What's my word against a lord's? Even Falconer hasn't enough credit to complain."

"Would he even try? He swears Rankin was not responsible for tearing up that parlor, though I've evidence otherwise." He kept his voice calm—almost toneless—as he turned the coin through his fingers. He had seen one of Mesmer's demonstrations and believed that it was the monotonous voice and seductive sway of the pendant rather than magic that put his subjects under a spell.

"That wasn't the only incident," George admitted. "He's smashed furniture more than once when servants don't show him proper respect. Falconer don't like him coming round, but who can stop him?"

"Not an innkeeper," agreed Blake. "And certainly not a groom. But I will stop him for all of us. I despise men who misuse their positions. Tell me about his tantrums."

The corner of George's mouth twitched. "That's what they be, all right. He's a great one for wanting his own way. I don't recollect all the times he's smashed a wine bottle against a wall or hurled a platter into the fire because service was a mite slow. I hafta warn new lads when they start here. Those prissy clothes hide the temper of a angry bull. He demands instant service and accepts no excuses."

"That fits the other tales I've heard, but sometimes even perfect service won't satisfy him. What can you tell me about the man he killed?"

George's leathery face turned white. "Nothing, my lord."

"I think you can." He raised his hand to eye level, turning the coin faster. "You know exactly what happened."

"Nothing happened." George's breath came in shallow gasps, but he couldn't tear his eyes from the coin.

"That's not true, George," said Blake softly. "A man died. You know how and why. If I found that information, others can as well."

George leaned weakly against the post supporting the eaves.

Blake smiled. "That's right. Jasper can find the truth if he looks. Helping me is the best way to protect yourself. So tell me about this death."

"I wasn't there," he insisted.

"But you know what happened. Tell me. I won't reveal the story until I can prove that Rankin committed a crime."

"Proof don't mean nothing." George glanced wildly around, calming only when he verified that no one could hear them. "He would never forgive me for hearing him that night. I would lose everything."

"I will protect you. If he tries to retaliate, you can join my staff."

"Leave the White Hart?" He made the prospect sound worse than death.

"Only if you wish. But I vow, on my honor as a gentleman, that you will not suffer." His instincts were alert. Every new protest underscored how damaging George's information must be. And it proved that George knew far more about Jasper than he'd revealed so far. Only a man who understood Jasper's ruthlessness would protect himself so well. "If Rankin killed a man, he must be punished. How would you feel if he killed another and yet another because you lacked the courage to speak?"

George flinched, then let out a long breath. "Yes, he killed a man. Killed two, in fact, though neither was intended. But I can't prove it. I weren't there."

"Tell me what you know. I can find evidence if I know where to look."

His voice dropped to a whisper. "Are you sure you can protect me? I've a mother to support."

"You won't suffer, nor will she."

George held his gaze for a long moment. Horses stomped, rattling bits of harness. Others wheezed softly or pawed the straw strewn beneath their feet. George finally nodded. "Very well, my lord. Your eyes got a look like that bay over there." He gestured to a distant stall. "Honest as they come, that horse. I can trust him with the most timid rider."

He sighed, seeming to shrink into himself. "I've never forgot a moment of that night. We was busy as bees, what with a dozen coaches going to London and Bath and several others headed for Plymouth for a boat race, or some such." He shook his head in disgust. "Young Rankin had been in the taproom since midafternoon, drinking and gaming. I heard later that he won more'n five thousand guineas from a stripling." Again the graying head shook, unable to comprehend either the amount or the sort of man who could risk it.

Blake grimaced. Had he coerced the groom into baring a tale he could not use? The man had little understanding of the upper classes. Gentlemen frequently wagered fortunes—Brummell had won and lost several, as had others he knew. Most accepted their fate, and no one blamed the winner.

"Several men witnessed the game," murmured George, his eyes again searching for potential listeners. "A few suspected Rankin had unusual luck that night, but no one dared mention cheating." He paused to bite his lip.

"So why did Rankin attack?" he finally asked.

"After the loser left, one of the spectators scolded him, swearing that a gentleman would have quit the game before stripping the lad of every farthing, especially since the boy was the sole support of a mother and two sisters."

Blake's imagination conjured the image of a boy putting a pistol to his head, leaving his family homeless, penniless, and broken in spirit. Despicable, if true—he had never condoned those who risked everything on the turn of a card, nor did he approve those who preyed on them—but nothing he could use.

"I didn't learn about the cards or the confrontation

until later," continued George. "All I saw was Rankin. He stumbled out here well past midnight. I stayed clear, not wanting to draw his attention when he was in one of his tempers—and that night was the worst I'd seen before or since. He often demands that his horse be kept ready to leave, so he didn't summon me."

"You mean he retrieves his own mount from the stable?" That did not fit the man's arrogance.

"Not as a rule. He just don't like waiting while we saddle Ajax. But that night he come out here. I was grateful, for we was busy, as I said. I was harnessing a curricle for another gent. The other grooms was out back with the carriages. Rankin didn't see me, for which I've always been grateful. He was in a wicked temper, muttering and swearing and blowing hot with plans I didn't think he meant. I was glad when he left."

"What plans?"

"I didn't understand most of what he said until I heard about the man what read him that scold on gentlemen's honor. The scold was bad enough, but embarrassing him in front of a dozen others made it worse. So he was grumbling. *No gentleman himself,* he says, and *no business of his.* He also said something about not being his brother's keeper. *But he'll be sorry,* he says, then follows it up with curses you don't expect from a gentleman. As he mounted Ajax, he muttered, *Maybe he'll stay out of my business if it costs him that team he sets such store by.* That got my attention real quick, though I'd no idea which horses he meant." His eyes again scanned the stable yard.

"But he made no move to harm any "

"No, so I thought it just talk. Many a man utters threats and curses while in his cups."

"And few carry them out," Blake said in agreement. He'd done it himself. Wine loosened tongues. But it also banished judgment.

A cat inched toward a bird that was pecking around the cobbles under the corn bin. George watched it pounce, then resumed his tale. "Rankin left. I finished harnessing the curricle and led it round to the door. Two men drove off in it, but they never made it home. An early traveler found them at dawn. The curricle had overturned into a ditch, killing the man who'd scolded Rankin, fatally injuring his passenger, and breaking the leg of one of the horses."

"But no one saw the accident."

George shook his head. "I told you I had no proof. The muttered threat of a drunken man means nothing."

"What do you think happened?"

"I think Rankin waited until the curricle left, then followed it. It had rained hard that day, stopping only an hour before Rankin collected his horse. The curricle tracks showed on the road when we drove out to retrieve the bodies, as did the tracks of the two horses pulling it. A single horse had also traveled that way. Its tracks veered into the curricle's a quarter mile before the crash."

"Was there any evidence that they were made at the same time?"

"I didn't examine them closely, but the horses changed from trot to gallop at that point."

"What do you think happened?" he asked again.

"I think Rankin tried to injure the team. Veering into the ditch where those tracks met would have strained a leg or two. But instead of shying, the horses bolted—they was high-strung tits that jumped at every little sound, and I saw no evidence in the tracks that the driver had control—dropped the ribbons, most like. He was three sheets to the wind that night."

"So the horses panicked, ran a quarter mile, and only then veered into the ditch?"

"With help. Twice more that single horse veered into the curricle's path. Where they finally swerved off the road, the ditch was deeper and rougher. The driver's head hit a rock. His passenger was still alive when we got there, but he died on the way back to town. We had to put down the injured horse."

"Two men dead, yet you said nothing about the tracks?"

George stared at his boot. "I tried, but the men with me was too busy loading the passenger into a wagon—we still hoped he'd live then. When we reached the White Hart, folks here was already claiming accident, and I'd had time to think. With both men dead, what purpose would it serve? Rankin would destroy me if I said anything."

Jasper would attack whether he was guilty or not. George's story carried no weight, for he was only a groom, but suggesting Jasper was guilty of wrongdoing would be an insult. The tracks might have contained evidence, but no one else had heeded them—unless the man who found the wreckage had noticed them.

"Who found the accident?" he asked. "Perhaps he can tell me more."

"He's gone, my lord. That's all he said at the time."

He would track down the traveler later, if necessary. Someone must recall the man's name. "Is there anyone else who might have heard Rankin's threats that night?"

"Squire Hawkins and Colonel Bangor, maybe. They followed him out of the inn. Then there was the passenger's story, though nobody heeded it. He was out of his head."

"The passenger?" It took every bit of control he could muster to hide his shock.

"Afore he passed out, he told the gent what found him about an attack by a horseman. But he was raving from fever and pain by then. Those who heeded him blame the ghost—that bit of road is haunted."

"But you believe him." He dropped his voice to a whisper as a man stepped out of the inn and crossed the road toward the cathedral.

"Maybe I hate Rankin too much." His eyes also followed the departing gentleman.

"I doubt it. What did the fellow say?"

"He swore a horseman swooped down and jerked the ribbons from the driver's hands. Then he whipped the horses into a frenzy, slicing into their forelegs—it's true the horses' legs was cut up, but those rocks was sharp. The horseman laughed when they bolted. Whenever the horses slowed, he whipped them again."

"Did he name the culprit?"

George shook his head. "His words weren't clear, and the tale was jumbled up with ramblings about Judgment Day and greenery and cats, or maybe it was cravats. He mighta mentioned names—Jack, Nigel, Shar—or mayhap they was groans. He was clearly out of his head. It is easier to believe the ghost spooked the team than to connect his words to Rankin. And easiest of all to suspect the driver lost control of a spirited team after drinking too much."

"So you kept quiet, even though two men died."

"If Squire Hawkins and Colonel Bangor saw nothing suspicious in his lordship's death, who would believe me? I don't interfere with the quality."

Blake froze. "Who were the victims?"

"Old Lord Seabrook and Vicar Parrish," he admitted.

Fear. He should have listened to his instincts. *Threatened to reveal his reprisals unless he left me alone.* If that's how Catherine had expressed her threat, it was no mystery why Jasper had attacked. Who would have understood Parrish's dying words better than his wife? Even if she'd heard them second-hand, she might have understood—or so Jasper feared.

Jasper's attacks on inferiors put him in no danger. He'd already admitted many of the incidents. If Catherine charged him with deliberate intent, he would twist her words until she appeared hysterical. But the death of a lord was a different matter.

He paced across the yard and back. As he'd reminded Catherine only that morning, a baron had precedence over a viscount's heir. Jasper might wish otherwise, but he was not the highest-ranking gentleman in the area yet. He remained a commoner, subject to the same laws that governed tradesmen and farm workers. In practice, that did not matter, for few held heirs to the same standards. But this was murder.

Could he use this incident to force the confession that would restore Catherine's reputation? He didn't know, but he finally had a place to start.

"All right, let's go over the tale from the beginning," he said, returning to George's side. Pulling out a pencil and a scrap of paper, he sighed. "What can you tell me about the men in the taproom that night? Let's start with the lad who lost his fortune."

Chapter Thirteen

Catherine jumped when Rockhurst strode into the morning room. Her nerves were still on edge from their encounter in the rose garden.

He had left her restless and unable to concentrate. Going to the nursery had been out of the question. Sarah would have noticed and demanded an explanation. Yet she couldn't remain in the manor, either. In her confusion, she might throw herself into his arms if they met unexpectedly in a hallway. So she'd gone to the village.

That visit had certainly cured her of any dreams about Rockhurst.

Jasper's poison had done its work even on the neediest parishioners. None of them wanted a kind word or helping hand. It was the first time the lower classes had shunned her, and it hurt. But even worse pain had followed.

Brad Lansbury cut her dead outside the Green Gull, though she suspected that assaulting her would have been more satisfying. Whatever Rockhurst had said to Mrs. Lansbury had yet to bear fruit, for Brad clearly believed Jasper's lies. Or maybe he remained angry over William's attack. One eye was swollen shut.

She was still reeling when she ran into Vicar Sanders.

"How dare you strut into my village and expose my parishioners to your obscenities?" he demanded without even a greeting.

"You are mistaken, sir." She tried to remain civil,

but his sudden concern for people he had ignored for two years swirled a red mist before her eyes.

"Don't contradict your betters, girl!"

It was too much. "How can you call yourself a man of God, yet condemn me on the unsupported word of one man? If you had paid the slightest attention to the parishioners you claim to serve, you would know that they have been fighting slander and worse from that same source for years."

"Harlot!" he snapped, overriding her voice. "Take your lies and excuses elsewhere. Debauchery has no place here. I must already purify the vicarage to remove your evil influence. Get you gone from my parish. I'll have you arrested if you dare set foot in my church again."

"*Your* church? *Your* village? *Your* parish?" Her fists clenched. "They belong to my brother. You might consider who controls this living before turning yourself into a spokesman for an arrogant fool."

"My duty to God transcends loyalty to a man nearly as corrupt as you." He gestured to a knot of people who were staring in fascination. "I must protect these innocents from contamination by the greatest sinner to walk the earth since Sodom and Gomorrah fell."

He continued his tirade, but she stopped listening. For whatever reason, Sanders had decided to make a public show of crucifying her. Perhaps Jasper had added new lies since the assembly. Or maybe Sanders had finally heard the ones Rockhurst refused to repeat. He might even relish the idea of driving off a person whose activities drew attention to his neglect. Not that his motives mattered. Her life here was finished. And the real losers were the parishioners. She had no illusions that Sanders would pay them any heed once she was gone.

She had stopped in the woods on the way home, staring at a spotted mushroom for hours as her mind grappled with her dilemma. She needed to leave. The people she had served for so long no longer wanted her aid. Sanders had barred her from entering the parish church, and asking William to intercede would only make matters worse. Replacing Sanders would give Jasper a new opportunity to revile them all. And his next target would be Harold's parishioners. He might already have begun, judging from today's reaction. So she must leave them in the hands of a vicar as priggish as William but a thousand times colder.

Yet Rockhurst was also right. She had no place to go and no way to support herself. While Harold had had distant ties to several respectable families, he had known none of them. His parents were dead, as was his only sister. Finding a decent position required a character reference from her vicar—an impossibility—and would force her to leave Sarah behind. Parishes only helped the needy from their own districts, and even the workhouses only took in locals—not that she would consider that, for Sarah would wind up in a mill, or worse. Which left her the choice of becoming a courtesan or leaving the country.

She'd finally returned to the house, her thoughts jumbled—and not just by Jasper's schemes. Every time she tried to focus, memories of Rockhurst's embrace distracted her. The heat. The excitement. The overwhelming pleasure.

Now here he was again, this time in the flesh. His amber eyes glowed like ancient gold as he shut the door firmly behind him. For a breathtaking moment, she thought he would sweep her into his arms.

"I found out why Jasper fears you," he said, taking the chair next to hers without waiting for an invitation to sit. "And this time there should be enough evidence to force a confession."

"What?" Both hands clutched her chest as her head reeled—with disappointment that he seemed unaffected by their kiss, with shock that anyone thought Jasper could fear a vicar's widow, with reluctance to admit that she'd decided to leave. She drew several quick breaths.

"Harry Fields discovered the incident. There is no way Jasper can pass this one off as high spirits. It was

deliberate malice, with witnesses. I've just spoken with
one of them, and there are two others, both gentry."

"Then why did they say nothing earlier?" She
forced her hands into her lap in an attempt to relax.
He was trying so hard to believe success was possible
that he must have overlooked something obvious. But
she could not afford dreams.

He frowned. "The others heard only part of his plans,
so they missed the connection at first. By then, other
people's assumptions had closed the matter, so they did
not question the verdict. Or maybe they found it more
comfortable to ignore their suspicions, since nothing
could have been changed."

"Then why would they reconsider now?" Her fists
crumpled her skirt.

"You are determined to be gloomy," he complained, "though I can hardly blame you after last
night. Perhaps I am overstating the evidence, for I've
heard only one man's story, but Jasper's guilt seems
clear."

"What happened?" She suddenly realized that he
was oddly reticent today.

His expression changed to one of sorrow. "One of
his revenges went awry. In trying to injure a team of
horses, he caused an accident that killed two men. The
witnesses overheard his threats against the driver. The
man who discovered the wreckage said the passenger
claimed that a horseman had caused the crash, but no
one believed him because he was delirious."

"Dear Lord! Not Harold!" Spots swirled before
her eyes.

His hand covered hers. "Forgive me for reviving
your grief, Catherine, but this is too serious to ignore."

She choked down sobs, fighting to maintain her
composure. She had not been braced for such news.
Several minutes passed before she could speak.
"What happened?"

As he described the card game at the White Hart
and her father's confrontation with Jasper, tears again
threatened, for she could imagine the scene so clearly.

Her father had never remained silent when others misbehaved.

"How like Father," she murmured when he finished. "He believed title holders had graver responsibilities than ordinary men, and he criticized anyone who harmed another. I can almost hear his lecture. *If a man wishes to risk his fortune, that is his business, but no gentleman remains in a game that might harm innocents. You should have protected West's family instead of taking advantage of his drinking to line your own pockets. You ignored your responsibility to those who lack your high station.*"

"If you are right, then he packed several insults into a short speech—ungentlemanly behavior, taking advantage of a stripling, greed, failure to uphold his duties." He shook his head. "And Jasper was already half seas over."

"I wondered why Harold was with Father that night. He'd said nothing about visiting Exeter or the manor, and his horse was at the White Hart when he d-died." She cursed the stutter, but shock still gripped her. "He must have accompanied Father to warn him of his danger."

"Do not jump to conclusions," he murmured, squeezing her hand, which remained under his. "We still have no real evidence. So far, I've heard only one man's tale of that night. Perhaps I should have waited to tell you, but I felt you should know. Did anyone repeat Harold's description of the accident?"

"Not that I recall—but I was in shock."

"You did not speak to the man who found the wreckage?"

"Mr. Berens?" She shook her head. "He was at the funerals, of course, but he said nothing about Harold being conscious." She shuddered, imagining the pain he must have suffered. By the time she'd learned of the accident, he'd been dead. Everyone had assured her that he had felt nothing.

"So you know his name. Do you also have his direction?"

The question pulled her attention back to the morning room and the hand clasping hers. "He died a month after Harold."

Rockhurst released a frustrated sigh. "How?"

"Carelessness." She shrugged, folding her hands to evade his touch. "He set a candle too close to his bed. The curtains caught fire, burning the house to the ground." She shook off a shiver. Jasper's involvement explained several of the oddities about Harold's death, though it raised other questions. "Who were the witnesses at the inn?"

"Squire Hawkins, Colonel Bangor, and one of the inn's grooms. Several others witnessed the card game, but if Jasper had threatened your father to his face, they would have said something at the time. None of them left soon enough to overhear his plans."

"But they might share Father's conviction that Jasper cheated Nigel West."

"I said nothing about cheating."

She shook her head. "Father would never have publicly berated Jasper if he thought the game was honest. He would have waited until they were alone to avoid embarrassing Jasper." Rising, she paced to the window and back. "I wonder if Nigel suspected cheating. He told his family that his father had lost everything—the man had died barely a week earlier. Jasper may have suggested the lie, threatening to do worse if he challenged him over the game."

"Or West might not have known the truth. He was so drunk he could barely stagger out to his horse that night, and he left the inn before your father accosted Jasper."

"I doubt many people know about that card game," she murmured, her mind following a different tack. "Father's death dominated gossip for weeks. I don't recall hearing a word about Nigel's losses, though that is no evidence," she added. She had been prostrate for days and then too concerned about Sarah and their sudden poverty to care about other problems.

"Where is Nigel now?" Rockhurst sounded interested.

"He moved to Plymouth, taking his mother and sisters with him. The last we heard, he was working as a clerk to a solicitor there."

"I must speak with him."

"Don't." She met his startled gaze. "Leave him out of this. Even if he suspected cheating, he can offer no proof, and his own actions belie the charge. He is rebuilding his life. One sister is keeping company with the solicitor's son. Revealing that he gamed away the family fortune could affect his job and terminate his sister's courtship."

"Don't exaggerate," he scoffed, stepping closer.

"I am not. What if the solicitor decides such poor judgment is intolerable in an employee and reflects on his entire family? There is no way to prove Jasper cheated and no way to recover the funds."

"Surely his family knows the truth by now."

"I doubt it. The Wests left within the week and spoke with few people before they fled. They were not really part of local society, you understand. The father had inherited the old Wilkins place from an uncle only a few years earlier."

"Are you saying that I should ignore Jasper's attack on your father because asking questions about that night might hurt West?"

"No. I am saying that whether Jasper cheated is irrelevant. The Wests are gone. Asking about the card game will start rumors that could easily spread to Plymouth. Why inflict new pain on a man who is already a victim? Concentrate on the accident."

"Very well. I will keep West out of it if possible. But I vowed to force Rankin into admitting he lied about you. If exposing all the circumstances of that night is the only way to succeed, I will do so."

"It is not worth the price."

"It is." He stared into her eyes. "What of Sarah? Jasper will not allow this scandal to die. He can't. Think about your words that day in the orchard. He believes you know what happened to your father, so destroying your credit is his only protection."

The shock drove her back to the window. Why had she not suspected this earlier?

I know what you are . . . you have destroyed too many people . . .

Her own words. She had been referring to Amy Carruthers and Jenkins, but his guilty conscience had thought she meant Harold and her father. So he had struck back, making sure that no one would ever believe her.

"I will speak to Hawkins and the colonel as soon as possible," said Rockhurst, pulling her away from her thoughts.

"You will learn nothing from Colonel Bangor. He fell on his head last month and has been unable to think clearly ever since. Besides, if he had entertained the slightest suspicion, he would have said something at the time. He would never pass up a chance to expose Jasper, for he has long hated him."

"Why?"

She shook her head. "That I don't know. But he would never remain silent after two deaths. His own explanation is ghosts."

"George mentioned ghosts."

"Which George?"

"The White Hart's groom. He claims that road is haunted." He led her back to her seat, turning his chair to watch her more closely.

She covered nervousness with a light laugh. "It is nonsense, of course, but the story persists. The ghost is supposedly a Frenchman who long ago washed up on the coast. A squire's daughter nursed him back to health. Naturally, the two fell in love."

"Naturally," he agreed.

She relaxed for the first time since morning. "The squire was upset, for he wanted his daughter to form a grand alliance—she was a great beauty. Also kind, generous, loving—"

"Talented, a paragon of every virtue, guaranteed to melt the hardest heart and sweep—"

"Stop that," she demanded, laughing.

"Why? Are you now claiming she was an antidote?"

"Whose story is this?" she demanded as her treacherous heart turned over. His eyes sparkled. Humor smoothed the lines from his forehead, revealing how anxious he had been since his arrival. His investigation weighed heavily on his spirits.

"Yours, of course. Pray, continue. I'm all ears."

No, he's all hard body and flashing eyes. She stifled the reminder. "As I was saying, the girl was worthy of a grand alliance. The stranger claimed to be noble, but his clothes were those of a pauper, so the squire dismissed him as a fraud—the man was French, after all."

"And we were undoubtedly at war with France."

"Aren't we always?"

His eyes twinkled, as he again claimed her hand. "If there is any basis for the story, he was probably a spy."

"No doubt." She wrenched her hand away, firmly reminding herself that touching him could only lead to trouble. "The squire had already begun marriage negotiations with a powerful lord, so as soon as the Frenchman could walk, he turned the man out."

"Thus forcing the lovers to elope. But the evil squire tracked them down and—"

"Quit interrupting!" she ordered, then cursed under her breath when she realized her face had twisted into a pout. Donning a sober expression, she finished the tale in a rush. "They planned to elope, but the girl's maid betrayed them to the squire. When the Frenchman approached the meeting place, the squire and his trusty footmen cut him down, then buried him and his horse where they fell. There is a cairn beside the road that supposedly marks the spot. The next day he learned that the Frenchman had been a duke of great wealth and power. The daughter cursed her father to eternal oblivion before flinging herself off a cliff. The duke still haunts that road, seeking her and attacking anyone who disbelieves his tale."

"Tragic, and possibly even true."

She shrugged. "I doubt it. There is no evidence the squire ever existed—believers attribute that to the daughter's curse. I suspect the story arose from the rock formations along the road. They cast odd shadows in moonlight and harbor patches of mist even on clear nights. More than one horse has panicked there. And there used to be a formation that resembled a rearing horse when glimpsed through mist from the right angle. It collapsed about ten years ago, but it might have once included a rider."

"Yet Colonel Bangor believes the tale."

"Colonel Bangor suffered an accident there many years ago. He found it easier to blame the Frenchman's ghost than his own poor driving. It soothed his pride, which was the only real casualty."

"And now he has suffered another accident."

"Happenstance. He slipped on a patch of moss and fell from his roof while verifying his housekeeper's claim that some slates needed repair—he has always insisted on checking everything personally. There were half a dozen witnesses. The doctor believes he will recover, but at the moment he remains confused."

"Squire Hawkins should recall that night." He rose to leave. "I will speak with him in the morning."

She still had misgivings. If no one had suspected Jasper at the time, raising the subject now had a better chance of hurting the Wests than of finding evidence against Jasper, but Rockhurst was in no mood to listen, so she nodded.

Once he was gone, she rose to pace the room. This news eliminated any hope of convincing him to leave. On the other hand, she now wondered if he might actually succeed in his attempt to expose Jasper. Could there really be enough evidence to force a confession?

She wanted to believe. Dear Lord, how she wanted to believe. The alternative was so painful. But there was more than hope behind her decision to continue this fight a little longer. Curiosity played a role—what had really happened on the coast road that night? And even stronger than curiosity was a burning need for revenge.

Shuddering, she paced faster. She hated to admit that she was reacting even a little like Jasper, though this situation was very different from his petty quarrels. He must pay for his crimes. In her family alone, there were two dead, one ruined, three besmirched, and no end in sight.

Poor Harold. Another innocent bystander cut down to serve Jasper's arrogance. Tears pricked her eyes. He had been a good man—sweet, kind, and genuinely caring. Love had come gently during their years of marriage, turning friendship into something deeper that sharpened her grief when she lost him.

She blinked back tears. Two years should have put this behind her, but he had not deserved such a fate. Dying because Jasper attacked another man made it worse.

Her father had been very different from Harold, though both had embraced justice and fair play. He was stubborn—a trait she had inherited—which had caused many an argument between them. She recalled the exhilaration that had accompanied her few victories. But even his stubbornness had had a certain charm. She missed their confrontations almost as much as she missed Harold's concern. Rockhurst reminded her of both men.

She sighed. She had never questioned the accident. One of her last arguments with her father had been over that team. He'd doted on that pair, though she'd considered them fractious. Flashy, certainly, but difficult to hold. She'd even predicted that they would bolt on the coast road after dark, which had raised guilt after his death. A storm had broken up that night, producing unexpected shifts in light as the full moon dodged in and out of clouds. When added to the eerie rock stacks and patches of fog endemic to that road, it was no surprise that a driver who had spent some time in a taproom would come to grief. Mixed with

her remorse for not fighting harder had been the fear
that he'd set his team at the road to prove her wrong.

But she had never understood Harold's presence.
They had been finishing dinner when he'd received a
summons from the ailing widow Green. She'd assumed
the widow was near death—the woman died a week
later. Now she had to wonder what the widow had
wanted.

Harold had gone from Mrs. Green's to the White
Hart, then accompanied her father home, leaving his
horse behind.

She shook her head. Nothing made sense. Mrs.
Green had lived only half a mile from the vicarage,
so Harold would have walked. Only after speaking to
her had he saddled his horse and gone to Exeter. He
must have intended to fetch her father to the widow's
bedside, then return to town.

Which brought her back to the widow Green. Since
her father had been the area's leading magistrate, the
widow must have been reporting a crime. But what
could a dying woman say that would demand a night
journey in foul weather?

Even as her curiosity stirred, she realized that she
was creating a mystery so she could forget Jasper's
plots for a time. But she needed a break from her own
problems, and maybe it was not too late to address
the widow's concern. Mrs. Green's housekeeper might
know what she had wanted. She was presently employed by Miss Mott.

But that must wait until morning. In the meantime,
she would check on Sarah, then find Laura. If Squire
Hawkins agreed with this tale, Rockhurst would leave
soon. Time was running out to attach him.

Laura was in the drawing room, seemingly blue-
deviled because Rockhurst had again spent the day in
Exeter. Catherine stifled her memory of that morning
kiss, reciting the familiar litany under her breath:
Laura deserved a good husband, and Rockhurst was
the best. It wasn't his fault that she'd tempted him

into forgetting his scruples. Even a saint could suffer an occasional lapse.

"Wear the blue gown this evening," she said, noting that the fire was nearly burned out. Laura should have summoned Rob to replenish it. "Blue shows your coloring to advantage and makes your eyes glow. Rockhurst has found evidence that might force Jasper to recant his lies, but that means he will soon leave us."

"I won't be coming down for dinner." Laura stared at her hands.

"Is something wrong?" Catherine joined her sister on the couch. Laura's eyes were still puffed from her night of tears, but brooding on the assembly would do her no good. "I know last night was difficult, but everything will be all right soon."

"It will never be all right." Her voice trembled.

"Of course it will. People will soon recognize Jasper for the villain he is."

"It won't matter." Breaking into sobs, she dropped her face into her hands.

"Shush," Catherine urged soothingly as the sobbing increased. "Nothing is worth such distress." Laura did not deal well with crises. No matter what happened— a cut finger, a shattered vase, the childhood prank that had broken Mary's leg—Laura's reaction was the same. To her credit, she rarely repeated an error, but her inability to talk until her own distress had been relieved by lengthy tears irritated her family no end.

Catherine let her cry on her shoulder, stifling a heartfelt sigh. If Laura didn't control herself soon, Rockhurst would find them.

"I've made a hash of everything," Laura sobbed.

Catherine patted her back and made soothing noises, though curses paraded through her mind. The last thing Rockhurst needed was to see Laura in the throes of tears. That contretemps at the ball was bad enough. But she had no hope of moving upstairs until the storm was past.

It took longer than usual for the storm of tears to abate, hinting that the problem was serious. She took

a firm grip on her composure. She could not afford
to lose her temper, for that would send Laura into
another outburst.

"Calm yourself," she murmured as the sobs turned
to hiccups. "It cannot be this bad."

"It is," mumbled Laura, keeping her face pressed
into Catherine's shoulder and her arms wound tightly
around her neck.

"Did you kill someone?"

Laura shook her head.

"Did you destroy someone's livelihood?"

Another shake.

"Have you burned down a house or sold a child
into slavery as a sweep?"

"No." Laura's arms relaxed.

"Then things could be much worse. I doubt you've
done anything that cannot be rectified, so tell me
the tale."

Laura sniffed, but sat up. Catherine pulled a handkerchief from her sleeve and handed it over, then
waited while Laura wiped her nose and dried her eyes.
She waited as Laura folded the handkerchief into a
neat square, smoothed every wrinkle from the damp
linen, set it on her lap, moved it to a table, moved it
back to her lap, licked her lips, returned the handkerchief to the table, arranged her hands into three different positions, and sighed.

"I cannot help until I know the story," Catherine
reminded her. "It will not improve with keeping."

"I know." She moved the handkerchief to the
couch, crossed her arms, pulled her knees nearly to
her chin, then burst out with, "Itriedtocompromise-
Rockhurst."

Catherine's heart stopped. "What exactly did you
do?" Keeping her voice steady was the hardest thing
she'd done in her life.

Laura returned her feet to the floor and relaxed
now that the truth was out and no one was screaming.
"I sent him a message to meet William in the library,
then sent William a message to meet Rockhurst there.

Since William was in the stables, I knew Rockhurst would arrive first. I messed up my hair and gown and planned to hide behind the draperies until I heard William in the hall, then throw myself on Rockhurst so William would find us."

"My God." Her hand shook. "How could you abuse the hospitality of this house so badly?"

Laura's face turned red. "I was desperate, Catherine. You saw how people looked at me last night. I needed to settle things, but Jasper's affairs kept distracting him. I thought a little push would remind him to declare himself."

"A little push? Forcing him to choose between an arrogant, unscrupulous wife and his place in society?" Her voice was rising.

"I'm not—"

"You *are* arrogant, Laura," she snapped. "You assume that beauty will bring you anything you want, but beauty alone won't hold a man, especially one like Rockhurst. He has his pick of beauties every time he visits London, most of them with large dowries. But he wants more. What did he do when you leaped out at him?"

"I didn't."

Catherine exhaled. Had Laura come to her senses in time? But she had barely formed the thought when Laura dashed it.

"He must have reached the library sooner than I had expected," she explained. "Apparently he saw me and understood my intention, though I did not know that until William arrived half an hour later. He was furious."

"Then he must have talked to Rockhurst."

She flinched. "Rockhurst not only complained, but charged William with condoning my plot."

"How often have I warned you to consider how your actions affect others?" Catherine demanded fiercely. Laura recoiled, but Catherine no longer cared. This was beyond heedless, ranking with Jasper's plots for unscrupulous manipulation. "By summoning

William, you involved him as surely as if he'd planned it. Rockhurst could blacken his name with a word."

"He won't. William was so furious with me that Rockhurst must believe him innocent."

"We can only hope. But it is no thanks to you if he refrains from destroying us. And you've forfeited any chance to attract the man."

"I never had a chance," said Laura in a small voice. "William says Rockhurst despises me, comparing me to London fortune hunters. He thinks me forward and obnoxious, and accused me of validating the rumors that you taught me to be a wanton." Again she burst into tears.

Catherine stalked to the window. It was the only way to keep from slapping Laura's face.

Damn the girl for ignoring her advice. If only she had behaved as usual—but it was too late for regrets. Rockhurst was probably disgusted with the entire family. No wonder he thought George's tale would force Jasper's confession. He was so desperate to escape Seabrook, he would exaggerate every bit of evidence. Even his vow would not keep him here much longer. He could not risk another attempt to trap him.

Returning to the couch, she forced Laura to face her. "I am disappointed in you, Laura. No matter how much you like a man, forcing him into marriage will guarantee a life of misery. He would never forgive such dishonor."

"I know." She rubbed away tears with the backs of her hands. "And I am more dishonorable than you know. William forced me to admit that I don't even like Rockhurst. I know very little about him and don't care for what I do know." She continued, but Catherine was no longer listening.

"You don't like Rockhurst?" she gasped, shocked at the unthinkable admission. How could anyone not want him? He was the ultimate gentleman, the embodiment of everything good in the world. But beyond his fairness, his intelligence, and his impeccable manners burned more passion that she'd ever encountered. Her cheeks blazed at the memory of that kiss.

Her heart took flight, lighter than it had been in months. Relief, she assured herself briskly. Relief that Laura's melancholy arose only from embarrassment and not a deep *tendre* for a man who had rejected her. She would not bear the pain of unrequited love.

"I don't," confirmed Laura, trying to laugh, though the sound was nearer a sob. "I have had little to do today but examine my feelings. Admitting that I don't want him makes my plot even more shameful. I wasn't seeking a husband but an escape from Seabrook. I cannot endure the cuts and rumors. I don't know how you remain so calm."

"One of the lessons that comes with age is that you can control no one but yourself. Weeping and wailing only turns others against you. And in my case, retaliation hurts Sarah."

Laura wiped another tear from each eye. "If only Jasper had left us alone. I was happy before this started."

Another fantasy, thought Catherine. Laura had long complained of boring days and provincial suitors. But she held her tongue. "Rockhurst believes he can force Jasper to confess his lies. I pray that he is right and is not rushing his fences to escape you." She felt a measure of satisfaction when Laura's face turned white.

"Make him understand that he is safe," begged Laura.

"I doubt he would believe me. Nor will he slow his efforts now. He has already set his plan in motion. You had best pray that he is not acting hastily. If he fails, the situation will be worse than ever—and impossible to overcome."

"What did he discover?"

She was angry enough not to care whether Laura was braced for the truth. "Jasper caused Papa's accident."

Horror drove away Laura's embarrassment. "Jasper killed Papa?"

"Not intentionally, but yes. He did." She repeated the main points of Rockhurst's report.

"We owe him so much," murmured Laura. "It makes my scheme even worse. How can I face him?"

"You will face him before dinner." She met Laura's eyes. "You will admit that you sought to attach his title and wealth. You will admit that you have no personal interest in him. You will vow to avoid him for the remainder of his stay. Then you will go to your room, where you will take all meals until he leaves."

Laura nodded. "William said the same thing. You will be with me?"

"I will remain in the room to protect him from further insult, but I will neither support you nor prompt you. Only Rockhurst will hear your apology, but if you do not confess everything, including your motives, you will know that your dishonor remains. Do you wish to live with that?"

"No. I will do what needs to be done." She picked up the handkerchief and left the drawing room. Catherine was pleased to note that her back was straight and her shoulders square. Maybe she had finally grown up.

Memory of Rockhurst's kiss drove Laura from her mind. Had it meant anything? He had seemed as horrified as she. Except for his touching her hand, their talk in the morning room had been aloof. But his touch had offered only comfort, she reminded herself. The doctor had done the same thing when informing her that Harold was dead.

Yet she sometimes suspected interest. Warmth often flashed through his eyes. She had ignored it, for amber eyes were naturally warm, and his turned a compelling gold when anything interested him. But it was harder to explain his stare the first time he'd spotted her in Exeter. And what about that blatant arousal in the rose garden?

Hope revived, spinning fantasies she had never

dared entertain—Rockhurst kissing her, touching her, even undressing her; Rockhurst sweeping her away to become his countess; Rockhurst falling madly in love with her. . . .

"Idiot!" she said, berating herself more strongly than ever. The most she could expect was to become his mistress. Earls wed young ladies of impeccable breeding, ladies with large dowries, ladies who were accustomed to moving in the highest circles. She would fail miserably if thrust into a London drawing room.

But you are in love with the man, whispered her conscience.

"No!" She forced the thought aside. Granted, it would be perilously easy to take that final step, but she was not stupid. Loving him would cast a pall over her life worse than Jasper's insinuations. He couldn't reciprocate. Especially now. He would never trust a Seabrook again.

Thrusting thoughts of him out of her mind, she hurried upstairs to dress for a dinner she could no longer skip.

Blake had never endured such an uncomfortable evening. When he reached the drawing room, only Catherine and Laura were there. He nearly retreated, but Catherine's eyes promised safety.

He shouldn't have believed them. She retreated to the window, leaving him to endure a halting, tear-filled apology that managed to insult him several times over. The high point of the evening was when Laura departed and he realized that she'd been confined to her room for the duration of his visit. Unfortunately, that left him alone with Catherine.

She was more aloof than he'd ever seen her, though he doubted that Laura's failed scheme was responsible. His revelations would have revived her grief and added anger over Jasper's attack. But the effect was worse than he had expected, casting doubts on his dreams.

His frustrations mounted as they conducted stilted conversation for the next half hour. Mary had unaccountably chosen to eat with Sarah. Even William's appearance as dinner was called did little to lighten the mood. Embarrassment blanketed the cavernous dining room in a gloom that candles could not penetrate.

The result was the worst two hours of his life. William was mortified to the point of incoherence, finally retreating into a wineglass so he needn't talk. His eyes never lifted from his plate. Catherine was remote, curtly changing the subject whenever he mentioned either Jasper or Laura.

He had hoped to learn more about the night of the accident, but it wasn't to be. Everyone scattered after Rob served the sweet course. But despite crawling into bed early, sleep remained out of reach. Plots, motives, and questions paraded through his mind for hours, often overlaid by memories of touching Catherine, holding Catherine, kissing . . .

Chapter Fourteen

Blake faced Squire Hawkins across the man's lit-tered desk, hoping the room's jumble of papers and stacks of books indicated inadequate shelving rather than a disordered mind. He hadn't admitted it to Catherine, but if Hawkins could not—or would not—help, he would have to concede defeat. Though he was convinced of Jasper's guilt, George's unsupported word was not enough to force a confession. Without a full confession, suspicion would forever attach to her name.

"I am investigating a complaint, not filing one," he said in response to the squire's question. Hawkins had been named a magistrate to fill the void created by Seabrook's death and Rankin's frequent absences.

"Then why come to me?" He reclined in his chair, folding his hands across an ample belly.

"For information. You've heard the rumors about Seabrook's sister, of course."

"Disgraceful affair!" His lips pursed.

"It would be if the tales were true, but they are not." He leaned forward, gazing directly into Hawkins's eyes. "In all the years I've known Seabrook, he has never lied, so when he begged my help to unmask the man who was fabricating stories about his sister, I had to agree."

"Commendable, I'm sure, though I fear he is blinded by family loyalty. You do yourself no good by listening to him. Only yesterday I heard one man comment on your gullibility and another question your intelligence."

"Suggestions first uttered by the same man who is attacking Mrs. Parrish." He kept his voice light with difficulty. Though he'd known that Jasper would try to undermine his credibility, the reality still hurt.

"But why?" Hawkins sounded bewildered.

"Longstanding habit, fury at anyone who opposes him, and fear that his earlier actions might come to public notice."

The squire frowned. "I presume you have evidence."

"Not as much as I'd like, though I am finding more each day. The culprit is crafty, but his actions form clear patterns that I find quite disturbing. His purpose is to avenge insults and repay anyone who annoys him."

"Are you saying that she annoyed him?"

"Definitely, though his retaliation far exceeds her insult. He fears her, for she recognizes his fundamental character and made the mistake of telling him so. The result is an unfounded attack on her credibility that is so pervasive few people note that not one shred of evidence supports it."

"Preposterous! A host of witnesses have stepped forward."

"Name one," he said in challenge.

"There's the man who found her with Lansbury—"

"What is his name?" Blake demanded.

"I— Well— I don't—"

Blake let him flounder a moment longer before interrupting. "Forget rumors for the moment and examine facts. Until last month, Mrs. Parrish was a respected, even beloved, member of the community. She ran her brother's house, chaperoned their sisters, ministered to the poor, and was welcomed everywhere. I've heard tradesmen refer to her as Saint Catherine."

"Not anymore."

"True. She is shunned by all classes now. But each class avoids her for a different reason. Society condemns her supposed misdeeds, but the lower classes know the tales are false. They avoid her to save themselves from similar attack.''

"You jest."

"Not at all." He shifted to a more comfortable position. "The rumors sprang up almost overnight, accusing her of unspeakable deeds, reprehensible behavior, and the deliberate ruination of innocents. Some of these purported acts date back years. One supposedly took place when she was fourteen."

"I know. But it was her success at hiding so much debauchery that is causing such a furor now."

"No one is capable of hiding such long-standing excess," he snapped. "Certainly not a woman like Mrs. Parrish. She lacks the social power to ostracize loose lips. She lacks the physical power to intimidate others into silence. And she lacks the fortune that might purchase a blind eye."

Hawkins frowned.

"And who revealed the tales?" he demanded, pressing his point. "She has no personal maid who might talk in a moment of pique, nor has any servant been with her for the entire period, so who would know so many details?"

"Once one person speaks up, others add their stories."

"But the more people who know a sensational tale, the less likely it will remain secret. And that is merely one reason I disbelieve the rumors. You are not the only man incapable of naming a witness. Not one gossip can identify a liaison. Not one gentleman has participated in even the least of her crimes or knows anyone who has."

"By George, that's odd." Hawkins sat up straight.

"Exactly. We have an enormous body of rumor, but it contains no names, no dates, no places, and no one can produce a living witness to any of it."

"You claimed habit, fury, and fear were behind this. Explain."

Blake let out a deep breath. "The culprit is Jasper Rankin," he began, then held up a hand to halt any protest. "Even a brief investigation turns up a long history of malicious attacks against anyone who irritates him. Tradesmen and tenants live in fear of his wrath. He is disliked in both Plymouth and Bath. His former schoolmates cite numerous incidents of misconduct, many requiring disciplinary action. In the end, he was sent down in disgrace. Guests at house parties he has attended report attacks on servants and threats against hosts. My own opinion is that he is unbalanced but cunning." He described a dozen of Jasper's local revenges.

"That proves nothing," objected Hawkins. "Those were youthful mistakes that he has long since rectified."

"Inadequately." He glared at the squire. "I would believe you if there were fewer cases, but even a heedless fool does not cause this much damage unless he does so by design. While I cannot climb into Jasper's head to prove his motive, I find it curious that every victim was someone who had embarrassed or insulted him. In every case Jasper threatened to make them pay. And every one of them suffered disastrous harm. The lower classes accept his guilt without question, which is why they are shunning Mrs. Parrish. They know from bitter experience that failure to follow Rankin's lead will draw his wrath onto their heads. They have watched him hand out this sort of justice since he was a child."

"Yet society knows nothing of it."

He saw the struggle in Hawkins's eyes. The man wanted to believe his high-ranking visitor, yet the images of a benevolent Jasper and a venal Catherine were firmly fixed in his mind.

"Society's ignorance arises in part because Rankin always has a logical explanation for the damage, but most of it comes from his carefully fostered perceptions. Rankin's reparations impress the upper classes, for they are not required. Too many gentlemen ignore any injury they cause their inferiors. Thus society considers him kind and generous. In reality, his payments are far less than he claims, and his threats warn his victims that complaints will bring further disaster. So few are willing to talk.''

The squire's face paled. "But what grievance does he have with Mrs. Parrish? Her birth is nearly as high as his.''

"True, yet she often works with members of the lower classes. She has helped them cope with Rankin's attacks. Thus she knows his ways. They argued last month. The subject is unimportant, but in a temper she revealed her knowledge. Knowing her birth was high enough that she could tarnish his reputation, he took the precaution of ruining hers.''

Hawkins drummed his fingers on the desk. "He is destroying her because she might tarnish his image? No one would believe her in the face of his charm. This makes no sense.''

"True, though he is remarkably sensitive. He can find insult in the most innocuous comment, and he cannot tolerate even one of his peers holding suspicions of him. Yet you are right that his charm could prevent most damage. Society cares little for the travails of the lower classes, and Mrs. Telcor would soon halt any talk.''

"Yet you still think him guilty?''

"Definitely, though not because of the cases Mrs. Parrish suggested. I thought at first he might be mad, but that is not true either. It wasn't until yesterday that I found the true answer. During their argument, Mrs. Parrish had claimed to know *all* his crimes. He believed her, though she actually knew only a few of his more innocuous revenges.''

Hawkins frowned so fiercely that for a moment his corpulent face resembled a hawk's. "He did something he can't explain away," he murmured.

Blake nodded. "Exactly. Nor can he buy his way out of it. One of his plots went awry. Not only did he kill a lord of the realm, but there were witnesses.''

The blood drained from Hawkins's face. "Are you imp-plying—''

"Think back, Squire. You stopped at the White Hart taproom two years ago. Lord Seabrook chastised Jasper for fleecing Nigel West that night. What did he say?"

His face turned even whiter. "He was in his cups—they both were. I was shocked when Seabrook spoke out, for he never humiliated people, even those who deserved it. But I passed it off as too much wine. Yet there was more to it than wine, or even the game with West." He frowned, drumming his fingers on the desk in an apparent effort to think.

"Was Parrish there?" asked Blake softly.

"That was it." He nodded several times. "Parrish had burst in half an hour earlier, in the devil of a hurry. He tried to drag Seabrook away immediately, but the man insisted that he explain his business while they finished the wine. I was across the room, so I've no idea what they said, though Rankin probably heard. He was at the next table." He shook his head. "Seabrook glared at Rankin several times as the tale progressed. He'd drained his glass and was rising to leave when West suddenly shouted that he was ruined. Seabrook exchanged a comment with Colonel Bangor as West stumbled out—Bangor was also rising to leave."

"Had he been at Seabrook's table?"

"No. He'd been playing cards with Rankin and West, though he'd declined to join that last hand."

"Did he win or lose?"

"I've no idea." Hawkins topped off their glasses. "West had barely shut the door when Seabrook jerked Rankin to his feet and tore strips off of him for continuing play when he knew West had a mother and sisters to support. The lad had buried his father the day before and was in no condition to think clearly."

Blake grimaced. "He actually laid hands on Rankin?"

Hawkins nodded. "Rankin was furious," he admitted. "I thought we'd have a mill for sure, but he only

clenched his fists—Seabrook was older and respected.
He murmured something we couldn't hear, then left."

"Did you see any evidence that Rankin cheated?"

"Certainly not!" The squire was clearly scandalized.
"He and West had been playing for hours before Seabrook arrived, with no complaint, though West looked
rather sickly."

"How much did he lose?"

"A few thousand guineas. He might have survived
that, but he'd also wagered his estate. Rankin lives
there now. It runs with his father's property. He will
likely combine them when he inherits."

So Jasper had acquired an estate of his own where
he could be uncontested master, and he had expanded
the family holdings in the process. For such a gain, he
might well have cheated. He would have thought nothing of forcing West to remain in the game until he
won what he wanted. A threat to ruin one or both of
the lad's sisters would have done it.

He ran through the scene in his mind. Catherine
claimed that Harold had known much about Jasper.
He might have discovered a new incident, one that
would allow a magistrate to move against him. If stubbornness was a Seabrook family trait—William certainly displayed it, as did Catherine—then the baron
would have demanded every last detail before acting.
No matter how low they'd kept their voices, Seabrook's glares would have suggested that they were
discussing Jasper.

So Jasper had felt threatened even before Seabrook
had laid hands on him and embarrassed him so publicly. He'd decided to take immediate steps to intimidate them into silence.

"What did Seabrook do after Rankin left?" he
asked.

"I don't know, for I also left. Rankin was just ahead
of me. I expected him to forgive some of West's losses,
or at least offer an extended payment schedule to protect West's family—that would have fit the image he
cultivates. But West was gone. Rankin headed for the

stable instead of calling for his horse—restless, I suppose; Seabrook's lecture had been brutal."

"He said nothing?"

"He was cursing under his breath—and who could blame him? He rode out a short time later."

Blake straightened. "What were his words?"

"What you would expect in that situation." He rubbed his chin with one hand. "He was humiliated by Seabrook's lecture and clearly angry. He made a few derogatory remarks about Seabrook's ancestry, his interference, and his high-handed arrogance. He might have said something like *He'll be sorry,* but I was not attending. It was late. I was anxious to be home. The yard was noisy. The colonel was just behind me, shouting for his horse. It had rained heavily, leaving water everywhere. A coach crawled in, its driver lamenting three hours lost digging free of mud." He shrugged. "I paid little heed to Rankin. He left before the lads brought 'round my carriage."

"Which way did he go?"

"South." His eyes widened. "That's odd. He should have headed out High Street if he was going home or following West."

"Instead he took the road to Seabrook Manor." Blake's heart raced. At last he had a real piece of evidence. His exploration of the area had proved that the few lanes connecting the south and west roads would have been heavy going for a horseman after a rain. There was no reason for Jasper to take the south road unless he had business there.

"But that means nothing," insisted Hawkins. "Perhaps he stopped at the Golden Stag. He often plays cards there. He may have muttered about making Seabrook sorry, but I thought no more of it than if he had cursed the rain for ruining the hay. No man of reason would kill someone for embarrassing him."

"But Rankin's reason is doubtful, and we don't know why Parrish was so anxious to take Seabrook away. The attack may have meant to silence the vicar."

"Dear Lord!"

"That is speculation, of course. And if it eases your mind, my evidence does not suggest murder. According to George—the groom who overheard the whole of Rankin's muttered plans—he meant to injure Seabrook's horses as a warning to leave him alone. Parrish's last words support that theory."

"That would have been an effective revenge," admitted Hawkins. "Seabrook set great store by that team. Bragged about them until many a man imagined strangling him. But Rankin must have known that he could never intimidate Seabrook. The man was a baron, not a tradesman, and would have struck back."

"I agree that it was a poor plan, but Jasper was half seas over that night and not thinking clearly. Mrs. Parrish is convinced that Seabrook would never have confronted him publicly if he hadn't spotted something havey-cavey about that card game, so Rankin probably had a guilty conscience to begin with. He had to protect himself from exposure, so he struck out in the same way he had done so often with others."

"If he attacked at all." Hawkins drained his glass. "Rankin might have been on the go, but Seabrook was three sheets to the wind that night, barely able to stand. And he was angry. The road was wet, with fog forming along the coast. Even a top sawyer would have trouble controlling a spirited team under those conditions, and Seabrook was no Corinthian."

"What about Parrish's dying words?"

"Garbled at best. If they meant anything at all, they described a local legend."

"The Frenchman's ghost. But I believe Jasper used that legend to mask his actions. By impersonating the Frenchman, he could disclaim culpability."

Hawkins looked troubled. Blake wondered if he was recalling other accidents along that stretch of road. When he said nothing further, Blake returned to his point. "A lord is dead. The circumstances are suspicious. I will seek additional evidence before acting, but I cannot ignore it. If asked, will you testify to what you saw and heard that night?"

"Of course. But I saw no evidence of cheating, and I can't put Rankin on that road. Where he went after leaving the inn yard is a mystery."

And that was that. Accepting that Hawkins would admit no more, Blake turned the conversation to Cavendish's penchant for faking ancient maps.

Catherine stopped in the nursery before leaving to call on Mrs. Stevens, the widow Green's former housekeeper.

"What are you sketching today?" she asked Sarah, frowning over the unfamiliar scene.

"Rockhurst's Abbey. He told me all about it while we were in the woods yesterday. It is huge, with seven wings and a big courtyard, and it has secret passages, and suits of armor in the halls, and his very own chapel where ghostly monks sometimes appear, and a lake with swans, and—"

"Enough! Why would he talk about his house?"

"I asked. We were studying trees. He is very good at leaves, and he knows almost as much as Mary about animals. He climbed an oak tree to fetch a nest. It is all right to bring down nests in autumn, because the birds are done with them and will build new ones in the spring. He says Papa was a very wise man, and I should remember everything he taught me—that was after I told him what Papa said about Mrs. Telcor's busy tongue."

Catherine blushed. Her new understanding of Jasper's past finally explained why Harold had considered Mrs. Telcor a tool of the devil for her blind devotion.

But she had little room for thought just now. Sarah's delighted prattle raised new images of Rockhurst. Did he really love children enough to spend hours every day bringing joy into Sarah's life? The girl had blossomed since his arrival, setting aside the last of her melancholy. Hopefully it would not return when he left.

But common sense suggested that his interest in Sarah was feigned. He had been annoyed by Laura's efforts to attract him. The nursery was the only place in the manor where he could avoid her. She could only thank fate that he had made the effort to hide his motives from Sarah.

"It was while we were talking about bird nests that I asked him about his house," continued Sarah, breaking into her thoughts. "Can we visit his abbey, Mama? He invited us."

"Perhaps," she hedged, taking back every kind thought about the man. He should not have issued an invitation he could not mean. Now Sarah would be hurt if they did not visit the wonders he had described.

Adding the incident to her other complaints—not least of which was that kiss she couldn't forget—she headed for the village.

Miss Mott's footman was reluctant to let Catherine in. Only when she made it clear that she had to see Mrs. Stevens did he step aside. The housekeeper's reaction wasn't much better. It required several protestations of innocence before the woman would even speak with her. But they finally settled down in the housekeeper's parlor with a pot of coffee and a tin of biscuits.

"I heard a most disturbing story yesterday," Catherine began. "In order to determine its truth, I must discover everything I can about the day my husband died."

"He was a good man," said Mrs. Stevens. "I can't believe he was involved in anything odd."

"Of course not, but someone claims that Jasper Rankin caused the accident that killed him. Since Harold had not intended to go to Exeter that night, he must have learned something from Mrs. Green that demanded my father's attention and threatened Jasper."

"Surely not." Mrs. Stevens was clearly shocked.

"That accident was caused by the Frenchman. Dear Mr. Parrish said so before he died."

"Did he?" Catherine frowned. "I know there were rumors to that effect, but no one told me anything Harold said. In fact, Dr. Lebrun swore he'd died without regaining consciousness."

"No." She shook her head vehemently. "Not to distress you, dear, but I had the tale directly from Mr. Berens himself, and who better to tell it, him being the one to find the wreckage and all."

"I know, but why tell you?"

"Mayhap you didn't know, being in mourning at the time, but after Mrs. Green passed on to her reward— and blessed she was to finally cast off her mortal pain—I went as housekeeper to Mr. Berens."

"I thought he only used day help." She tried to hide rising excitement. Perhaps Mrs. Stevens would know Harold's dying words.

"He did, but finding that accident changed him." She paused for a long swallow of coffee. "Terrified, he was, expecting the Frenchman to attack him next. I rarely saw him after he hired me. At night he flitted from window to window, peering into the dark for any glimpse of the ghost. He slept only by day, drawing both shutters and draperies tight and demanding that a footman remain in the hall outside his room, armed with a poker."

"What good would a poker do against a spirit?" She was having trouble picturing the confident Mr. Berens huddled in his house in terror.

"None, as his end proved." Her voice dropped to a whisper. "The ghost struck him down, then burned the place to the ground in warning." She glanced over her shoulder and shuddered.

"Surely not!" But her mind was working at top speed. Berens would never fear a ghost, but he may have expected a more tangible attack. One that would arrive in the dark to escape detection from his neighbors.

"I saw the Frenchman myself that last night," Mrs.

Steven swore. "Muffled in a great black cloak with a cowl pulled low over his eyes. He was riding an enormous black horse. I locked the door tight and checked every last window, but I'd a done better to drag Mr. Berens away. He might still be alive."

"It wasn't your fault," Catherine said soothingly. "Did Mr. Berens ever repeat what my husband said?"

Mrs. Stevens shook her head. "Not exact-like, though he was telling the tale to a friend the day I took up my duties. It was definitely the Frenchman, furious because he wasn't getting the respect he deserved. He swooped to the attack again and again, according to Mr. Parrish, shouting that his name was Jacque or Josh or something like that, and he was a high-ranking lord—as if we didn't know he was a duke."

Josh . . . ranking. Catherine stifled a gasp. Jasper Rankin. If Berens had understood Harold's meaning, he would have known his danger and shifted the blame to the Frenchman to protect himself—he had been a close friend of Carruthers. But Jasper had taken no chances.

She didn't dare start new speculation by displaying interest in the fire. Rockhurst could question Mrs. Stevens if necessary. She would concentrate on Harold.

"We should let the duke rest in peace," she said, accepting another biscuit. "I am more interested in Harold's last night. Mrs. Green summoned him. Have you any idea why?"

"Nay, Mrs. Parrish. She didn't say."

Catherine slumped in exaggerated disappointment. "I was hoping you might have overheard part of their conversation—not that you listened," she hastily added when Mrs. Stevens stiffened with indignation. "But your duties would keep you close. I know you acted as butler because the staff was so small, and you had charge of her cordials and nostrums."

"Well, yes, I did hear a snatch or two—they weren't keeping their voices down. Mrs. Green claimed that something had been bothering her for some time. I didn't hear what because I had to take Cook to task for setting out broken biscuits for the dear vicar."

"He would not have minded," Catherine said, smiling in recollection. "He was like a small boy when it came to sweets."

"That he was." Mrs. Stevens also smiled. "Later I heard him praying with her—she'd had another spell that morning and knew her time was at hand. But that's all."

"Did you know what had been troubling her? You were as much her companion as her housekeeper after Mr. Green's death."

Mrs. Stevens was quiet so long, Catherine thought she would refuse to answer, but she finally spoke. "There was one matter she'd fretted over. Maybe she decided to reveal the tale rather than take it to the grave, particularly since she knew she'd soon be beyond his reach. And if you are right about the accident, it might fit. It concerned Jasper Rankin." Taking a deep breath, she began talking.

An hour later Catherine hurried toward Seabrook, anxious to find Rockhurst.

Chapter Fifteen

Though he would rather have paced, Blake forced himself to sit quietly in Rankin's study. Nervous energy made him jittery, but he had to project confidence despite his reservations. His evidence was mostly conjecture, yet there was no time to look for more. Too many people knew his purpose by now. Delaying would give Jasper a chance to strengthen his defenses. So he must bluff.

"Lord Rankin is not hearing cases this week," a toplofty butler had informed him half an hour earlier. "He is suffering a malaise of the spirit and requires calm. If you are in urgent need of a magistrate, Squire Hawkins will help." The tone had implied contempt for the squire's elevation to the post.

"Rankin's malaise will worsen if he refuses to see me," Blake had countered sharply. "My problem concerns his heir. If I take the matter elsewhere, the name of Rankin will be blackened from here to London and beyond."

The threat had worked. The butler had escorted him to the study, though he'd grumbled under his breath in a most unbutlerly display.

Blake didn't care if his demands disrupted the household. It was past time for Rankin to exert some control over his son.

Once the butler left, Blake had made a single circuit of the room, searching for clues to Rankin's character. This would be his one chance to win the viscount's support, so he must play his cards very carefully—not that he would ignore Jasper's crimes if Rankin refused to cooperate, but the man's help would make forcing a public confession easier.

The study offered little information about the viscount beyond what he already knew. Mrs. Telcor had suggested that he reveled in poor health, a charge supported by the butler's protests and by the many well-thumbed herbals stacked on the shelf nearest the desk. Catherine had claimed that his family name was important, a fact borne out by the ornate stand supporting a large Bible that was open to reveal generations of Rankin births, deaths, and marriages. Someone had transcribed the names onto an artistic family tree that hung on the wall above.

Little else was obvious. Nothing in the study revealed Rankin's interests or his feelings for his son. Aside from the herbals, the shelves contained only a standard set of the leather-bound books sold to gentlemen who wanted an instant library. He might be trying to appear more educated than he was, or he may have acquired them because libraries were the current mode, like Egyptian furniture and racing curricles. The desk was bare. Was Rankin tidy and methodical, or too intent on his various ills to work?

Movement drew him to the window. A groom trotted hurriedly down the drive. Rankin had probably sent for Jasper. Thus he had agreed to a meeting.

Returning to his seat so he could present a relaxed, assured façade, he waited. The clock struck three, the butler brought wine, and still he waited.

Catherine had accosted him the moment he'd returned from interviewing Squire Hawkins that morning, as lighthearted as he'd ever seen her. She had uncovered information that implicated Jasper in another death. Even more important, Mrs. Stevens's tale proved that Jasper's revenges dated back to childhood and explained his attack on Seabrook and Parrish.

Mrs. Green had summoned Harold Parrish shortly before her death, having decided to share her information while she still could. Her fear of heavenly judgment finally outweighed her fear of earthly retribution,

so she had described the day she had come across ten-
year-old Jasper killing a cat.

Not just killing it, Blake emended, recalling Catherine's white face as she repeated the tale. He had tortured it first and was systematically dismembering it
when Mrs. Green arrived.

"It scratched me," he'd explained with a shrug. "I
am the heir. Nothing is allowed to hurt me."

"No one has absolute power or absolute privilege,"
she'd tried to explain. "Not even the king. You are
heir to your father's title, but that position carries
many responsibilities, one of which is to protect those
lower and weaker than yourself."

His response had been crude, then he'd launched a
garbled version of history purporting to prove that
lords exercised unrestricted authority over their pos-
sessions and were guaranteed freedom from every annoyance. Finally he'd added a threat she'd never
forgotten. "Anyone who bothers me must be punished. Even you."

The menace in his voice had reminded her of Mrs.
Carlton's broken leg, suffered in an unexplained fall
the day after she'd scolded Jasper for throwing rocks
at her geese. She'd never mentioned the boy again,
though she'd complained about him often enough before. So Mrs. Green said nothing about the cat. A
month later, Mrs. Telcor had been praising Jasper's
kindness and maligning Lord Rankin's disinterest in
his son. Mrs. Green had agreed that Rankin's neglect
was disgraceful. She'd agreed that Jasper's current
tutor was slothful. Then she'd added that the boy
needed a better understanding of his future responsibilities and firmer discipline to prepare him for assuming them. That night her own cat had turned up on
her doorstep, mangled. Heeding the warning, she had
never discussed Jasper again.

The story explained much. Harold Parrish had long
tried to help his parishioners—a thankless job, for Jasper preyed on them with impunity. The moment he'd
heard Mrs. Green's story, he had seen a chance to act.

Here at last was a witness to Jasper's motives, someone who could offer proof positive of the patterns
obvious in his behavior. So he'd fetched Seabrook.
He'd probably intended to visit the hardest-hit victims
after Seabrook listened to the widow's tale.

But Seabrook's stubbornness had allowed Jasper to
overhear part of these plans. Both had to be intimi-
dated into silence.

Blake had wanted to comfort Catherine when she'd
finished her tale, but it hadn't been necessary. She'd
been fighting mad rather than grieving.

"We have to stop him," she'd said, skirts swirling
as she strode about the room. "Three men dead by
his hand, and God alone knows how many more."

"I agree, but we can't charge him with murder,"
he'd reminded her. "There isn't enough evidence."

"Why? Mrs. Stevens saw him."

"Do you expect me to go before the assizes and
claim that Jasper murdered Mr. Berens? Jasper's motive would be an accident that Berens himself claimed
was caused by a ghost. My evidence would consist of
a housekeeper who saw the ghost in the yard and
checked to make sure every door and window was
locked."

She'd sagged. "You don't believe me."

He'd pulled her close enough to drown in her eyes.
"I do believe you, Catherine. I am as convinced as
you that Jasper started that fire. He probably struck
Berens on the head first so he couldn't escape."

"But the windows—"

"Maybe Mrs. Stevens was wrong. Or maybe Jasper
broke one to get in—the fire would hide a broken
window. But I can't prove it. Besides, we are not trying to send Jasper to the gallows. We want a confession."

"But he has to pay something." She'd trembled.

"Because he killed your husband?"

"In part, though it helps to know that Harold died
trying to help others. But if he deliberately killed Berens, what's to stop him from killing someone else?"

"What, indeed?" he repeated now, as footsteps approached the door. Jasper might consider murder a tidy solution to a growing number of problems.

Blake rose as Lord Rankin entered the study. The man did not appear ill. Nor did he appear cooperative. Anger blazed in his eyes, reddening his face. His fists were clenched.

"How dare you drag me from a sickbed to complain about a young man's prank?" he demanded, throwing himself into his desk chair.

The question removed all doubt about which approach to use. Abandoning the notion of appealing to the father, he addressed the magistrate. "I said nothing about pranks, Lord Rankin, though a man of twenty-six is too old to indulge in juvenile behavior. I wish to present evidence of a crime. It is your duty to hold the accused until the next assizes." He resumed his seat.

"You needn't preach duty to me, Rockhurst," growled Rankin. "I have been magistrate of this district for thirty years."

"And Jasper has been terrorizing it for twenty." He met Rankin's angry face, confident that his own was set in implacable certainty.

"Pranks," snorted Rankin. "You, better than most, should know that young men will sow their oats. I read the London papers."

So Rankin knew about the turkeys he'd smuggled into Lady Horseley's bedchamber last year. Not one of his better ideas, as he was the first to admit, but he'd wearied of her attempts to malign him. In the end, she'd seen the humor of it. He had repaired the damage, and they had declared peace. He acknowledged the irony of decrying Jasper's behavior as juvenile when the lad was his junior by four years.

"I am not discussing pranks," he repeated. "I am discussing crimes—deliberate damage to property and deliberate injury to people and animals."

"Then why have I heard nothing before?" Rankin drummed his fingers on the desk top.

"Because everyone knows you have turned a blind eye to his shortcomings since childhood. The tutors at Harrow recognized them, as did his fellow students. You must have received letters when he was sent down."

Rankin frowned, but his eyes revealed the disbelief he must have cultivated to protect his family name.

"Locally, he intimidates the victims into silence," continued Blake. "They know that disclosing his deeds will draw retaliation."

Rankin's expression grew troubled. "How do you come to know of them, then?"

Blake softened his tone. "Until recently, his victims were unwilling to fight back. Most are from the lower classes and know their word will never stand against his. Many are your dependents and thus will one day be under Jasper's thumb."

Rankin flinched.

"And though his actions are deliberate, they are designed to look like high spirits or carelessness. He is arrogant enough to believe that he is immune from censure."

"Arrogance is hardly a crime."

"Not in itself. But his conceit has twisted history to convince him that he is above the law."

"Nonsense," sputtered Rankin. "I admit I've had to chastise him for the friends he keeps, but he hasn't a malicious bone in his body."

"Hasn't a malicious bone? Tell that to the cats he tortured and dismembered in childhood," snapped Blake, angry enough to reveal his loathing. "Tell it to the merchants he ruined, the tenants he punished, and the girls he seduced—not because he wanted them, but merely to hurt their loving families. Tell it to the innocents his lies besmirched and the friend whose eye he put out. And tell it to the men he murdered."

"I-I-" Rankin's hand clutched his chest. His face had gone from purple to white.

Cursing himself for succumbing to temper, Blake poured wine for his host. He hadn't believed the man

was truly ill, but this was more than shock. And it was
not at all what he wanted. Causing a fit that killed
Rankin would elevate Jasper to the peerage, making
it a thousand times harder to defeat him.

He resumed his seat as Rankin drank, then waited
until the viscount's color returned.

Rankin shook his head, inhaled deeply several
times, then stared at his visitor. "You are sure?"

"The evidence is clear."

"I will listen, but I want Jasper here as well. He has
a right to face his accuser."

"It is not a right he accorded Mrs. Parrish when he
savaged her reputation, but I believe in fair play,"
he agreed, relaxing. It was far better to catch Jasper
unaware, with a witness at hand, than to grant him an
opportunity to prepare excuses. He only hoped that
Rankin's pride in his position as magistrate would balance his obsession with the family's good name, keeping him impartial.

"Thank you. I have already sent for him. He should
arrive shortly."

In fact, he did not arrive for another hour, but
Blake remained silent. Rankin was arranging excuses
and honing his disbelief. His eyes flicked often toward
the family tree, usually accompanied by a grimace or
a flinch. But that would make the disclosures more
shocking and his condemnation of Jasper harsher. Yet
conjecture, hearsay, and logic would not be enough to
guarantee that shift, Blake reminded himself as Rankin poured more wine. Somehow he must push Jasper
into admitting guilt.

He suppressed a grimace, hoping Rankin knew
about him only from London's society pages. He
might be an earl, but many lords considered him a
dangerous heretic for his support of the reformers in
Parliament. They knew he demanded equal justice for
all classes—which was why Jasper's crimes infuriated
him.

This case cast shame on England's justice system.
A merchant or laborer would have been transported

long ago had he committed any of Jasper's crimes, even inadvertently. High spirits excused harming others only in the aristocracy. No tenant could claim that trampling a lord's fields was a boyish prank or careless mistake. No magistrate would listen. Only the result mattered. Yes, the aristocracy deserved privileges in return for the responsibilities attached to their positions. But those privileges should not include preying on those they should be protecting.

Jasper embodied the worst traits of the aristocracy—arrogance, heedlessness, and a conviction that he could do anything with impunity. He must be taught a lesson.

"What is so important that I must cancel my plans?" demanded Jasper, slamming the door behind him.

"Lord Rockhurst has filed a complaint against you," said Rankin, motioning Jasper to a chair. "As magistrate, I must investigate his charges."

Blake drew in a breath to steady nerves still jumping from Jasper's explosive entrance.

Jasper gave him a look of pure loathing. "I should have known he would make trouble when I learned he was Seabrook's friend. You can ignore him easily enough. He is a weak-minded fool who has been deluded by a schemer. And he incited that brawl at the assembly rooms, though I've not yet discovered his purpose."

"Insults won't erase your deeds," said Blake mildly, holding his temper firmly in check—he suspected that Jasper was trying to trigger it. "Nor can excuses hide your intentions forever. The more victims you create, the easier it is for others to see the truth. Too many people now know that you punish any irritation, no matter how insignificant."

"Lies, my lord. Plots conjured by greedy men who hope to use your sympathy to force favors from me."

"Favors, sir?" asked Blake, feigning surprise. "What favor could I seek from you?"

"Not you," sputtered Jasper. "The fools you've

been talking to. Carruthers. Jenkins. Seabrook himself."

"Odd that you can name so many victims before I've even begun," he murmured softly. "As to favors, I've found no one willing to accept your favor, save Mrs. Telcor, but there is ample evidence of your misdeeds."

"Then perhaps we should examine this evidence," suggested Rankin. His face slipped into a frown as he cast another furtive glance at the family tree.

"Seabrook has known me since school. I've had some small success discerning the truth behind certain incidents and have served several years as a magistrate in Oxfordshire, so when the rumors harming his sister began, he asked me to investigate. He swore they were lies."

"He is hardly an impartial judge," snapped Jasper.

Rankin raised a hand. "You will have your say in a moment." His voice had turned to ice.

Jasper opened his mouth, but thought better of it when he met his father's gaze. He subsided.

"My lord?"

Blake nodded. "Seabrook has always been honorable and truthful, so I agreed. The first fact that struck me was the timing. Dozens of rumors appeared, almost overnight. And though they claim witnesses to each act, not one person admits to being one of those witnesses. Nor can anyone name a soul who is."

"Why would anyone admit they'd kept such scandal secret, leaving others vulnerable to her corruption?" sneered Jasper.

"Hold your tongue!" Rankin was as angry at the interruption as at the charge.

Blake ignored them both. "In the course of my investigation, I talked to people of all classes," he continued. "Many revealed other tales, all falling into the same malicious pattern." He repeated several, pointing out the common theme. "There are more. And if a stranger can discover a dozen in less than a week, they must be legion."

"Fustian!" Jasper leaped to his feet. "It is a plot by that harlot to discredit me."

"Jasper!"

"Don't you see how he's twisted the facts, Father? I have long since admitted fault for these so-called crimes and done my best to atone. As for the chandler's daughter, the silly chit interpreted friendly greetings as flirtation and threw herself at me. I refused to court her, finally spending a month in Bath to avoid her. But she was so determined to rise above her station that she got herself with child, then claimed an affair that never existed, hoping her father could force me into wedding her."

Blake shrugged. "Your word. Her word. It matters not, for it is merely one of many. And I can produce witnesses to your misdeeds dating back to that cat you tortured at age ten."

"Old lady Green is dead." Jasper snorted.

Blake met Rankin's eyes, satisfied that he had heard the admission. Though he'd named no names, Jasper had known exactly what he'd meant. "Every incident fits a single pattern," he continued. "If someone irritates or insults you, intentionally or not, disaster follows. And you are always there. But I digress." He held up a hand to halt further protest. "These cases merely establish your character. My real complaint is murder."

Rankin sighed, shaking his head.

"Murder!" squeaked Jasper.

"Murder. I hereby accuse Jasper Rankin, son and heir to Viscount Rankin, of killing the late Lord Seabrook and his son-in-law Harold Parrish by deliberately and repeatedly attacking Seabrook's curricle until it veered into the ditch, dashing the occupants against the rocks."

Jasper's jaw hung slack in shock.

"I further accuse the aforesaid Jasper Rankin of killing Gerald Berens by burning his house down around him to prevent him from disclosing the attack on Seabrook."

Jasper's face had taken on a green tinge.

"Why kill Seabrook?" asked Rankin.

"Several reasons. He embarrassed Jasper by chastising him for fleecing Nigel West of everything he owned. A dozen men overheard the confrontation. But beyond that, Mrs. Green had just told Parrish about seeing Jasper torture cats in childhood. At age ten, Jasper had not yet learned to disguise his motives, so he admitted that anything causing him the least harm must be punished, because he was the heir, so his every desire must be granted."

"My God," murmured Rankin.

Blake continued. "Mrs. Green also described how Jasper coerced her silence. Parrish had long sought evidence that would stop the attacks on his parishioners, so he asked Seabrook to listen to her story. Jasper overheard their discussion. To keep his activities quiet among his peers, he had to silence both men. Three witnesses overheard him plotting to force Seabrook's curricle off the road. Berens heard Parrish's description of the accident before he died."

"Then why has no one come forward in the two years since?" demanded Rankin.

"Two men found it easier to accept tales of ghostly manifestations than to examine their suspicions. The other remained silent out of fear. He knows that Jasper strikes out against anyone who utters even innocuous criticism. How could he accuse him of murder?"

"You are doing so."

"I believe in justice. A lord is dead, cut down to protect sordid secrets. Two others also died. Condoning such atrocities undermines the very foundation of the system you and I are sworn to uphold." He held Rankin's eye.

Jasper snorted. "Ignore him, Father," he said, shaking his head. "He seeks only to restore innocence to the village harlot. Somehow he thinks this plot will accomplish that impossible goal. Either he devised it himself, or he is gullible enough to believe liars and cheats. He cannot know whose word is trustworthy and whose is not. What right does he have to impose his wishes on your district?"

"A charge has been made," said Rankin slowly. "I cannot dismiss it without examining the evidence."

Blake relaxed. "Mrs. Green's staff overheard her conversation with Parrish. She had previously told the same tale to her housekeeper. Colonel Bangor, Squire Hawkins, and Squire Pott were among those in the White Hart taproom when Seabrook arrived that evening. Jasper, Colonel Bangor, and Nigel West were playing cards. The colonel is unable to answer questions right now, as you know, but Squire Pott recalls that West tried to withdraw from the game several times. Jasper convinced him to remain." He had spoken to Pott on his way to Rankin Park.

"He could have left if he'd really wanted to," muttered Jasper.

"I did not suggest otherwise," said Blake smoothly. "I am merely setting the scene. Parrish arrived during the last hand, his conversation clearly audible at the table you shared with Bangor and West. Pott also heard their words. Bangor sat out the last hand, for you offered West a double or nothing chance to recoup heavy losses. You won everything he had, including the estate on which you now live." He flicked a glance at Rankin, satisfied to note the man's frown, then returned to Jasper. "All the men agree that Seabrook chastised you for not ending the game sooner. He believed that a true gentleman would never have suggested that last bet."

"He insisted," snarled Jasper. "He knew quite well what he was risking."

"That is beside the point, though Pott's memory is rather different. You were already seething over Parrish's attempt to punish you for your reprisals, so when Seabrook labeled your behavior ungentlemanly, you vowed that he would regret interfering."

Jasper shrugged.

Rankin's eyes revealed new anger.

"As you strode toward the stables, you uttered further threats against Seabrook and his prized horses. Colonel Bangor and Squire Hawkins overheard you."

"Impossible. They stayed in the taproom."

Blake smiled. "No, they did not. They were barely ten feet behind you. Drink made you careless, so your voice carried."

"Everyone grumbles when angry. No one takes it seriously."

Rankin nodded.

"Agreed. I doubt anyone is immune from angry outbursts," said Blake. "But you took it further. You had ordered the White Hart grooms to keep your horse ready that night—a common demand whenever you suspected you might need a speedy exit. By the time you entered the stable, you were plotting in earnest."

Jasper snorted.

"Unbeknownst to you, a groom overheard every word. He tried to speak up when he arrived at the accident scene the next morning, for the tracks on the muddy road clearly showed your attack, but no one listened. By the time they returned to town, he'd had time to remember your habits, so he kept quiet for fear of reprisals."

Rankin's frown deepened as he gazed at his son.

Blake continued. "You took the south road out of Exeter when you left the stable."

"That is not a road that leads here," said Rankin.

"He lies," snapped Jasper.

"Hawkins watched you leave as he waited for his carriage." He switched his gaze to Rankin. "There is no doubt he took the south road. He probably waited in that copse half a mile out of town, for Seabrook did not spot him until he raced up from behind and jerked away the ribbons. Then he whipped the horses into a frenzy, slashing at their legs. Naturally, they bolted. Twice over the next quarter mile, they slowed. Each time, he returned, slashing at the horses until they finally veered into the ditch. The curricle overturned, killing Seabrook and fatally wounding Parrish."

"They weren't supposed to die," Jasper swore, then choked when he realized what he had said.

"My God!" Rankin blanched.

"I didn't do anything," shouted Jasper, jumping to his feet. "We were all shocked at their deaths. That's all I meant. No one is supposed to die driving home after an evening with friends."

"Sit down," Rankin ordered. "Have you more evidence, my lord?"

"Parrish's last words, which describe the repeated attacks of the horseman. He tried to name Jasper, but lost consciousness. Yet his words echoed in Berens's head. Whether he recognized their meaning at once or only realized it after Jasper threatened him, I don't know. But within the week, he knew his peril. For his protection, he told everyone he knew that the Frenchman had caused the accident, then took the extra precaution of locking himself in his house. His housekeeper heard him repeating Parrish's dying words over and over. And she saw Jasper approaching the house just before the fire started."

"Lies!" shouted Jasper. "All lies. You've heard Berens's stories, Father. He swore it was the Frenchman's ghost."

Rankin shook his head. "You forget that I was summoned when the accident was first discovered. I interviewed Berens while others retrieved the bodies. He repeated Parrish's words, but said nothing of ghosts. That story did not begin until later. If Parrish had been less crazed from pain, we would have paid more attention, but he seemed to be raving. Now I know he was not. He tried to tell Berens to ask Mrs. Green about the cat, and he claimed that West had been forced into that game. But we did not understand." He let out a long breath. "I have overlooked your arrogance for too many years, Jasper." His voice broke. "I should have taken you in hand after your first tutor swore you'd pushed him down the stairs.

But I let Mrs. Telcor convince me he'd lied to cover drunkenness. I am as responsible for staining our name as you, for it was easier to ignore you than to train you properly." He turned to Blake. "Did he mean to kill Seabrook that night?"

"I don't believe so. He had previously employed intimidation, using schemes that inflicted severe and lasting pain on his victims. He meant to cripple or destroy Seabrook's horses, but he pushed too far and killed the men instead. Berens was deliberate, though. I cannot ignore that."

Rankin shakily drained his wineglass. "You have placed me in an untenable position, Rockhurst," he said on a sigh. "How can I bind over my only son? Conviction would demand hanging. Seabrook was a lord."

"Father!" Jasper's face turned white.

Blake frowned, pretending to consider Rankin's dilemma. Trying Jasper for murder was not his goal. As he'd told Catherine, the evidence was too weak to assure a conviction. Seabrook had been too drunk that night to control his team even without Jasper's attack. And Mrs. Stevens had not seen nearly as much as he'd implied. Only Jasper's weak protest had convinced him that the fire was indeed deliberate.

"I have long championed justice, regardless of rank," he began slowly, watching terror leach the last color from Jasper's face. "I possess sworn statements from all the witnesses. This is a clear case of a malicious attack that resulted in the death of a lord."

"But you know his death was an accident," protested Rankin. "You can hardly call it murder when he did not intend to kill."

"The law makes no distinction," Blake reminded him. "He sought to cause harm. His victim died." He paused to let that sink in, watching Jasper out of the corner of his eye, then nearly smiled. He would wager a monkey Jasper was soiling his breeches. "Ask Jasper if motives matter," he suggested. "He has avoided

paying for his crimes for twenty years by asking people to judge appearances and ignore his real motives."

Rankin moaned.

"But perhaps we should consider true justice and
not just the letter of the law. Seabrook, Parrish, and
Berens are dead. No punishment can bring them back.
But the wrongs Jasper perpetrated against others can
still be set right. If he repairs that damage, perhaps a
lesser penalty will suffice. Overseeing your Caribbean
estate for ten years might teach him responsibility."

Rankin slumped in relief. "What must he do?"

"Father!"

"Would you rather stand trial for capital murder?"
Jasper sank back into his chair.

Blake relaxed. "His most recent victim is Mrs. Parrish. While fighting off his unwanted advances, she
revealed knowledge of his other crimes. He ruined his
reputation so no one would believe her. Since the day
William requested my help, Jasper has extended his
rumors to include the entire family."

"Despicable!" Rankin drummed his fingers.

"I agree. He must publicly admit that he started
every one of the rumors, that every one is a lie, and
that his goal was to discredit her so no one would
believe that he killed her father and husband. He must
admit that his other attacks were not inadvertent high
spirits but deliberate attempts to hurt the victims. And
he must repay the damage he has done to those victims. For example, without the income that should
have come from those ruined crops, Jones's family will
starve this winter. Jasper's so-called reparations were
an insult."

"Arbitrating the damage claims will take years."

"No doubt, but better you than a court."

He nodded. "I will see that it is done."

Blake let the subject of reparations drop. They
could resume it later. "I will call on Mrs. Telcor tomorrow. If she does not accept the truth, I will give
my evidence to another magistrate." He named a man
known for despising arrogant young men.

"Agreed." Rankin glared at Jasper. "We will visit Mrs. Telcor immediately. A ship leaves Plymouth on Thursday. He will be on it."

Blake waited until Jasper met his eyes. "If I file these statements with a court, you can never return. No matter how many years pass, you would be arrested the moment you set foot in England. Keep that in mind while making your calls. Even acceding to your father's honors will not protect you from a murder charge."

Jasper nodded.

Satisfied, Blake bade farewell to Lord Rankin. With luck, it would be over by morning.

"You are free," he told Catherine in the drawing room before dinner, having described his meetings with Pott and the Rankins.

"Do not celebrate too soon," she warned. "I know Jasper. He will find a way to twist this to his advantage. And now that he knows his true peril, he will destroy you."

"I've taken steps to deal with every contingency," he insisted, wondering why she remained wary. "Even Rankin believes him guilty. And Jasper knows that if his confession is inadequate, I can have him tried for murder."

"It won't be enough," she insisted. "The man has an uncanny knack for protecting himself. He has probably warned people that his father intends to disown him or even kill him so the viscountcy can pass to someone else. Whatever he actually says, some will believe that he is caught in a trap and will utter any lie to escape with his life."

"That is insane!"

"Is it?" She tried to glare, but her gaze softened when it met his. "You agreed that Jasper is unbalanced. If you expect to defeat him, you must think in unbalanced ways."

"I'm not sure I can." He examined the wineglass in his hand. "What do you think he will do beyond depicting me as a weak-minded, delusional fool—which he has already done?"

"That I can't say. But he will do something. You had best be prepared."

"He is too concerned about his own future to bother with mine," he insisted.

"Have it your way." She threw up her arms in exasperation. "But at least do me the favor of saying nothing about this until we learn which of us is right. I'll not have you raising hopes that will immediately be dashed."

She left him when Mary arrived, giving him no chance to question her further. But his mind fretted as he chatted with William. Her words had made too much sense. Jasper left no insult unavenged. His investigation had been an insult even before today.

Chapter Sixteen

Catherine completed another circuit of the drawing room, then cursed herself. Rockhurst had left for Exeter two hours ago, and no matter how hard she tried, she could not keep hope buried. If anyone found her here, they would know something had happened, but she couldn't talk about Jasper just yet. The others would assume that Rockhurst had erased the unpleasantness of these past weeks, which would cause more pain when they discovered that little had changed. Doubts would remain in most people's minds. It was always safer to assume the worst, which was why losing one's reputation was permanent.

She only hoped that Rockhurst's own reputation wouldn't suffer. And maybe suspicion of Laura and Mary was not yet fixed. If they recovered, she would be content.

In the meantime, no one must see her nervous fears, and the best way to accomplish that was to avoid everyone. Mary was with Sarah in the schoolroom. William was meeting with the steward in the library. But the servants were everywhere, and Laura could appear at any time.

Donning a warm cloak, she headed for the rose garden, seeking its peace. Hope had been battering her defenses since last night. If she allowed it free rein, learned that she remained an outcast would destroy her. She could not afford to collapse in front of Rockhurst. He would feel guilty and insist on trying again to redeem her.

But the rose garden proved to be a poor refuge.

Not only was it visible from the upper windows, but it was too imbued with Rockhurst. It was here he had kissed her, devouring her in a surge of desire she needed to forget.

So she fled to the orchard. It was a barren place in November, but that was exactly what she needed. A brisk walk would burn off energy, and a brutal reminder of the facts would finally banish hope.

The facts were clear, she insisted to herself, striding through drifts of leaves. Rockhurst did not have enough evidence for an arrest, which Jasper must know. And he was acting hastily, spurred by his need to escape Seabrook before Laura could stage another compromise. When Jasper called his bluff, Rockhurst would lose.

She pulled her cloak tighter as anger replaced her restlessness. If Laura hadn't pushed him into haste, they would not be facing this disaster. This was not the first time Laura had precipitated a crisis by ignoring potential consequences, though it was by far the worst. Jasper would plant some new calumny before leaving England, and the gullible Mrs. Telcor would spread it far and wide. They would suffer for years to come. Even if people doubted the tale, they would hesitate to accept a Seabrook. It was easier to avoid anyone of questionable virtue.

Tears overflowed. They were tied to the estate, so they would have to endure the inevitable ostracism. Laura would never wed, nor would Mary. She even doubted if William could ever find an acceptable wife. Would he settle for a title-hungry merchant's daughter or allow a distant cousin to inherit the barony? Not that it mattered. Society would shun them once Jasper's poison did its work. Even helping the poor must cease, for they would lose too much by allowing her to care.

Sarah would also suffer.

And it's all your fault!

She sank onto a stump, dropping her head into her hands as the tears fell in earnest. She was wrong to blame Laura. In the end she had caused this tragedy all by herself, and through the same selfish blindness. In this very place, she had let temper rule, insulting Jasper despite knowing what the consequences would be. She had enjoyed flinging his offer back in his face. Remembering Amy Carruthers had lent extra force to her knee, and she had relished the pain exploding through his eyes.

Stupid woman. Two minutes of pleasure had destroyed her family.

"I won't be long," Blake told his coachman as he descended from his carriage. Taking a deep breath, he rapped on Mrs. Telcor's door.

Doubt had clouded his mind since Catherine's outburst in the drawing room last evening. It had cast a pall over his satisfaction, keeping him awake much of the night and restless the rest of it. Nor did morning produce calm. Catherine had flatly refused to accompany him today.

"I can't face another round of cuts," she'd claimed over breakfast. It was the first time they had shared that meal.

"You won't," he'd sworn. "News of Jasper's confession should have reached every drawing room in the area by now."

But she had refused to listen, reiterating her previous claims. Her utter certainty was contagious—so much so that he dreaded this call. If Catherine remained under suspicion, he would have to file formal charges against Jasper, knowing that his evidence was not strong enough for a conviction. Jasper might well arrange a fatal accident for his father. The evidence was even less likely to convict a viscount.

He was reaching for the knocker a second time when the door opened.

"Welcome, my lord," said the butler, motioning him inside. The man seemed harried.

Blake soon realized why. The drawing room was crammed with nearly as many people as had been at

the assembly. Chairs, benches, stools, and even a flour
keg had been pressed into service to seat every gossip
from miles around. A score of gentlemen leaned
against the walls. No one cared about the proper
length of calls this day. He suspected some had been
here since breakfast.

Everyone fell silent as he squeezed across the room
to accept tea from his hostess. A footman handed him
refreshments as a maid rushed another tray from the
kitchen. He could almost feel the cook's panic at having to produce so much food without notice. The items
on his plate looked decidedly odd—a bit of bread
topped with blancmange and a nut, another sprinkled
with coarse sugar.

Miss Crumleigh uttered a meaningless comment on
the weather. Miss Ander added a remark about the
price of coal. Desultory conversation on topics of no
interest soon filled the silence. Blake wondered how
long they could avoid the subject they were here to
discuss. Even the observation that Cavendish had
closed his stationer's shop and disappeared raised no
excitement.

Blake smiled to himself. Hawkins must have started
asking questions.

"Did Jasper Rankin really make up the stories
about Mrs. Parrish?" demanded a new arrival as she
walked through the door. Her question freed tongues
paralyzed by his presence.

"He said so, didn't he?" scoffed Hortense Peters
from her seat at Mrs. Telcor's right hand. "I heard
him myself in this very room."

"But he had no choice," declared Mrs. Telcor. "His
father dragged him to town and forced him to say
those dreadful things. The poor boy has feared for
some time that Rankin's wits were wandering, and this
proves it. Why else would he ruin his own heir? Even
he should know that the next in line is a vulgar fool
who would call all manner of ridicule onto the title."

"I saw no sign of weak wits when we spoke recently," said Blake. "While Lord Rankin is naturally

concerned about his health, that hardly indicates senility." He locked eyes with an elderly lady he suspected was Miss Mott. Frail and wrapped in several shawls, she had nonetheless come out on this momentous day to discuss Jasper's fall from grace.

"Of course it does not," she answered. "Lord Rankin is as rational as any of us."

"And he has ample reason to lock Jasper away," added Hortense. "Ruining Mrs. Parrish is bad enough, even without the rest."

"He didn't ruin her," swore Mrs. Telcor. "Rankin forced him into that falsehood. Why would he wish to harm her?"

"To keep her quiet about how her husband and father died, of course." Hortense glared.

"That is absurd. We all know how they died. Seabrook was so drunk that the Frenchman's ghost startled him into driving into a ditch."

"Hah!" snorted Mr. Fester. "Jasper killed them because they'd discovered what a swine he is. When he found out Mrs. Parrish knew the truth, he destroyed her reputation so we wouldn't believe her."

"I've never heard anything so preposterous in my life," spat Mrs. Telcor. "Where did you hear such nonsense?"

"From Jasper." He shrugged.

Hortense cast a triumphant smile at her rival, ignoring the fact that Mrs. Telcor was the hostess.

Miss Ander nodded. "I was in the confectioner's shop yesterday when he came in. And I must say I've long distrusted him. He tried to force my maid last year, for all she's over fifty. He is a spoiled little boy who wants his own way in all things and punishes anyone who impedes him. Seabrook fell afoul of his temper, so Jasper forced his curricle off the road."

"Lies his father placed in his mouth," insisted Mrs. Telcor.

"Truth even you must accept," snapped Hortense.

"You wouldn't recognize truth if it bit you in the ankle." Mrs. Telcor turned away in a direct cut.

"Are you blind, Hermione Telcor?" demanded Clara Peters, looming over the woman like an avenging Fury. "That boy has twisted you 'round his finger since he was a lad, but you refuse to see it. Open your eyes. How many times have you believed his excuses even when witnesses claimed differently?"

Mrs. Telcor blanched. "But his father gloated."

"No." Hortense motioned her sister back to her chair. "I sat here during every minute of their call, as did others." She glanced at several ladies, who nodded agreement. "Lord Rankin showed no triumph over Jasper's downfall. He was shocked and heartbroken. For a man proud of his breeding, discovering that his son is a lying, seducing murderer was a terrible blow. Yes, he is forcing this confession. But only to atone to Jasper's victims. Jasper agreed because he wants to avoid being hanged. There was no trace of remorse in his eyes, only defiance, tinged with fear."

"Of his father," insisted Mrs. Telcor, though uncertainty had crept into her voice.

"For his life," said Hortense. A dozen heads nodded.

"You needn't rely only on Rankin's word," added Fester. "Jasper's confession has unleashed a host of tongues. This morning alone, I've spoken with a dozen witnesses to other incidents, from the boy who was punished for damage Jasper caused, to the groom who watched him ride after Seabrook that night. Jasper is an arrogant tyrant who uses intimidation and brutality to enforce his will. No one is safe from his spite. Three deaths and countless injuries have already been laid to his account, and that doesn't begin to address the other damage he's caused."

"He left the chandler's girl with child," said Miss Ander.

"And stripped the West boy of everything he owned," added Clara.

"What about the tailor?"

"And Farmer Lansbury?"

"Sally Parker's broken arm."

"Peter Winslow's shattered wrist."

"Those dismembered cattle last year were his doing."

"So was Mr. Howard's favorite terrier."

Mrs. Telcor moaned, sliding to the floor in a faint. Blake leaped to assist her, for the collapse was genuine. No trace of color remained in her face. She must finally believe that Jasper had tricked her. Scooping her up, he followed the butler upstairs. By the time he returned, the Peters sisters had carried the day. Opinion had shifted firmly against Jasper, with voices vying to outshout one another with yet another example of the man's dishonor. Blake paused outside the door to listen.

"I feel sorriest for Mrs. Parrish," Hortense was saying. "She's lost her husband, her father, her friends, and her reputation to that man's spite. We cannot continue blaming her for his sins."

"I shouldn't have cut her without evidence," a matron said with a sigh.

"I should have known there was something wrong with those stories," said another. "She's always been kind. The bazaar she arranged last year raised enough to start a school in the village."

"And she's selfless," someone added. "She skipped part of Christmas with her family to soothe my grief after poor Jimmy died in Portugal. The villagers call her Saint Catherine."

"He should hang for what he's done to Seabrook's family," murmured a gentleman.

An enormous weight lifted from Blake's shoulders. Success. Justice was served. Smiling, he slipped outside. He would stop at the White Hart long enough to thank George. Then it was time to consider the future.

Catherine fumbled for her handkerchief. Cursing the past was useless, as was crying. But she couldn't seem to stop.

"Are you hurt?"

She jumped to her feet, frantically scrubbing away tears as Rockhurst strode closer. "I am fine."

He turned her to face him, his hands burning into her shoulders. "You act like you've lost your last friend."

"Haven't I?" His expression finally penetrated her gloom—joy rather than defeat.

"You are free, Catherine," he said softly. "Truly, forever free. Jasper's reputation is in shreds. His downfall is being celebrated both high and low."

"He actually confessed?" Shock made her voice squeak. "I was certain that he would offer new lies."

"He tried. As you expected, he had laid the foundation for his mad father's attempt to destroy him. He also blamed William for your father's death—supposedly William schemed to wrest control of the barony."

"My God! Even I had not expected such calumny."

"Relax." His thumbs stroked her neck. "It was a stupid attempt concocted without thought by a desperate man. Miss Ander remembered that William had been away at the time."

"He was in Plymouth. We had to send for him." Her head spun.

"Exactly. Jasper miscalculated badly. His father is furious. He is sending Jasper to the Caribbean under guard. Instead of running the estate when he arrives, he will be kept under close supervision and locked up if he misbehaves. The Misses Peters were so eloquent in your defense that even Mrs. Telcor now accepts the truth."

"Mrs. Telcor believes me innocent?" She was having trouble breathing.

He slid an arm around her shoulders, tucking her against his side as he walked toward the house. "Yes. It was a shock, of course—she actually fainted when the truth penetrated her stubborn head. When I left her, she swore she'd been uncertain of the tales for some time, though I suspect she is saving face by revising her memories. She will soon recall incidents that prove Jasper was a sneaky liar even as a boy. She'll have to. Already his confession is bringing victim after victim into the open. By tomorrow he will be credited with every misfortune to befall anyone since the day he was born. If she expects to retain her credibility as a gossip, she will have to go along."

She laughed. "I cannot believe they would turn on him so fast. They considered him a saint only yesterday."

"Public opinion is fickle," he reminded her, shrugging. "The higher a person starts, the farther he has to fall—which explains your own problem. Saint Catherine started on a pedestal so high it scraped heaven."

She actually blushed at his foolishness.

"But that works in your favor now," he continued. "No one enjoys feeling gullible. Admitting that he pulled the wool over their eyes implies that they are fools, so they need an explanation that absolves them of guilt. Thus Jasper must be a tool of Satan with evil powers that go beyond human comprehension. If he fooled everyone, then no one is to blame."

"Profound. So we will vilify him, and our children will remember him as Evil Incarnate. Ultimately, he will dwindle to an ogre used to scare toddlers into behaving."

"The important thing is that you are free," he repeated, squeezing her shoulder.

Rob met them at the manor's side door. "You have callers, madam."

"Callers?"

Rockhurst smiled.

"They asked for you, madam, but I thought it prudent to summon Lord Seabrook and your sisters as well."

Rockhurst's hand tightened, preventing her protest, though she swore silently at Rob's temerity in exposing Laura and Mary to another round of unpleasantness. Rockhurst kept his arm in place until they reached the main entrance hall. The loss of heat when he freed her seemed more real than the voices floating out of the drawing room.

Another knock drew Rob to the front door. Rockhurst slipped into the drawing room when Mrs. Telcor entered. As her carriage moved away from the steps, Catherine spotted a dozen others trundling up the drive. Several horsemen accompanied them, including Vicar Sanders.

"Forgive me, child," Mrs. Telcor begged shakily, pulling Catherine into a desperate hug. "I was a blind fool."

"Never a fool," she murmured. "Jasper can be most persuasive." She raised a brow to Rob, who nodded. "Come sit and have some tea. I would like to put this incident behind us as quickly as possible."

"Bless you for your forgiving heart."

Catherine walked through the next two hours in a daze. It seemed that everyone she knew stopped to pay their respects. Some apologized; others simply picked up where they had left off before the rumors started. All repeated increasingly shocking tales of Jasper. She tried to change the subject, but finally gave up.

William was similarly besieged, as were Laura and Mary. In the rush to condemn Jasper, people overlooked their part in the brawl.

Only Alicia's arrival caused any strain. William rebuffed her attempt to resume their courtship, and two ladies cut her for the vulgar manners she'd displayed at the assembly. Whispers behind fans revealed that none of her pearls had been returned. No one criticized their disappearance, for she had often adopted airs and graces above her station.

But Catherine ignored the murmurs, too intent on her churning emotions to worry about lost pearls. As the afternoon wore on, only Rockhurst's presence kept this outpouring of goodwill from overwhelming her. Whenever she caught his eye, she relaxed. He was a rock who kept her from drowning, a miracle worker, an archangel sent from heaven to rescue her from Satan's plots. What had she done to deserve such largesse? She wondered, then blushed to think she had harbored dreams about such a paragon.

"I can't believe they all called," she told him once the last lady left. William had returned to the library after sending Laura and Mary upstairs. "Did you put them up to it?"

"Not I, but I am glad they did. Wrongs should be addressed as soon as possible. Postponement creates new grievances that can fester, forever barring forgiveness. But this has cleared the air, so you are truly free."

But she wasn't, she admitted, glancing around her brother's drawing room. Her reputation might be restored, but she would never be free. She was tied to Seabrook. For now, she ran the house, but even that would stop once William married. And Sarah's future was even bleaker. Without a dowry, the best she could achieve would be a post as governess or companion. She moved to the window to avoid intruding on him any further. It was over. He would be gone in the morning.

"What is troubling you now?" He slipped behind her, resting his hands on her shoulders.

"Nothing." The denial sounded feeble even to her ears. "I was merely considering the instructions I must give Mrs. Moulding. Cook would appreciate setting dinner back an hour. She wasn't anticipating this crowd."

"I know you better than that, Catherine," he said softly. "You were reminding yourself that nothing has really changed. You are still tied to your brother, anticipating life as a poor relation." He turned her, forcing her to meet his eyes. "But you are indeed free— free to choose whatever future you wish. You can stay here and run the manor for a time. Or you can dedicate your life to helping those in need—to redress Jasper's crimes, Lord Rankin will offer you a yearly stipend equal to Harold's living. Or you can marry me."

Already dizzy at the thought of independence, she

stumbled away from him in shock at his last statement. "You cannot be serious. Your vow is fulfilled. My reputation is intact and my life restored. There is no need to sacrifice yourself in a misguided attempt to elevate me. That was never part of our agreement."

He caught her as she tripped. "Don't put words in my mouth, Catherine. I am very serious. Yes, my vow is fulfilled. More than fulfilled, for I never expected to win reparations. I can walk away with a clear conscience. But leaving would be painful. I love you and I want you by my side forever."

"No, you don't. You are a man of great compassion, but don't confuse that with love. I am not a charity case to be whisked away to a life of opulence as amends for Jasper's slurs. Think, my lord. I would make a terrible countess. I have no experience with society, and my breeding is barely adequate. You would be laughed out of your clubs for allowing a greedy upstart to snare you into marriage. I won't tarnish anyone's reputation. I know the pain too well."

His eyes darkened with anger. "I warned you about putting thoughts in my head. You are free to argue with me if you wish, but don't tell me my feelings don't exist. I love you. Accept it. I have enough experience to distinguish between love, lust, and compassion. If you don't care for me, then send me to perdition. But don't deny my love."

She opened her mouth to send him away, but no words emerged.

He relaxed and took her hands in his. "Let's try this again. I love you and I love Sarah. My life would be greatly enriched by including both of you in it. Will you marry me?"

"It wouldn't work." She freed her hands, unable to think when he was touching her.

"You are not the sort to flee from truth." He shifted to face her fully, clasping his hands behind his back.

"I need to think," she muttered, then cursed herself when he grinned. Those quirking eyebrows revealed yet another side to a character she already found too fascinating—a fun, slightly naughty side, at odds with his saintly image.

"You think too much, Catherine. There is nothing wrong with your breeding. With apologies for raising an embarrassing subject, it is exactly the same as Laura's." He held her eyes, nodding when she blushed. "Your father was a baron, and your mother descended from a viscount, which gives you better blood than my best friend's wife, and he is heir to a marquess—not that I care. I would love you if your family sold trinkets or raised sheep."

"That is not—"

But he ignored her protest. "As to social graces, or whatever poppycock you've lodged in your head, London society is little different from Devonshire society, not that it matters. I've no great love for either."

"Perhaps not, but you should consider what wedding a vicar's widow would mean to your family. You might not care about a tarnished reputation, but they will."

"*They* who?" he demanded, looming over her. Though he carefully restrained himself from touching, she was irritated that he scrambled her wits even more in this position. "My mother splits her year between the dower house and Bath. I've no brothers or sisters. Most of my cousins despise me for refusing to finance their idleness. And frankly, my reputation is so tarnished already that marrying you can only improve it."

"I don't believe it. William thinks you walk on water."

"He hasn't seen me in twelve years, and it's obvious he doesn't read the society columns." He paced to the window and back, running his fingers through his hair in a way that lodged heat in her womb. "You probably could have improved my reputation even before vanquishing Jasper. It is very like the one we just rid you of," he admitted when he returned. "I've been rather wild the last two years—not an attractive trait in a man my age. Then there is my scandalous insistence on running my own affairs—including a brief stint in trade that I dare not mention in polite company—and some pranks I blush to acknowledge." He explained.

"Turkeys?" she burst out, falling into gales of laughter. "You stuffed a flock of turkeys into a gossip's bed?"

"There were only four." He nibbled the tip of one finger, his expression making him look six years old. "Then there is my problem with politics. I hold reformist notions, which some people consider more scandalous than my other vices. In fact, I'm not exactly welcome in some circles."

"My lord, I—"

"Blake. I've put most of that behind me—had done so before coming here, in fact. You must believe that."

She nodded, amazed to realize that he was nervous. She was also surprised that these supposed foibles actually made him more likable than ever. Less intimidating, perhaps. Less perfect. And thus more approachable.

"But it will take a few years to live down some of the wildness. I'm hoping you can overlook it. I love you, Catherine. That's all that matters to me. Perhaps I should have waited, but I thought you might care, at least a little. Was I wrong?"

"No." When her hand stole upward to touch his cheek, he pressed a kiss into her palm, then circled the spot with the tip of his tongue. "Are you sure, Blake?"

"Yes." He cradled her head between his hands. Her arms circled his waist as he pulled her closer. "What is your answer, love?"

She nodded. "I love you, Blake. Who would not?"

"Catherine." It was more of a sigh than her name. His hold tightened, pulling her into a kiss even headier than the one they had shared in the garden. He was everything she had dreamed of, promising love, tenderness, protection, and more passion than she could imagine. She returned it all, vow for vow, touch for touch, and finally accepted it as real. She didn't know how or why, but her most secret fantasy had come true.

Blake reveled in his relief. He needed her. Wanted her more than anyone he had ever known. He had not planned to propose this soon, and for a terrifying moment he had feared that his impetuous words had driven her away. She could be extremely stubborn.

But it was all right. Very much all right, he admitted, pulling her closer as her hands explored his body. No timid virgin here. He would be hard-pressed to stay out of her bed until they were married. Only when need threatened to overwhelm his honor did he pull away.

"You will never regret this," he vowed, placing one last kiss on the end of her nose. "We belong together."

She nodded, too lost in emotion to speak.

Smiling, he led her toward the door. "We must see Sarah. She should be the first to know."

"Right." She started to say something, but shook her head instead.

He wondered if her thoughts were as scattered as his. "Shall we wed at Christmas?"

"That's only a month away."

"Enough time—barely. I'd do it sooner, but it will take almost that long to get a special license and send for my mother. Though it is quite tempting."

"That it is."

The anticipation in her voice stopped him at the foot of the stairs. "I love you, Catherine," he managed before pulling her into another embrace. Her mouth opened eagerly to meet his.

Only the creak of the servants' door finally sent them scurrying toward the nursery.

For only $3.99 each, you'll get to surrender to your wildest desires....

LORDS OF DESIRE

A special romance promotion from Signet Books—featuring some of our most popular, award-winning authors...

Arizona Gold by Maggie James
❏ 0-451-40799-7

Bride of Hearts by Janet Lynnford
❏ 0-451-40831-4

Diamonds and Desire by Constance Laux
❏ 0-451-20092-6

PENGUIN PUTNAM INC.
Online

Your Internet gateway to a virtual environment with
hundreds of entertaining and enlightening books
from Penguin Putnam Inc.

*While you're there, get the latest buzz on
the best authors and books around—*

Tom Clancy, Patricia Cornwell, W.E.B. Griffin,
Nora Roberts, William Gibson, Robin Cook,
Brian Jacques, Catherine Coulter, Stephen King,
Jacquelyn Mitchard, and many more!

**Penguin Putnam Online is located at
http://www.penguinputnam.com**

PENGUIN PUTNAM NEWS

Every month you'll get an inside look at our upcom-
ing books and new features on our site. This is an
ongoing effort to provide you with the most
up-to-date information about
our books and authors.

**Subscribe to Penguin Putnam News at
http://www.penguinputnam.com/ClubPPI**